The Blood Moon
Sealed My Fate

Book One in The Blood Moon Series

By: Rhonda Partin-Sharp

2018

CLEEPs Authors

ISBN 978-1-947216-03-7

Published By:
CLEEPs Authors
P. O. Box 5334
Cincinnati, OH 45205

Author's Information:
Facebook Page: Author Rhonda Partin-Sharp
Blog: *https://ronisharp.wixsite.com/mysite/blog/*

Cover Photo by Lisa Coorey-Gerard
Cover Design by Lisa Coorey-Gerard and Rhonda Partin-Sharp

WARNING
This book contains adult topics and may not be appropriate for young readers.

Dedication

I dedicate this book to my parents, Estil and Cloma Partin, because they taught me to have enough strength and compassion that I was able to hear and not just listen when I was told the story that inspired this novel. I love them. Every ounce of good that resides in me is due to their love, both the profound effect that love had on me directly as well as how their love taught me that a loving Father in heaven could not be cruel and judgmental even if some of his followers portrayed him that way. Their love taught me to seek and find a God of love, mercy and compassion. Since their passing, I miss them every day. I feel like I lost the only two people who see the world the same way I do because of our unique shared experiences. I love them both unconditionally.

Acknowledgements

I am grateful to my father, Estil Partin, who encouraged me to write this story and who taught me that we can overcome anything. He epitomized the saying, "What doesn't kill us makes us strong." He was always better than where he started even when others didn't see it, and he soared above where he started in his last few years of life.

I am grateful to my mother, Cloma Partin, who encouraged me to write even when the many trials we experienced made it almost impossible to find time to do so. When she was alive, I told her the song "Wind Beneath My Wings" by Bette Midler must have been written to tell the story of the impact she had on my life. That was our song.

I am grateful to Dr. Deborah Andrews. She stood by me and some of my family as we learned to embrace the culture my family migrated to when they left the mountains. She also stood by us as we learned how to set boundaries that our new culture quickly taught us we were lacking.

I am grateful to Pastor Robert Keefer and his wife Kathleen, Pastor and Author Thom Shuman, and Priest Hawley Todd. They helped me release negative religious beliefs and grow to understand the love of Christ. That understanding increased my happiness and added flavor to this book.

I am grateful to Linde Grace White who is my dear friend and editor. To say she is my editor is not sufficient – She is an editor extraordinaire. My book flourished under her painful red ink marks that I sometimes feared and even resented, but she was usually right. My book was greatly improved under her guidance just as the quality of my life has improved due to her very patient, nurturing and never-failing friendship. Her own writing against child abuse can be found at LindeGraceWhite.org.

I am grateful to Wayne Holmes of Religious Recovery Press for his literature, which helps people expand their minds beyond the religious boxes so many people get trapped in. I am impressed with his literary skills. I am also grateful for what he has taught me about publishing.

I am grateful to my husband, David, for assisting with computer software and technical issues, especially those that arose in the last hours as we prepared for publication. I appreciate him supporting me in writing this story and making this dream come true even when it took time away from him and other responsibilities.

I am grateful to the owner(s) and staff of College Hill Coffee Company in Cincinnati, Ohio. They allowed Linde Grace White and I to park there for hours each Wednesday afternoon for many months while we edited this book.

I am grateful to everyone who helped me strengthen my boundaries, whether that happened through their support or through painful life lessons that provided the opportunity for me to dig deeper and find strength I did not know I had. When I began my journey of personal growth, a beloved boss and friend named Rosemary told me personal growth would resemble peeling away the layers of an onion. With each layer I peeled away, I would be better than I was before. Each new layer; however, would provide new opportunities to get even stronger. The new layers would be easier than the ones that came before, both because of my increased strength and the higher quality of people each level of growth would bring into my life. This is exactly what happened. I'm still working on boundaries, but I'm much better at it than when I started. I do have a higher quality of people to help me recover when I repeat a boundary mistake and have a new lesson to learn. I am grateful to both those who gave me support and those who gave me a painful life lesson that gave me the opportunity to grow. I still and probably always will be concerned for others those who inflicted harm might hurt, but I have learned from any pain they caused and moved on. Now that I'm on the other side of it, I am grateful for those lessons.

The Blood Moon
Sealed My Fate

CHAPTER ONE
A MOUNTAIN MURDER

I wasn't sure if it was my Ma grabbing my wrist that startled me awake or her screaming, "What ya be doin' in yer brother's bed, ya filthy lil' slut? Such things be fer married folk!"

In my half-awake state, I murmured, "Do that be meanin' I be married to Pa, since he be comin' to my bed?"

I hit the floor before I finished the sentence. I wasn't fully awake until I hit the floor. Had I been awake, I probably wouldn't have said what I said about my Pa. I wished I was still asleep while she drug me across the floor and under the curtain that served as a door for my brother's and my room. I looked frantically around for Pa. He must have gone to work already, because I didn't see him any place.

As she drug me toward the front door, she yelled, "I done told ya about gettin' into bed with yer lil' brother, ya filthy lil' slut."

"He be havin' hisself a bad dream," I said, my words coming out in a frantic whine that I didn't even recognize as my own voice. "I just be tryin' to be makin' him be feelin' better."

Ma whirled around and yanked me to my feet. I soon forgot the pain in my shoulder, because the back of her hand striking my face gave me another pain to think about. She held my wrist so tight that I thought my hand would fall off as she whirled back around and led me out of the house. I was not able to get away no matter how hard I fought. I was five and a half years old. I was looking forward to turning six, if Ma didn't kill me first.

It wasn't just the painful grip she had on my wrist as she led me across the yard. It was the look in her eyes. One minute they looked like they had fire in them. The next minute they looked black as coal. Her body was so stiff that every step looked like it hurt her. It didn't matter that she was only five feet tall. It didn't matter that she wore the typical feed sack dress that made all of our mountain women look innocent. When she got in these moods, she looked like a vicious giant. The gray that was already conquering her dark hair and the lines that were already invading her young face combined with those moods to make her look like a wicked witch.

I knew no one would help me. My little brother, Eamon, was the only person at home that day. No one lived near enough to know what was happening on this isolated, rock-infested mountain farm. The sheriff almost never came around. When he did, he always believed whatever your folks said, especially your Pa. The preacher was even worse than my folks, and the neighbors were too afraid to get involved even if they knew.

The only people who cared about us were Uncle Teagan and MawMaw Tierney. MawMaw Tierney was Ma's Ma, but she wasn't anything like Ma. MawMaw Tierney was the kindest grandma a girl could have. Uncle Teagan was her brother. Everyone said you could tell they came from the same seed, because they were the two kindest people on this mountain.

They couldn't help us much. Everyone on this mountain believed what a man did to his family was his business. I've heard so many people say, "H'it be yer property, ya be doin' with h'it as ya be seein' fit." If Uncle Teagan and MawMaw Tierney helped us, they would lose the support of everyone on this mountain. They wouldn't be able to help us in small ways anymore.

I looked back at Eamon as Ma led me toward the barn. He was watching from the bottom of the porch steps. My heart hurt when I saw the fear and pain on his face. He took a couple of slow steps toward me. I focused my gaze on him and mouthed the word "No" repeatedly until he sat on the steps. I was grateful that I had seen him sit on the steps before she led me into the barn. This would be much harder if I was worried about him.

I fought harder as she led me toward the storage room at the back of the barn. I had been in there before. She often left me in there for days without food or water. I had not forgotten that suffering, so my heart began to race when she led me toward the door.

She threw me into the storage room so hard that I hit the back wall. As I slid down the wall, I heard the chain going across the handles. I jumped up and ran to the door. I threw myself on it, but it didn't budge. I leaned my back against the door and slid down it until I was sitting on the floor. I wept.

For the remainder of the day, I watched light streaming between the wall boards. The light went away. The light returned. The light went away again. I didn't remember it coming back a second time. Everything seemed dark. Maybe it was night. Maybe it was day. I had been lying on a pile of hay for quite a while now. The first day I had been able to tell when the light of day peeked through the boards. Now, I couldn't tell. I thought it must be night, because I was cold. I used the hay for a blanket.

· · · · ·

I was half asleep and half awake when I heard a small voice say, "Sinead."

I drug myself to my knees and touched my hand to the wall. I imagined I felt my little brother's hand on the other side of the wall as he said, "H'it be me, Eamon."

Eamon was past three and half years old. He would soon be four years old, if he made it to his next birthday. I could picture him on the other side of the wall – his thin frame, tattered shirt, overalls with one broken suspender, and thick curly black hair. I became afraid he would be beaten if she found him here.

"Git yerself on back to the house," I said as I leaned my forehead against the wall.

I saw my long black curls hanging on each side of my head. My hair looked just like Eamon's even when it was matted like it was then. I pressed my hand harder into the wall.

"I be wantin' to be with ya," Eamon said.

3

I looked between the boards and saw his small palm pressed against the outside wall.

"Git yerself on back to the house. She be beatin' ya if'n she be findin' ya out here."

"Do ya be a'right?" Eamon asked.

His voice was raspy. I knew that voice. He was choking on tears he was too afraid to shed.

"Yas," I said. "I be a'right. Right as rain. Git yerself on back to the house now. Please."

"MawMaw Tierney done said I be growin' up to be a big strong man. She won't be hurtin' ya nary more when I is," Eamon said.

"When I git big, they won't be hurtin' ya nary more neither," I said as I pressed my cheek against the wall. "Please, git yerself on back to the house."

As I heard his feet squishing across the wet ground of early winter, I looked between the wallboards to watch him. I was soon distracted by the moon. It was red like blood. When I saw it, I knew my time was short. Preacher Skaggs told us the moon would turn to blood before the last days. He told me the last days would be hard for me if I didn't do everything he told me to do, but I didn't do everything he told me to do. I ran from him when he touched me like Pa touched me, because I was afraid Pa would beat me if he found out. Preacher Skaggs was right. I was getting my come-uppance. The blood moon sealed my fate.

I knew this was the winter of my life. I didn't know how long I had been lying here. I was cold. I was hungry. I was thirsty. I had been scared. I wasn't scared anymore. That was when she always came back, just when I stopped being scared.

The fear returned when I heard the chain being removed from the door. As I looked around frantically for a way to escape, I noticed that light was beginning to stream through the wall boards again. I pushed myself as far into the corner as I could. I hugged my knees and covered my head with my arms as I prayed for the darkness again. I imagined an angel pulling me through the wall boards to safety, but Ma grabbed my arm and yanked me back into the barn before the angel rescued me.

I fell on my stomach so hard that it knocked the wind out of me. When I caught my breath enough to roll onto my back, Ma was standing above me holding a stick in her right hand. She bounced it off

4

her left palm as she walked around me. I braced myself to be hit, but she kicked me in the stomach instead. I gasped for breath and rolled into a ball like a pill bug.

My breath returned when I felt the stick across my back. I think my screams were coming from someone else as she hit me again, and again, and again. Each kick was a welcome break from the stick. I lay like a pill bug with my hands over the back of my head during the entire beating. When she finally stopped, I crawled toward the door. Ma rapped the stick across my back several times as I crawled. Just when I thought I would make it through the door, she yanked me up by the back of my dress. As soon as my feet touched the ground, I tried to run. She was still holding onto the back of my dress, so it ripped.

"Clothes nary be growin' on trees," she yelled as she grabbed me around the waist, spun around and threw me back into the room. As I flew across the room, I felt like she was a tornado who had picked me up like a tree in a field. I knew I would spin with her until she had destroyed everything, including me.

When I hit the wall, I felt the worst pain I had ever felt. When the pain stopped, I was looking down at my own body. I saw myself lying on my back. My arms and legs were bent in ways I had never been able to bend them. The pink floral dress Pa had bought me was covered in blood stains. One cheek was smashed into the floor. My long black hair was plastered by blood to the other cheek. The hair that hung down my back was tangled like a rat's nest. My blue-gray eyes were wide open.

Ma was still yelling about the dress being torn as she stormed over to my body and grabbed my wrist. She only held it for a second before she knelt beside me and pushed one of my eyelids closed. Whatever she felt at that moment seemed to free her from her tornado. As she ran out of the barn, she screamed, "I be goin' to be hangin' fer this!"

A few seconds later, I returned to my body. I felt my heart weakly beating before I felt the pain return, and when it did, I wished I was still looking down at my body. I didn't move. I watched dust dance in the light that streamed between the wall boards. When the light went away, I listened to the crickets chirp and the tree frogs begin their song. Then, I heard Eamon's voice.

I forced my head to turn. I saw one of Eamon's eyes peeking between the wall boards. One beautiful blue-gray eye that shone like the sky reflecting off Uncle Teagan's pond.

"Eamon," I said with a voice so hoarse I barely recognized it as my own.

"Ya be a'right?" he asked with a quiet voice that almost sounded like a song.

"I be a'right," I answered.

I knew my weak raspy voice proved that to be a lie when Eamon said the words that were forbidden in our house. "I be lovin' ya, Sinead."

I knew he was telling me goodbye.

"I be lovin' ya, Eamon," I said, hoarsely. I coughed lightly. After the pain from the cough finished tearing through my body, I asked, "Will ya be doin' somethin' fer me?"

"Yas," he answered.

"Ya be doin' what they be sayin'," I said. Every word hurt, but I continued to force out what I had to say. "Ya be tellin' them ya not be knowin' nothin' about what they be doin'. Nary be lettin' them know when ya be feelin' mad. H'it be makin' me sad when they be hurtin' ya. Ya be keepin' yerself safe fer me."

"Ya be goin' to be with God?" he asked.

I heard him choke on a tear.

"Me and God be watchin' over ya together. We be gettin' them back one day."

"Can I be goin' with ya?" Eamon asked, pleading.

"I be goin' to be askin' God to be watchin' over ya. Ya be needin' to be goin' on back to the house now. They be hurtin' ya if'n they be findin' ya out here. Please, git yerself on back to the house."

"A'right," he said. I heard his feet squish across the early winter ground a few steps and stop. I heard the sound returning. He whispered through the wall boards, "I be askin' God to be keepin' ya safe whilst ya be with him."

"Much obliged," I said, gurgling.

The sound of feet squishing across the early winter ground kept getting farther away.

6

I gurgled a few more times before I was looking at my body again. The angel came to pull me through the wall boards. She was later than I had hoped, but she came and wrapped her arms around me. I looked down at my body as we rose into the air together. I saw how pretty I would have been. My long black hair curled all the way to my waist. I had the same blue-gray eyes Eamon had. My fair skin looked pretty next to my dark hair. My body was long and thin like Pa's. I had Pa's high cheek bones instead of the flat featureless face of that woman who called herself my Ma.

When I realized how much I looked like Eamon, my thoughts returned to him. I couldn't leave him. When we got to the ceiling, I stretched my arms out to stop the angel from taking me through. When my head went through any way, I screamed, "Stop!"

The angel looked into my eyes and said, "There is no reason to be afraid. We are going to a better place. No one will hurt you there."

I believed her. She was beautiful. She looked like a woman, but she was much taller than any woman I had ever seen. Her whole body glowed like her long wavy golden hair. I wanted to go with her. Everything about her shining eyes and her glowing smile made me want to go with her, but I could still hear Eamon's feet squishing across the early winter ground. I told her no.

I was on the ground next to my body again. I tried to wipe the blood-matted hair off my body's face, but my hand went right through. I pulled my hand away and looked through it. Only then did I know I was really dead.

CHAPTER TWO
WHEN PA GETS HOME

I didn't know where to go or what to do. I sat next to my body until I heard Pa's wagon rattling home behind the clomp of horse's hoofs. I wanted to run to him, but I didn't know how.

Pa was no angel, but he was good enough to me. His blue-gray eyes often looked dark and hard, but they softened and looked full of light when he looked at me. I remembered Ma yelling, "Even the wrinkles on yer ol' weather-beaten face be softenin' when ya be lookin' at that child. Ya nary be lookin' at me that way. Ya nary be lookin' at the child I done bore ya that way?"

Pa was tall as a tree. He showed me that even a tiny mouse like me can melt the heart of a tree like Pa. I will never forget that mop of straight black hair falling over his blue-gray eyes when he looked down at me. I often wished he would look at Eamon the same way. I wished that even more now that I was gone.

I heard all the familiar sounds. Pa called 'Whoa!" to the horse, climbed down from the wagon, stomped across the gravel in front of the house and up the porch steps, dropped his boots and coveralls onto the floor, stomped back down the porch steps and across the gravel to the spigot, splashed water as he washed the coal dust off his hands and face, stomped back across the gravel and up the porch steps, opened the creaky door and entered the house. Seconds later I heard the front door slam followed by Pa's heavy footsteps as he ran across the porch, down the steps and across the gravel. Seconds after the gravel stopped announcing his approach, I saw him come into the room where I sat next to my body.

He ran across the room and knelt next to me. He pulled my body into his arms and screamed, "Naw! Naw! Naw! Naw! Naw! Not Ruby's child! Naw! Not Ruby's child!"

Ma stormed into the barn a few seconds later. Her bloodshot eyes glared hate at Pa as she screamed, "This here be yer fault as much as h'it be mine. If'n ya nary be treatin' her so much better just cause she be Ruby's bastard, this nary be happenin'."

Pa jumped up and ran across the room as fast as a bolt of lightning. He slapped Ma's face so hard she fell down. As he looked down at her, he screamed, "Yer damn jealousy be what kilt that child! H'it nary be her fault I be lovin' her Ma. Ya nary be callin' her a bastard again! I be marryin' her Ma outta love! She be more my child than anythin' what be comin' outta yer belly ever will be!"

I had seen him beat Ma many times. It was hard to believe the man who delivered those beatings was the same man who never beat me, bought me toys, laid the last biscuit on my plate when everyone else was hungry, sneaked into my room one night and laid a rag doll under my folded arm, and bought me the pink floral dress I was wearing when Ma killed me.

"But," Ma said.

That was all it took to unleash Pa's rage. He beat her like she beat me earlier that day. When he finished, he returned to my side and embraced my body.

Ma crawled across the room and through the door into the main barn. A few minutes later, I heard the sound of Pa's hunting rifle slide across the wagon bed. Fear taught my ghost body to move to the door and see what Ma was doing. With the rifle in her hands, she jumped on the seat of our wagon. As soon as she had the wagon turned toward the road, she rode away at a pace that was much too fast for a wagon.

I knew where she was going. She ran to her brothers every time Pa beat her. I thanked God her brothers didn't live with MawMaw Tierney anymore. I didn't think her heart could take knowing how her children turned out.

I turned back to Pa. He continued to rock my body. His apparent helplessness reminded me of a time when he had come to my bed. He smelled of moonshine and was crying like a woman. He held me close and rocked me while he said. "I be lovin' ya, child. Ya surely do be remindin' me of yer Ma. I surely do be missin' her. That wife I be havin' now be havin' the same crazy eyes my own Ma done had when she be goin' crazy. I be knowin' how that be, child. I done gone through h'it myself. My Ma nary be bigger than a bunny rabbit, but she be havin' the heart of a bear when her eyes be lookin' that way. When I be gittin' too big fer her to be overpowerin' my body, I be learnin' she be more sneaky than I nary be able to be. I be preferrin' the beatin's. Havin' a bruised body be easier than bein' sneaked up on. Once a beatin' be over, h'it be done. Havin' someone sneaky after ya be makin' a body a'feared all the time. I sometimes be havin' a hard time huntin', cuz I be knowin' what h'it be like to be hunted. Ya nary be knowin' what direction h'it be comin' from. Ya be in the belly of the beast. Ya nary be knowin' how to be fightin' back. If'n ya be fightin' in this direction, h'it be gittin' ya from the other direction."

Pa said too many words that night for me to remember them. The feelings are what I remembered. I knew exactly how he felt as he had described his Ma to me, because that is how Ma made me feel. I knew what he had been talking about without having to remember the words.

I didn't cotton to beatings too much, because I knew what they felt like. But, I never got upset when it was Ma being beat. I knew Pa was right about her. It was usually her sneaky ways that brought it on her. She was like a snake in the grass, and that is why I knew Pa was right when he said the serpent was the devil.

Whenever they were holding snakes at church, I knew they misunderstood the scriptures. Those who got bit had hands that were twisted like my heart had been twisted in life. I still couldn't believe they forgot that the snake in the Garden of Eden was the one who defied God. They would never tame the serpent. Maybe they didn't understand that, because they didn't live with Ma. I had tried to shake the devil off my hand like the apostle Paul had shook the snake into the fire and lived, but my snake never let go. I hadn't been as lucky as Paul.

CHAPTER THREE
CLAN PROTECTION

Pa kept rocking me even after I heard the sound of horse's hooves. He didn't give any sign that he was aware of the sound even though it kept getting louder. Tears were just starting to spill out of his stubborn eyes when the horses stormed into the barn.

One of Ma's two brothers yanked his horse to a halt just outside the storage room door. He was so large that I wondered how his horse carried him as I watched him dismount. The only time I saw him was when Ma ran to him for protection, so I couldn't even remember his name.

Ma walked through the barn door while I watched her smaller brother dismount. She paused for a second when she saw Pa and asked. "What in hell ya still be doin' here?"

Pa just kept rocking me and crying.

The large brother put his big hands under Pa's arms and lifted Pa to his feet. Pa hugged me to his chest like I used to hug my rag doll. The small brother pried me out of Pa's arms and gave me to Ma.

The large brother grabbed the front of Pa's shirt and pushed him backwards into the wall as he asked, threateningly, "What in hell be goin' on over here tonight?"

When Pa's back hit the wall, he pulled the large brother's hands off the shirt, pushed him away and said. "Buck, I nary be knowin' what that woman be tellin' ya, but I nary be havin' a part in this."

I was surprised Pa had the courage to stand up to Buck. Pa was a tall man, but he was a thin man. Buck was the same height as Pa and three times as wide. He had some fat on him, but his wide shoulders were muscle. His forearms were so swollen with muscle that he'd had to cut the sleeves off his shirt. Even though he was a young man, his face was already getting wrinkles and his dark curly hair was already salt and pepper just like Ma. His skin was so dark from working in the sun that he almost looked like a black man, but no one was going to say that to this mountain of a man.

The small brother looked almost like Buck except his hair was not so dark and wasn't gray. He was small enough that he could wear a shirt without busting out of it, and his skin was much lighter. Other than that, there was no doubt these two were brothers. He looked at my body and asked, "Do ya be tellin' me this lil' woman done hurt this child this bad?"

Pa looked at him and said, "Ya be knowin' how she be, Carl."

"Yassir, I reckon I do be knowin'," Carl said as he walked toward Pa. When his face was right in Pa's face, he said, "Pokin' girls that nary be wantin' to be poked by a stranger be doin' that. H'it be makin' 'em sour ol' women. Ya done made yer bed when ya forced yer manhood on my virgin sister. I reckon now ya be layin' in h'it."

Pa swallowed hard before Carl pointed at my body and asked, "Do rape be how ya be gittin' that young'un? Ya be doin' this to be gittin' rid of the proof?"

Pa grabbed Carl around the neck and pushed him toward the opposite wall as he yelled, "Ya be knowin' that child be belongin' to my beloved Ruby!"

Buck wrapped his arm around Pa's neck from behind and said, "Ya need to be lettin' him go. If'n ya don't, I be chokin' ya to death."

"Ya both be knowin' h'it nary be me what done kilt that child," Pa said as he removed his hands from Carl's neck.

"How we be knowin' that?" Buck whispered into Pa's ear from behind. "We nary be here to be seein' h'it. H'it be yer word against that lil' wife of yers. Nary a person be believin' that lil' slip of a gal be strong enough to be killin' that child."

Even though Pa was fighting for air, he said, "When y'all done forced me to be marryin' her, ya be tellin' me what a two-faced lil' whore she be. H'it nary be makin' no sense y'all bein' on her side now?"

"She be our blood," Buck said as his face turned red. "Blood be thicker than water. We nary be lettin' blood swing fer killin' a child that nary be havin' our blood in h'it."

Carl got so close to Pa's face that he was spitting on Pa as he said, "H'it be a pity that Eamon be havin' some of our blood. That be makin' ya kin, so we be obliged to be lettin' ya live, if'n ya be doin' what we be tellin' ya to be doin'."

Buck pushed Pa into Carl. Carl grabbed the front of Pa's shirt and continued to hold Pa close to his face as he said, "Ya nary be tellin' a soul what Mabon's done. If'n ya do, we be tellin' the sheriff we done see'd ya be beatin' that poor child to death. We be tellin' him ya done gone plum crazy, and we nary be able to be stoppin' ya."

Buck came up behind Pa and said, "I nary be above hittin' my brother to be convincin' the Sheriff ya done beat the hell outta him when he be tryin' to save Sinead."

Carl laughed and said, "I done gived my brother a few bruises in the past. I nary be above givin' him a few more."

Carl pushed Pa backwards when he let go of his shirt. Pa fell into Buck.

As Buck pushed Pa forward, he asked, "Ya be understandin'?"

Pa nodded as he regained his footing.

"That nary be all," Carl said as he pulled a pocket knife out of his pants pocket. He opened it slow as he looked at Pa. After holding Pa's gaze for a few seconds, Carl began to shave the ends off his fingernails as he said, "If'n any harm be comin' to our sister, they be findin' yer body down in the mines."

Buck laughed and said, "The stupidest varmint be knowin' ya be havin' to be takin' a bird down in them there mines. Ya be havin' to be makin' sure there be no gas that can be killin' ya. Folks be sayin' what a poor stupid bastard ya be fer nary takin' one down. Folks be thinkin' h'it be a pity yer own ignorance done kilt ya."

Carl put his arm over Pa's shoulder like they were best friends as he said, "If'n Ma ever be findin' out about this, ya be regrettin' the day ya be borned. Knowin' the truth would be killin' Ma, and we cain't be havin' that."

Pa stared into Carl's eyes as he asked, "Since when do ya be givin' a damn about yer Ma? Ya never be visitin' her after yer Pa done died and she done moved in with her brother Teagan. Ya be lettin' her and Ol' Teagan struggle to be makin' their ol' bodies be doin' all the work with only his three frail daughters to be helpin'. Ya nary be givin' a shit. Y'all only be wanderin' over there when ya be wantin' somethin'. Anyhow, yer Ma nary be stupid even if she done raised nothin' but stupid young'uns. She be knowin' her grandchild be gone."

Carl's face got a deeper shade of red with every word Pa said. Carl put the tip of his knife under Pa's chin and said, "That girl nary be her grandchild. We nary be wantin' her to be knowin' y'all be child killers. We nary be wantin' her worryin' about Eamon. She nary be findin' out about this. Ya be findin' a way to be makin' h'it look like Sinead done died of sickness. If'n ya nary be doin' that, they be findin' yer body down in them mines. Ya be understandin'."

When Pa didn't answer, Buck got right in his face and asked, "Ya be understandin'?"

Pa swallowed hard before he nodded.

Buck and Carl walked toward the door. Just before they left the room, Buck said, "We be checkin' on Mabon tomorrow. Look what ya done did to her. She better not be lookin' no worse."

After the brothers left the room, Ma walked across the room like she did on any ordinary day and laid me in the hay. As she did, I heard the familiar rattle of her brother's tacks as they mounted their horses. The sound of hoofs soon filled the air, getting softer as they rode away.

Ma pushed the bloody hair off my face and said, "She be cold, Caelan."

Pa walked over and knelt next to Ma. He laid his hand on me for less than a second before he jerked it away.

Ma laughed and said, "Ya be holdin' her all that time and nary be noticin' she be cold, ya ol' fool."

He looked at Ma and said, "Mabon, ya done kilt her." Tears welled in his eyes again as he asked, "Why ya be killin' my lil' girl? Why ya be havin' yer brothers be throwin' threats before she be in the ground?"

"Ya be thinkin' I be goin' to be lettin' ya kill me over a child what nary be mine? Ya done saved yer skin by marryin' me when ya done forced Eamon into my belly, but my family's honor still be stained. If'n ya be tellin' the sheriff, my brothers be tellin' him with tears in their eyes how they done tried to be savin' poor lil' Sinead from ya. If'n ya be beatin' or killin' me, my brothers be doin' the same to ya."

"Ya be just like my own Ma," Pa said before he stood up. He paced for several minutes as he asked repeatedly, "How we be makin' h'it look like sickness?"

Ma began to follow Pa as he paced. When he clasped his hands behind his back, she did the same thing. As I watched her, I wondered why I had ever been afraid of her. She was too small to look threatening. Her legs were so short she was soon panting from trying to keep up with him. She looked like what she was: a tiny woman whose youthful dark curls were being stolen by gray and whose youthful skin was being stolen by wrinkles.

Pa reeled around and slapped her face so hard with the back of his hand that she tumbled over backwards. As she sat on the ground looking up at him, he yelled, "What have ya done to us?"

In spite of the tears that filled her eyes, she laughed as she moved her hand to her cheek and said, "Ya need to be worryin' about what my brothers will be doin' to ya."

As she looked up at him through tear-filled eyes, I thought about the hundreds of times I had seen Pa hit her in the same way. I remembered all the times he had hit Eamon. Was Carl right? Was Pa the reason Ma was so hateful? I remembered the suffering she had caused me, and the pity I felt for her returned to the darkness of my own thoughts.

She wiped the tears from below her eyes as she said, "I was just bein' a good Christian woman. Preacher be sayin' not to be sparin' the rod or ya be spoilin' the child."

"Is Preacher gonna be gittin' this body outta here fer us?" Pa asked, yelling.

She crawled to my body and picked it up before she said, "I be gittin' rid of h'it. I reckon I be the only one what be man enough to be doin' what's got to be done."

I watched her carry my body out of the barn. She cradled it in her arms like I so often longed to be cradled when I was alive. She stared into my body's cold dead eyes as she walked toward the woods.

15

I followed her. When I got to the barn door, I saw Eamon watching from the side of the house. I moved quickly to him and said, "Git yer self inside!" He ran into the house.

When I knew my brother was safe, I turned and watched Ma carry my body into the woods. I felt sad, because I didn't know if I would be able to go on without the body that was so familiar to me.

I moved to the door of the house and grabbed the door knob. My hand went right through it. I stared at my transparent hand for a long time before I tried again, and again, and again. I was still trying when Pa walked right through me, grabbed the door knob and opened the door.

I heard two creaking footsteps before he asked, "What ya be doin' outta bed, Eamon?

I didn't have a heart anymore, but it felt like it quickened. I tried to follow Pa in before the door was closed all the way. To my surprise, I hit the almost closed door and went right through the wood. I fell right through the door without damaging it or myself. I was surprised to see that there wasn't a hole in the door. I looked at my hands. They were still transparent. My eyes followed my arms to my body, and I realized everything was transparent. I wondered what else this new transparent body could do.

I heard the floor boards creak and realized Pa had made a step toward Eamon. I whirled around and saw Pa was taking his belt off as he walked. I moved quickly across the room and stood between him and Eamon. To my surprise, Pa stopped. For a moment, I thought he saw me. As he began to latch his belt again, he said, "One dead child be enough fer this day."

I felt Eamon shaking behind me. I turned and saw that his skin was white and clammy, and his lower lip was quivering. I lay my hand on his shoulder. It went through, but Eamon looked toward where my hand had tried to touch him. He only looked for a second, but during that second, he stopped shaking.

Pa moved slightly, but it was enough to make the floor boards creak. Eamon began to shake again, and his eyes shot back to Pa. The heart that was no longer in my body began to beat faster. What was I going to do if Eamon got so scared he pee'd? I was always the one who cleaned him up. If I couldn't clean him up, would they kill him, too?

I lay my hand on his shoulder. It was scary to see my hand moving into him each time I didn't hold it steady, but I kept it there any way. Eamon looked toward where my hand was touching him as I said firmly, "Git yer self to bed!"

Eamon looked at our Pa one more time before he turned and walked toward the curtain that served as a door to the bedroom he and I had once shared.

I had been dead long enough to learn that living people could not see me. My folks had no idea I was in the barn with them earlier that evening. But, somehow, it seemed like Eamon could understand me when I talked to him.

I looked at Pa to make sure he wasn't following Eamon. I was relieved to see that Pa continued to walk away. I was relieved to hear the floor boards creaking with each step. I would be relieved to hear the creaking of the chair on the other side of the room when he settled onto it.

I stood between them as they walked in opposite directions away from each other. I saw Pa lumbering away like a horse tired from a day of plowing. I remembered him always carrying himself like he was tired. His hard-earned muscles seemed to weigh him down instead of strengthening him. The thick black hair on his head seemed to be only inches from the ceiling despite the tired stoop of his shoulders.

My little brother was already walking with the same tired lumber at only three and a half years old. His body was so close to the floor that the tired stoop of his shoulders made his limp arms look like they should be dragging something heavy. He didn't have strong muscles. He was so thin it looked like his bones could hardly hold his skin up. His skinny bottom barely held up the pants he'd been wearing for days. By the time he had muscles, Pa's muscles would be old and withering. I wondered if Eamon would get revenge then.

I watched my helpless brother walk through the curtain before I looked back at Pa. I felt a rage so big I couldn't wait for my brother to get big and strong enough to get even. I ran at Pa, fists flailing. My fists went through him like air. He didn't look at where I was touching him like my brother did. He just sighed deeply, reached under the table for a jar of moonshine, unscrewed the lid and took a big gulp.

When my hands went through Pa, I felt a sadness so deep that I understood the tired stoop both of the men in my life had. As I floated toward the room that now belonged only to my brother, I carried myself with the same tired stoop on my transparent shoulders.

I stopped halfway across the main room and looked around. I had been afraid every minute I was alive. This creaky old cabin never knew a coat of paint. The boards were almost as gray and weatherworn on the inside as they were on the outside. The furniture seemed to be made from the same gray wood. The table and chairs where Pa was sitting allowed him to stare through the wide opening that led to the small kitchen where Ma cooked for only him. That table and chairs were as gray as the walls. The gray cabinet that leaned on the wall next to the kitchen door almost disappeared into the gray wall behind it. The wooden bench that faced the fireplace on the other side of the cabinet was almost invisible as it blended into the gray. I wondered how people sat on it without missing it and falling to the floor. The wooden bench on the other side of the room had a coffee table and two rocking chairs between it and the fireplace. All of that furniture also blended into the walls.

This house seemed to be designed to make sure there was no comfort. The oil lamp that burned on the table in front of Pa didn't create light as the flame danced. Even the flame seemed dark. It only made the gray more visible. It only reminded us that there was no comfort.

Comfort could not survive here. Ma once got a glass figurine at the company store. The only purpose it served was to cut her when the pieces shattered off the wall beside her head after Pa threw it in a fit of rage.

I looked his way when Pa moved and made the chair creak. That was another thing that made this house so scary. Every time you moved, the house creaked. Our folks always knew what you were doing, so you always had to be afraid. Even over the noise of the fire or Ma cooking, they could hear the creaking. Sometimes the creaking would make Pa stop yelling and come after us instead. We knew he was coming, because we could hear the creaking as his feet raced across the floor boards. We learned to fear the creaking almost more than what the creaking would bring on us.

18

I moved toward the curtain that led to where my brother slept. There was no creaking as I moved. Before I floated through the curtain, I looked back at the old man sitting at the table and thought, "This place nary be so scary now."

CHAPTER FOUR
MAWMAW TIERNEY

When you're dead, you don't sleep in the way living people sleep, but everyone needs a break. It's no different for the dead. We enter a sleep-like state where we separate from everything. It's like floating in a safe bubble that only you can get in. I wished Eamon could go to that safe bubble with me.

When I left my safe bubble the next morning, I was lying on the bed next to Eamon. I had gone to his bed every time we felt unsafe when I'd been alive, which had been most of the time. Therefore, waking up next to him seemed normal to me. I didn't remember I was dead until I realized my movements weren't making the bed creak. I didn't have to tiptoe back to my own bed feeling scared. I didn't have to worry about what my punishment would be if I got caught before I made it to my bed.

I had trained myself to wake up early and return to my own bed when I was alive. If our folks caught us in bed together, they screamed that we were filthy mongrels worse than animals. They screamed that brothers and sisters don't lay together. They screamed that lying together was for married people. The worst beating I ever got was when I asked Ma if I was married to Pa since he sometimes laid on my bed; I shook as I remembered that was why she killed me. I had whispered that before she pulled me off Eamon's bed. I remembered being in a lot of pain. I remembered flying into the wall. I remembered lying in the straw unable to move. I remembered seeing Eamon's beautiful blue-gray eye looking through the boards. I remembered being afraid they would see him. I knew he was safely in bed with me, but I jerked my head quickly in his direction to make sure.

My body slowly stopped shaking when I saw his tiny body next to me. He was wrapped in the tattered quilt he slept with every night. MawMaw Tierney made that quilt for him out of her old dresses. She was very fond of the color brown, so it was splattered across the quilt in many different patterns from solid to flowers to gingham. Everyone knew to give her any feed sacks that had brown in their pattern.

My folks had tried to keep the quilt for themselves, but MawMaw Tierney wouldn't hear of it. She made sure my brother had that quilt every time she visited. It was the only thing he owned that was protected. He hugged it so much that it was already becoming threadbare.

A tuft of black hair was sticking out of the top of the quilt cocoon he wrapped himself up in at night. I felt comforted when I saw him wrapped up in that quilt, because it looked like he was giving himself the hugs no one else ever gave him. I leaned over to see his precious face peeking out from between the quilt and the tuft of hair. I began to shake again when I saw his eyes were open and tears were slowly rolling out of them.

I snuggled closer and laid my arm across him. I didn't notice this made him cry harder, because I was shocked by the image of my transparent arm going through his body. When the shock wore off and I realized it, I said, "Shhh, Don't ya be lettin' 'em hear ya cry." I rubbed my hand up and down his back. It was still difficult for me to watch my hand be partly inside his body as I moved it. I kept doing it anyway, because it seemed to calm him.

I heard someone knock on the front door. I knew Pa was going to answer it, because his heavy footsteps caused the floorboards to creak much louder than Ma's tiny feet did.

As soon as I heard hinges creak a signal that the door was opening, Ma yelled, "Who in hell do h'it be?"

"H'it be yer Ma," Pa answered, grunting, before he said, "Bring yer self on in, Tierney."

I heard MawMaw Tierney's light footsteps creaking across the floorboards as she entered the house. "H'it be lookin' like y'all be havin' a bit of a lie-in this mornin'," MawMaw Tierney said as I heard the hinges creak and the door slam shut. "H'it be nearly nine o'clock in the mornin'. Y'all be livin' on city time."

I leaned my head against the wall, so I could hear what they were saying better. I had done this many times before, but this was the first time my head went through the wall. I found my head in the living room, but my body was still on the bed. I wasn't just listening to them; I was watching them.

MawMaw Tierney pulled her thick green shawl off her shoulders as she walked across the room. When I had been little more than a baby, a peddler came through the mountains selling wares. He had green, brown and gray yarn. It was much prettier than the natural color yarns MawMaw Tierney made from her wool. The colors were much brighter than the yarns MawMaw Tierney sometimes dyed from plant dyes. I liked the green, so MawMaw Tierney bought enough to make a matching shawl for both of us even though I knew she would rather have the brown. It took her an entire season to patiently crochet those shawls. I sat with her every time she worked on them. While she crocheted, she told me stories about when she was a young girl. That was the happiest summer of my life.

She folded the shawl and laid it across the back of the bench before she sat down. She looked down at the old gray coffee table that sat in front of her and said, "That there table be lookin' a darn sight better with a cup of coffee on h'it."

"Mabon," Pa yelled as he sat next to MawMaw Tierney. "Ya need to be gittin' yer Ma a cup of coffee. Ya need to be gittin' me one, too."

Ma emerged from behind the curtain that covered their bedroom door. That door was so close to the fireplace that MawMaw Tierney told them time and again they shouldn't have a curtain on it. They didn't listen to her anymore than they listened to anyone. The curtain caught in Ma's arm as she threw the gray shawl MawMaw Tierney had crocheted for her across her shoulders. Ma almost threw the bottom of the curtain into the fire as she got her arm loose from it. MawMaw Tierney gasped when the curtain got near the fire.

"I be gittin' some water to be heatin' now," Ma said as she walked toward the wide kitchen door that opened on the other side of the fireplace.

"Y'all really do be havin' a lie in," MawMaw Tierney said as she watched Ma walk across the room in her long gray and white gingham night gown. "Do everythin' be a'right?"

My folks glanced at each other. I knew the look in their eyes, because I had seen it in my brother's eyes so many times. They were afraid.

They released each other from the glance before Pa said, "Sinead be real sick fer a few days now. We nary be gittin' much sleep these last few nights."

MawMaw Tierney started to get up as she said, "Well, lemme see the poor darlin'."

She was only halfway up when Pa said, "Doc be thinkin' she might be catchin'. The boy be still in bed. H'it be lookin' like he be gittin' h'it, too."

MawMaw Tierney sat back down so fast it looked like her bottom was on springs. She stared at Pa as one eyebrow raised, which was followed by a crinkled forehead. "When do Doc Jones be by?" she asked.

Pa stammered a few times before Ma came out of the kitchen and said, "The water be on the boil. We nary be seein' Doc Jones. We nary be able to be findin' him. She be so bad last night we be gittin' real worrisome. We be takin' her over to Ol' Crow, the ol' Snake Doctor, the Indian Guy."

"He nary be seein' whites," MawMaw Tierney said, surprised. "He nary be talkin' to most of us."

"When he be seein' she be a child and how sick she be, he done see'd her," Ma said so naturally that I almost believed her lie. "He be sayin' we nary be tellin' nobody he be seein' her. He nary be wantin' the whites to be makin' nary habit of comin' to him. So, ya be havin' to be keepin' that a secret." Ma paused for a minute while shaking her head before she said, "I nary be thinkin' many folk be goin' to him no how. We be havin' to pay him ten percent of our crop this year, or he be sayin' they be comin' to git h'it." She shook her head again as she said, "Tisk Tisk." She took a deep breath before she finished by saying, "Ya be thinkin' he be the good Lord hisself, wantin' us to be tithin' to him. Ya be doin' anything when h'it be yer young'uns though."

I watched mesmerized for a good minute. I had never realized Ma was such a good liar. I almost believed I'd been to Ol' Crow myself after listening to that well-spun yarn. When I finally snapped out of her spell, I screamed "Liars!"

I burst the rest of the way through the wall. I stood in the middle of the room, still wearing my blood stained pink floral dress. I expected a reaction. I kept looking from one face to the other when I didn't receive one. I had to remember I was dead. They couldn't see me.

"I cain't believe ya be takin' that child to that dark skin," MawMaw Tierney said. "The poor thing more than likely to be dyin' now."

MawMaw Tierney looked at Pa when he said, "We be prayin' fer the best." He wasn't nearly as good of a liar as Ma. He used the same tone when he discussed the weather.

I ran across the room and stood right in front of MawMaw Tierney. I looked deep in her eyes and yelled, "They be a-lyin'!"

I turned so I could look from face to face. It was obvious no one had heard me. I fell on my knees at MawMaw Tierney's feet. I tried to wrap my arms around her legs like I did every time my folks picked me up from her house, but my arms went right through her. When they did, she looked down at me.

When her eyes caught mine, I yelled, "They be lyin', MawMaw Tierney. They be storyin'. They be tellin' ya stories."

MawMaw Tierney looked back at Pa.

I grabbed for her arm, but my hand went through it. She looked at me again, and I yelled, "MawMaw Tierney, ya gots to be gittin' Eamon outta here! Please!"

MawMaw Tierney's whole body shook like she had been hit with a draft. She scooted away from Pa and leaned on the arm of the bench as she said, "I ought to be takin' Eamon with me before he be catchin' what be ailin' poor Sinead."

"Ma, that nary be a good idea," Ma said in a voice so sweet I was surprised to hear it come out of her mouth. "Eamon done been around her. He likely to be gittin' sick. Ya be an ol' woman. If ya be catchin' whatever they be havin', h'it be likely to be killin' ya."

MawMaw Tierney laughed and said, "Yer house done be filled with h'it. If'n I be gonna git h'it, I be gonna git h'it. The boy be safer at my house. If'n he be with me, y'all can be gittin' some rest. Ya done been up with the girl all night. Lemme be takin' the boy, and we be gittin' outta here before anyone else be gittin' sick."

"We cain't be takin' no chance on gittin' ya sick," Pa said, harshly.

MawMaw Tierney walked toward the curtain that led to Eamon's room as she said, "Quit talkin' nonsense. I be takin' the boy with me. Anybody who be in their right mind be knowin' ya be havin' to keep young'uns away from other sick young'uns."

Pa jumped up from his seat and stood in front of MawMaw Tierney while he said, "Ya be an ol' woman, Tierney. I nary gonna be lettin' ya be killin' yerself."

MawMaw Tierney put her hand on his upper arm and tried to push him out of her way as she said, "Nonsense." When he didn't move, she shrugged and said, "Ya nary be no mountain. I can be walkin 'round ya just as well."

As MawMaw Tierney walked around Pa, Ma ran across the room and blocked MawMaw Tierney's way.

MawMaw Tierney looked right in Ma's eyes and asked, "What in hell be goin' on with y'all this mornin'?"

"I reckon we be havin' to tell her," Ma said as she looked over at Pa.

A look of surprise stole Pa's features for several seconds before he said, "I reckon we do."

MawMaw Tierney looked back at Pa and asked, "What on God's earth do she be talkin' about?"

"Ya best be comin' back over and be sittin' down," Ma said as she took MawMaw Tierney's upper arm in her hand and led her back to the bench. MawMaw Tierney sat down and Ma sat next to her before she said, "We nary be wantin' to be worrying ya. We be knowin' how much ya be lovin' that lil' girl."

MawMaw Tierney clasped the collar of her dress as she asked, "What be happenin'?"

Ma swallowed hard and wiped an imaginary tear from under her eye before she said, "Sinead done wandered off into the woods last night. We nary be findin' her. We be lyin' in this mornin', because we done been out all night lookin' fer her. We not be tellin' Eamon yet. We not be wantin' to worry him. Ya cain't be takin' Eamon with ya or he be knowin' somethin' be wrong."

MawMaw Tierney clutched her collar tighter as she said in a quivering voice, "I be knowin' somethin' be wrong. Them boys of mine be out last night kind of suspicious like. I be knowin', because they be wanderin' 'round our place half drunk in the middle of the night. They be staggerin' 'round with their arms over each other's shoulders, holdin' each other up whilst they be mumblin' about Caelan. I nary be gittin' a straight answer outta neither one of 'em. When I be seein' the red clay on the horses hooves, I be knowin' they done been over this way. I be figurin' somethin' done happened to Caelan. I be right surprised when Caelan be answerin' the door this mornin'"

"They be helpin' us look fer Sinead," Ma said.

"Drunk?" MawMaw Tierney asked, surprised.

"I reckon they be so upset they took to drinkin' after they left," Ma answered.

"Oh, good Lord," MawMaw Tierney said as she started wringing her hands. "Them there boys be wanderin' 'round my place half the night. Why they be leavin' y'all when ya be searchin' fer that child?"

Ma swallowed hard before she said, "They be sayin' we nary be havin' any luck in the dark. They be sayin' they be comin' back by this mornin' to be helpin' us look fer her."

MawMaw Tierney stood up as she said, "They ought to be back here then. I bet them good fer nothin's be lyin in this mornin', too. I be goin' over to their place to be wranglin' them up and settin' them on over here. We gots to be findin' that there child before critters be gittin' her."

MawMaw Tierney picked up her shawl off the back of the bench and wrapped it around her shoulders as she walked toward the front door. She didn't say anything else as she let herself out.

When the door closed behind her, I felt like I lost my breath even though I didn't have a body to breathe with. I always felt safe when she was visiting. I felt safe for Eamon today when she was in the house. Safety was walking off the porch with her, and I couldn't let it get away. I ran through the door.

When I caught up with her, she turned and looked in my direction. Looking toward me didn't even slow her down. She was like a train steaming toward its destination. Every muscle in her body was tense. Her stiff arms moved back and forth in harmony with her legs. She was moving so fast that her salt and pepper hair was starting to come out of its bun and hang around her face. She blew a dangle of hair out of her eyes and kept on moving.

Blowing seemed to release something from inside her. She began to speak rapidly to herself, "Them two be goin' to be killin' them young'uns. Cain't even be keepin' up with that child to be keepin' her safe outta them there woods. They may as well be grindin' her up to be feedin' her to the wild animals theirselves fer all they seem to be carin'. Only God be knowin' why he be choosin' to be givin' young'uns to the likes of them two. Mabon may be my daughter, but she nary be fit to be a Ma." She paused and slowed her pace steadily until she came to a full stop. She looked up in the sky and said, "Good Lord, I just be havin' to be leavin' them young'uns with ya. I nary be thinkin' there be a soul on this here mountain can be helpin' them two."

I didn't walk with her when she started walking again. I stood where she had stopped and watched her bottom bounce off toward the woods. She wasn't going to do anything. She was going to leave it up to God. Too many people on this damn mountain left important things up to God no matter how many times they saw it hadn't helped. People kept telling me that God helps those who help themselves, but as soon as the going got tough, they left it all up to the Man upstairs. I was already over here where they told me God was going to be, and I hadn't seen any sign of Him. Eamon was on his own if I didn't find a way to help him myself.

When I got back to the house, I ran through the wall into Eamon's room. I didn't even have to think about how to run through the wall this time. It just happened. I sat on the bed next to him, hugged my knees and rocked as I tried to think of ways to keep him safe. I sat that way while I heard Ma make breakfast and Pa suck it in like a hog at a feeding trough. A good hour passed before they finished their morning ritual that we were never invited to, and I still hadn't thought of any way to keep Eamon safe.

Just as Ma came into the room to throw a biscuit at Eamon for breakfast, I heard the sound of horse's hoofs riding hard into the front yard. I looked through the wall and saw Buck and Carl rein their horses to a stop and hop off almost as if it were one movement. They ran across the yard and through the front door without knocking.

I changed the wall I was looking through just in time to see Pa jump up and ask, "What in hell y'all be doin' here?"

"Ya lyin' sack of shit," Carl yelled as he ran toward Pa. "Ya done told Ma a big ol' sack of lies that be causin' her to be yankin' us outta bed and boxin' our ears before she be demandin' we be gittin' on over here to be helpin' y'all find Sinead."

"Ya nary be tellin' her nothin', do ya?" Pa asked and then stood there with his mouth hanging open.

"We nary be tellin' her nothin'," Carl answered.

"Well, don't be worryin' about h'it, then. Sit yerself on down and be lettin' Mabon be makin' ya some breakfast. We be figurin' out what we be tellin' her."

"She be on her way over in the buggy. What be yer big plan now?"

"I nary be knowin'," Pa said as he collapsed back into his chair. He just sat there shaking his head back and forth really slow.

Ma came out of the kitchen, wiping her hands on a towel as she walked. She slipped the corner of the towel into her skirt waist and said, "What in hell would y'all men be doin' without us women? Why in hell do ya be thinkin' I done carried Sinead to the woods last night fer? Come on. Ya be needin' to be followin' me."

All three men followed her to the door. Just before they exited, Ma turned to Pa and said, "Ya gots to be stayin' here with Eamon, Ya gots to be makin' sure he nary be sayin' nothin' to Ma when she be gittin' here."

Pa shook his head and went back into the room while Ma and her brothers left.

I followed them onto the front porch and watched them disappear into the woods. They were only out of a sight a few minutes when MawMaw Tierney's buggy pulled into the front yard.

Pa went out onto the porch to meet her.

As she climbed down from the buggy, she asked, "Where do them boys of mine be?"

"They be out lookin' fer Sinead with Mabon," Pa answered.

"Already?" she asked as she walked across the front yard and up the porch steps. "H'it be seemin' like they be just a few steps ahead of me."

"Mabon be already out lookin' fer the child, so they done went out to be joinin' her."

"I hope we be knowin' somethin' soon," MawMaw Tierney said as she walked past Pa and into the house. She walked to the bench and sat down before she said, "A cup of coffee would be right nice."

Pa sighed deep, but he went to the kitchen and made her a cup of coffee with the water Ma had heated that morning. As he was sitting the cup on the table in front of MawMaw Tierney, we all jumped in response to a scream that sounded like a whole pack of coyotes wailing at the same time.

"What do that be?" MawMaw Tierney asked, yelling, as she jumped up and ran to the front porch.

Pa followed her, and I followed Pa. We got outside just as Mabon was walking out of the woods carrying my body. It had been in bad shape when she carried it into the woods, but a night among the wild animals took an even greater toll on it. Mabon was holding it close and screaming like a crazy woman. Halfway across the yard she stumbled and fell to her knees, letting it fall to the ground in front of her.

MawMaw Tierney ran across the yard and fell to her knees on the other side of my body. "Lord, please be helpin' us," she said as she twisted her hands in front of her chest in a manner that made it look like she was praying.

Pa didn't join in on their wailing when he ran across the yard and fell to his knees next to MawMaw Tierney. He just stared at my body, and his breath became very shallow.

I stood behind Pa and looked at my body. I felt like I was split down the middle. One half of me couldn't understand that this had once been mine. The other half was so connected to it that I couldn't understand why I didn't feel the wounds.

After a few minutes, MawMaw Tierney looked at Pa and yelled, "Ya be gittin' a blanket to be coverin' this child with. Nobody be needin' to be seein' her like this!"

Before she could finish her sentence, I heard Eamon gasp behind me. He fell to his knees and started crying.

"Ya be gittin' that damn blanket, NOW!" MawMaw Tierney screamed as Pa struggled to get to his feet.

I ran to Eamon and put my arm around his shoulder. I wasn't sure if he was aware of my presence until I said, "Don't be lookin'; ya needs to be lookin' away," and he obeyed.

My uncles came out of the woods and ran across the yard. Uncle Carl grabbed Eamon and carried him into the house. I followed him as he carried Eamon to his bed and laid him on it. He looked like a giant as he carried my brother's small body, but he looked even more like a giant when he sat on the edge of the bed and tried to comfort Eamon.

Eamon grabbed the corner of his quilt and pulled it over his head. He quickly cocooned himself into the blanket, rolled away from Carl and stared at the wall.

"Git yerself outta here," I yelled at Carl. "I be the only one who can help him."

I guess in moments of deep emotion, the living can still hear us. Uncle Carl got up and left the room. I lay next to Eamon and put my arm across him.

No one bothered us again that day.

CHAPTER FIVE
MABON'S STORY

I laid next to Eamon with my arm through his shoulder as I tried to think of ways to protect him after Pa went to work. Eamon was cocooned in his blanket, but we learned a long time ago how little protection that cocoon offered.

On a typical day, Ma worked Eamon and me just about to death. When Pa wasn't home, she sat and relaxed more than any mountain woman I'd ever met. By the time I was three, I was standing on a chair in the back yard hanging laundry. It was very hard to lift the big things like sheets and blankets, but I learned a long time ago what happened if I dropped them or let them drag the ground. When I thought of all the work Eamon and I did when Pa wasn't around, I became afraid she would try to make Eamon do it all by himself. I was afraid he would be beaten if he couldn't.

When Pa was around, he wouldn't let Ma work us so hard. If she sat down for a minute, he called her a lazy whore and barked orders at her. The morning after MawMaw Tierney had visited, Pa barked orders at Ma even worse than usual. It was his first day back at the mines since Ma killed me, and he was particularly snarly that morning.

I peeked through the wall and saw that Ma was already in the kitchen when Pa came out of the bedroom dressed in a t-shirt and denim pants. He always wore them under his one piece work coveralls when he went to the mines. Ma kept shoveling wood and coal into the belly of the iron cook stove and clanking heavy iron pans on top of it.

Despite the busy noise of preparing his meal, he sat at the table outside the wide kitchen door, stared at Ma and yelled, "Ya needs to be gittin' off'n yer ass and be gittin' me some vittles to et, woman!"

I returned to Eamon's side and listened.

Ma didn't say anything, but the cooking noises seemed to gain speed. A few minutes later, I smelled the food cooking. I knew before I smelled it that she was cooking biscuits, gravy and bacon. That was usually the only thing Pa would eat.

As soon as I heard his plate hit the table, I heard that old man scarfing down food with animal-like grunts and groans that sounded like when he came to my bed and lay with me.

Even my ghost frame shivered from that memory. Eamon must have felt it, because he shivered too. He rolled over in bed and looked into my eyes so intently that I thought he must be able to see me.

I put my hand over his mouth and said, "Don't be sayin' nary a thang. They be sure to be beatin' ya if'n ya do."

I thought Eamon nodded at me. Was it my imagination, or did he see me? Whichever it was, I knew he wasn't going to make any noise. I removed my hand.

When the animal sounds stopped, I heard Pa push his plate away as he yelled, "Ya better be havin' me somethin' to be takin' with me. H'it be a long day down in them there holes."

Ma didn't say anything, but I heard his lunch bucket hit the table. I heard his chair creak, the floor boards creak as his big feet clomped across them, the door opening, the creaking of the porch and its stairs, and the sound of work boots on gravel until Pa was far enough away to take the sound with him. Eamon's body relaxed when the sound disappeared, but he tightened every muscle in his body when Ma's movements made the floor boards creak again.

I could tell by his tight muscles that he was afraid she was coming to pull him out of bed and put him to work like she usually did after Pa left. Eamon and I looked at each other with surprise when we heard her footsteps creak to the front door, across the porch and across the gravel until she was far enough away to take the sound with her. I stuck my head through the outside wall and saw that she was walking toward the barn. She was still in her gray and white gingham nightgown. Her gray shawl was loosely wrapped around her shoulders and was flapping in the wind.

I pulled my head back through the wall, looked at Eamon and said, "She be goin' to the barn. Ya be stayin' here. I be goin' to be seein' what she be up to."

When I said the word barn, Eamon's eyes got wider. I didn't know if he was remembering what happened to me or if he feared for what could happen to him. I was still haunted by the look in his eyes when I got to the other side of the wall, so I stuck my head back through the wall and said, "Nary need fer bein' afeared. H'it gonna be a'right. I be goin' to be findin' out what she be up to. There nary goin' to be more surprises."

He nodded, so I pulled my head back through the wall and began to follow her. I felt my heart rate and breathing quicken even though I no longer had a body. The next thing I knew, I disappeared from where I'd been standing and appeared in the room where I'd lost my life. Was it my heart beating faster that allowed me to do that? Was it the strong emotions I was feeling? I didn't know how it happened.

It made me sad to look around the last room I knew life in. The thought of her walking into this room when I was already here reminded me of the last time I waited for her here. That memory made my non-existent heart beat even faster.

When she got to the door, she stopped. I went to the door to see what she was doing. She reached out and touched the chains that hung from it like they were an animal she was petting. She stood that way for several minutes before she pushed the door open and looked inside.

I held my breath until she whispered, "Sinead."

"What?" I answered, but she gave no sign that she heard me.

"Do I be makin' ya be leavin' yer ghost here?" she whispered and stepped into the room.

All of my life I had been told to be careful about where I left my ghost. I couldn't believe she cared about my ghost now. All of my life she had beaten me, starved me, and allowed Pa to come to my room. In spite of that, she stood in the room where she killed me acting like she cared about what happened to me in the next life.

The only memories I had of my folks showing concern for me was when they tried to warn me about the afterlife. They told me to leave my ghost on the mountain, or I would have an unhappy haunting. They gave me dire warnings about hell while they forced me to live it on earth. They taught me that the only power I had to stop horrible things from happening in my life was to pray about them. They must have believed this, because I never saw either of them try to make any change on their own no matter how much change was needed. All they ever did was pray that change would come, but it never did. Even MawMaw Tierney chose to pray for Eamon instead of taking him to safety just yesterday. Remembering all the dire stories they told me about the afterlife made me shudder when I thought of where the angel would take me if she returned.

"I be reckonin' there be worse places to be leavin' yer ghost," Ma said loud enough to pull me from my thoughts. "Ya could be leavin' h'it in the big city or down in the mines. That would be bad." She walked to the middle of the room and looked around as she said, "There be better places, too."

I didn't want to watch her deal with her own demons when those demons killed me. It was like MawMaw Tierney said when we watched a gossiping crowd gathered around an old man who was thrown from his horse: "H'it be like watchin' a train wreck. Ya cain't be turnin' away till ya done see'd the impact." I couldn't turn away.

Ma knelt by a spot of my blood that hadn't been absorbed by the dirt floor. She touched it with her long bony middle finger. She jerked her finger away like the blood had burned it. She held that hand in her other hand and rocked back and forth like she was rocking an injured child. When she spoke, it seemed like the injured child she was rocking was herself.

"H'it nary be no secret. I nary be lovin' ya, child. How could I be lovin' ya when ya nary be mine. That ol' man be makin' h'it hard fer me to be lovin' my own child. I be swearin' on all that be holy that I nary be meanin' to be killin' ya."

She started sobbing. Her tears were coming so fast that she was unable to speak for several minutes. When the tears slowed, she said, "I just be madder than hell. I be the one what be havin' to be takin' all the shit. Ever body else be gittin' the love. He be lovin' yer Ma so much h'it liked to kilt him when she done went away. He nary be workin' her near to death like he be doin' me. He be buyin' her gifts from that there

34

company store. He be buyin' her store bought dresses and face paint. When his Ma be askin' how he be goin' to be payin' for h'it, he be sayin' the company store could be havin' his soul. He be sayin' they could be livin' in that minin' camp forever if'n that be how long h'it be takin' to be payin' off the bill. Now, she be gone, and I be workin' my ass off to be payin' fer what she done got whilst I be wearin' dresses I be makin' outta feed sacks. The money from sellin' my eggs be goin' to that damn store. The money from my quilts be goin' to that damn store. What do I be havin' to show fer h'it? What do my Eamon be havin' to show fer h'it? Yer Ma be makin' sure we nary be affordin' ya when she be takin' all that stuff from yer Pa. H'it be as much her fault ya be dead as h'it be mine, but I gots to be worryin' about the noose goin' around my neck. She always be the one what be winnin'."

Ma dropped her face into her palms and sobbed so hard that her whole body quaked. Even though she killed me, I was tempted to put my arm across her shoulders and comfort her. I didn't, because I realized she lied even to herself. She didn't gather those eggs or make those quilts. I gathered those eggs. MawMaw Tierney made quilts to keep her from beating me or a dime would have never entered this house on the stitches of a quilt.

Even if I wouldn't have realized she was a liar, I couldn't have comforted her. She taught me in life to stay as far away from her as possible, so I didn't know how to approach her now. I was also too in shock to approach her. The only emotion I thought she had was anger. I didn't know she could feel anything else. This display of emotion was too shocking for me to process.

She cried until her body was so weak from crying that she fell over on her side and curled up in a ball. Her eyes were inches away from my dried-up blood. When she realized that, her tears stopped and her eyes grew wide. She quickly moved to a seated position and scooted backwards until the wall of the barn stopped her. She hugged her knees and stared at the crimson mud that had been born from the mingling of blood and earth.

Her voice was ragged when she said, "Ya nary be knowin' what h'it be like, child. Ever time he be bringin' ya a present, I be knowin' he still be lovin' yer Ma through ya. I be knowin' he nary be treatin' my young'uns as good as he be treatin' ya. I be knowin' he nary be treatin' me as good as he be treatin' ya." Her voice trailed off. She was quiet for a long time before she said, "I be knowin' h'it be wrong when he be comin' to yer bed at night. I be knowin' I ought to be stoppin' him, but I be knowin' he be showin' ya love. I be hearin' him comfortin' ya when ya be cryin' about h'it. I be wishin' I could be so lucky."

Her voice trailed off again. She lowered her forehead to her knees. Her breathing became so shallow that I wasn't sure she was breathing anymore. I was just about to touch her to see if she was still alive when she lifted her head and said, "H'it done happened a few weeks after yer Ma went away."

She leaned her head back against the wall and looked up at the ceiling. Her eyes were glazed. Her body was in the room, but she was seeing something very far away.

"I be walkin' down the Ol' Orchard Road," she said while she looked at the ceiling like it was a movie screen. "I just be a young girl. I be maybe ten years older than ya be now, I mean than ya be when I, well, ya be knowin'." She swallowed hard before she continued. "I be havin' on a new dress Ma done made me outta feed sacks. H'it must a been the pertiest dress I ever be seein'. The flowers on h'it be big and bright red. There be two matchin' feed sacks, so Ma be havin' enough to be puttin' a ruffle along the bottom and around the neck. Ma even be lettin' me be puttin' on some of her red lipstick. She be sayin' that perty red be bringin' out my dark hair and be makin' me be lookin' like a movie star. I be feelin' like an angel. Tryin' to be actin' like an angel be what done got me in trouble when I be runnin' into yer Pa that day.

"Like I be sayin', I be walkin' down the Ol' Orchard Road. Yer Pa be sittin' on a big rock under that giant oak, ya know, the one what be sittin' right up next to the road. He be cryin'. I be startin' to walk on by, but I done stopped to be askin' him what he be cryin' fer. He be sayin' he done lost his precious Ruby.

"I be thinkin' he be sad, because losin' a ruby be makin' someone poor again. I be knowin' how awful h'it be to be poor, so my heart just be wellin' up with sadness fer him. I be sittin' on that rock next to him and be taking his hand. I be tellin' him h'it be a'right. I be tellin' him the good Lord be takin' care of him even if he nary be havin' his rubies no more.

"He be sayin' how perty I be before he be reachin' up and touchin' my cheek with his fingers. He be runnin' his thumb across my red lips. He be tellin' me how his Ruby done had red lips. That when I be knowin' Ruby be a name. I be tryin' to be gittin' up. I be feelin' like I be needin' to be gittin' away from him.

"He be grabbin' my arm and be tellin' me nary to be leavin'. He be strong. I nary be leavin' then no matter how bad I be wantin' to. He be wrappin' his other arm around my shoulders and be pullin' me close to him. He be puttin' his big lips on my red lipstick. I be tryin' to be pushin' him away with my free hand, but he be kissin' me so hard. I barely be breathin'. How I be movin' his big ol' body when I done be outta breath? The more I be fightin' him, the harder he be kissin' me. My lips and cheeks be hurtin' he be kissin' so hard."

She took a deep breath before she continued. "He be pullin' me closer to him. He be wrappin' his arms around me so tight I be feelin' like a caged animal. When he finally be pullin' his lips off a-mine, I be smellin' booze. I reckon I be tastin' booze all along, but I be so a'feared I nary be understandin' that till then. I nearly be throwin' up the smell be so strong. I be feelin' weak. I nearly be swoonin'. When my body done gone weak, he be layin' me on the ground. I be feelin' his weight be layin' on top of me. My strength be comin' back, so I be tryin' to fight. I just be so short and tiny, and he be so tall and strong. Once he be on me, there be no gittin' him off me."

She broke away from her view of the ceiling and looked at the spot of blood on the floor again before she said, "I reckon ya be knowin' how that be feelin'."

She crawled to the spot like a cowering dog. She stayed on all fours while she stared into the blood like it was a crystal ball and said, "Crazy as h'it be soundin', my next thought be of my dress. He be gonna ruin my new dress rollin' me 'round in the dirt like that. The red flowers be on white material. The kind of stains he be makin' nary wash outta white. When he be yankin' the bottom of my dress up by the ruffle, I be thinkin' he better not be tearin' that ruffle as hard as Ma done worked to be puttin' h'it on there. I still be thinkin' about my dress when he be raisin' h'it up and unzippin' his breeches. I still be thinkin' about my dress when he be pullin' his hard snake out of his pants. I be thinkin' he be gonna piss on my dress and really ruin h'it.

I'd a been fightin' harder if I be knowin' he be gonna push my underpants outta the way to be forcin' that big ol' piece of meat into my private parts."

She began to pant, and this really made her look like a cowering dog. She sat on her lower legs and clutched her hands to her chest as she rocked herself. After a while, she rose to her feet and started pacing back and forth next to the blood. She looked like the tiger that had paced by the bars of his cage when the traveling circus passed through town. Just before she knelt next to the blood again, she began to fan her face with an open hand.

She fell so hard when she knelt next to the blood that I expected to see skinned knees when she stood up again. She leaned closer to the blood and whispered, "I nary be feelin' so much pain before. I be feelin' like I be about ripped in two. I be thinkin' I be screamin', but I nary be sure. All of me be held prisoner by that pain. H'it be happenin' fer so long I be thinkin' I be gonna die. When h'it be endin', I nary be sure h'it be over. I be feelin' like I nary be in my body anymore. I be feelin' like I be standin' next to my body watchin' him be doin' this to me.

"When he be rollin' off'n me, he be layin' next to me just pantin' like a dawg. I be too afraid to be movin'. I just be layin' there listenin' to his heavy breathin' slowly be comin' back to normal. When h'it did, he done looked at me and said, 'Ya nary be my Ruby. Who do ya be?' I be gittin' up and runnin' away.

"Ma done see'd somethin' be wrong whilst I still be on the road. Before I be gittin' to our property, she be runnin' across our yard. As soon as she be gittin' to me, she be kneelin' in front of me and askin', 'What be happenin' to ya, child?'

"I be knowin' her comforts nary be lastin' long when I be seein' Pa be walkin' up behind her. When he be gittin' about halfway to where we be, I be hearin' him yell, 'What in hell be goin' on got ever' one runnin' 'round like a bunch a crazy people?'

"Ma be gittin' up and standin' next to me with her arm across my shoulder. She be lookin' down at the ground instead of lookin' at Pa.

"Pa be stoppin' fer a spell and lookin' at me before he come runnin' at me screamin', 'Ya be ruinin' that perty dress yer Ma be workin' so hard on.' He be grabbin' my arm and draggin' me toward the big oak tree in our front yard. The whole way he be screamin', 'Ya be gittin' on up here and breakin' off a switch from that there tree.'

"I done been through enough that day, so I be tryin' to run away from him. Whilst I be runnin' away, Ma be grabbin' his arm and sayin', 'Let her be. We nary be knowin' what be happenin' to the child.'

"Pa be wrestlin' his arm away from Ma and pushin' her to the ground. Whilst she be tryin' to git up, he be chasin' me down and grabbin' my wrist just like Caelan had done. He be draggin' me toward the tree whilst he be orderin' me to be breakin' off a switch. I be feelin' like I be out of my body again, so I be doin' what I be told.

"When I be handin' him the switch, he be pullin' my skirt up and hittin' my arse and the back of my legs with h'it. He be hittin' me several times before he be noticin' the blood streamin' down between my legs.

"I must a been outside my body. I be swearin' I be seein' him drop the switch and stagger away from me, but I be facin' away from him. My eyes be fillin' with tears. His eyes be growin' big, and his mouth be fallin' wide open. He be yellin', "That be yer womanhood rollin' down between yer legs. Ya be rollin' in the dirt like a bitch in heat in that beautiful dress yer Ma be workin' so hard to be makin' fer ya.

"I nary be rememberin' what be happenin' next. I reckon I done told 'em enough fer 'em to be knowin' h'it be Caelan what be doin' that to me. The next thing I be knowin', we be standin' in front of Preacher Skaggs gittin' married."

She sighed a broken sigh that revealed the tears she was trying to hold in before they began to spill down her cheeks. Her body quaked with the tears that were so strong she was unable to speak for several minutes. When her tears slowed, she wiped her eyes and nose on the sleeve of her nightgown before she said, "That be the worst day of my life. The day they be forcin' me to be marryin' Caelan be even worse than the day he be rapin' me. I be knowin' as I be standin' there answerin' the preacher the way I done been told to be answerin' him that my life be nary better than my Ma's life done been.

"My Ma be dreamin' that I be havin' a better life than she done had. She be makin' me perty dresses, because she be wantin' me to be perty enough to be findin' a good husband. She nary be wantin' me to be marryin' a man like my Pa. She be wantin' me to at least be peaceful even if'n I nary be happy. She be tellin' me to be marryin' a man like her brother. She be tellin' me he be proof that not all men be like my Pa and my brothers.

"I be understandin' fer the first time why that be her dream fer me. I be wantin' to be throwin' up I be feelin' so sick from the thought of spendin' my life bein' trapped in the same house with the man what done raped me. I be knowin' he nary be better than Pa. I be knowin' my life gonna be hell from here.

"I be feelin' a rage like I never be feelin' before whilst I be standin' in front of that preacher. I be seein' clear that bein' like my Pa and my brothers be the only way to be safe in this here world. I be knowin' from that moment on that I cain't be lettin' nobody else be matterin' above myself, not even my children."

She stood up and started walking around the spot of blood. She walked like she was trying to outrun the memories. When she finally stopped, she spat on the blood before she said, "So, I be stuck with a man who be lovin' another woman who be long gone whilst she be leavin' me with her young'un. I be stuck with the bills he be makin' buyin' fer both a ya. All I be gittin' be that ol' bastard ridin' me ever night like he did on the Ol' Orchard Road. I be gittin' him slappin' me when I cain't be gittin' his breakfast on the table fast enough. He be doin' that even when I be laborin' to bring forth the child he done put in my belly. Now, I prob'ly be gittin' the noose fer all my troubles. The only thing I be havin' to look forward to be the day Caelan be dyin' and leavin' me alone like Pa done left Ma alone. Ever' one be sayin' how Ma's life be gittin' better since Pa done died and she be movin' in with Uncle Teagan" She paused for several seconds and sighed deep before she said, "H'it just not be happenin' fast enough. H'it prob'ly nary be matterin' anyhow. My brothers done been ruin't by Pa. I nary be havin' a kind-hearted brother like Ma be havin' in Teagan. My brothers be just like Pa. I reckon there nary be escapin' this wicked ol' mountain fer me."

She wiped the tears off her cheeks with her dirty palms, leaving streaks of dirt across her face, as she said, "The only thing I be missin' about ya be the times when ya be givin' my body a rest from bein' pounded into the mattress."

As she stared at the spot of blood with the hard face and cold eyes I was used to, I felt pity for her. A part of me understood why this young woman already looked old. She hadn't looked so old when she had softened her features to tell her story to the blood. I was just about to forgive her for what she had done to me until she stormed out of the barn saying, "God only be knowin' what that thing he done put in my belly be gittin' up to whilst I be out here."

I thought about Eamon with all of my heart. I learned that was one key to taking me immediately to another place, because I was transported to his bed where I thought he would be. He was not there. I moved through the wall into the main part of the house. He was not there. I looked around frantically. I was again surprised by how fast my heart could beat and my breath could come in my ghost body. My ghost organs seemed to function on emotion. I heard a noise in the kitchen and ran to it. Eamon was standing on Pa's chair in front of the hot iron cook stove that still had a fire burning inside it. My fear that he would get burned was quickly forgotten when I saw he was dunking a biscuit in gravy that sat in a pan on top of the stove.

"Hurry," I yelled. "She be beatin' ya fer stealin' if'n she be catchin' ya."

He shoved half the biscuit in his mouth and dunked the other half in the gravy again. As he finished the last half of the biscuit, we heard Ma's footsteps on the porch. He stopped chewing and looked at me with scared eyes.

"Swallow h'it before she sees h'it."

He was chewing really fast when the front door opened. I thought "Stop" so loud that the word echoed in my head. The door slammed shut on her. She screamed my name and ran off the porch.

"Ya needs to be gittin' yerself to yer room!"

Eamon was cocooned in his blanket and faking sleep before Ma found the courage to open the door again. When I heard her open it, I giggled. I guess she had the answer to the question she asked in the barn. Now she knew where she left my ghost, and I would use her fear to protect Eamon any time I found the power to do so.

She went to the kitchen, picked up a biscuit and carried it to Eamon's bed like she always did. She usually barked a list of work at him while he ate whatever morsel she gave him for breakfast. Today,

41

she threw the biscuit at him and walked out of the room. He didn't pick it up off the quilt and start eating it until the curtain closed behind her.

I peeked through the wall and saw that she was sitting on the bench in front of the fireplace. She had wrapped her gray shawl around her shoulders and was staring at the fire. Long after it burned out, I stuck my head through the wall again. She was still sitting there. It looked like she hadn't moved all day.

CHAPTER SIX
LOVE???

Eamon stayed in bed all day. Maybe he didn't know what to do when he wasn't being worked like an old mule. Maybe he was grieving my death. Maybe he was in shock from what parts of my murder he'd seen. Maybe he was already worn out at three years old. I lay next to him all day. I didn't see any reason to leave him. After all, he was the reason I stayed here instead of going with the angel.

I was lying on the mattress next to Eamon when I heard the porch steps creak, followed by the familiar creaking of Pa clomping across the porch, stopping outside the front door, taking off his coveralls and laying them across the porch railing, taking off his hardhat and boots and putting them under the bench that extended the length of the porch, his bare feet leaving the porch and shuffling across the gravel, the hand pump splashing water as he rinsed his hands and face, and the returning steps to the house. Even though I didn't have a heart anymore, I felt it beat faster. I hated to hear him come home. I hated Ma, too, but it was easier to be with one crazy person than two.

I looked at Eamon. He stared at me from inside his cocoon. His eyes were wide with fear. I always suspected he felt the same way about Pa coming home, and now I knew he did. I hovered a little above the mattress, so I could lay my arm across him without it going through him. My touch, or whatever it was my ghost body offered, seemed to comfort him. His eyes became less wide, but his muscles remained tight.

I felt a sensation like my own muscles were tightening when I heard Pa returning from the pump, but I didn't understand how my ghost body could do that anymore than I understood how my heart rate and breathing could still quicken. The sensation grew worse as I listened to the creak continue up the steps, across the porch, and in the hinges of the front door.

The hinges sounded like the hinges on Grandpa's coffin when the preacher closed the lid: a slow steady creak that ended with the thud of pine hitting pine. That sound was followed by the family mumbling praise to the box for locking the old man's hatred away for eternity. I understood the mumbling, because every time our door thudded against the frame, our folks' hatred was locked inside the house with us.

My thoughts became louder than the creaking. Would I have a pine box? Would I have a funeral? Would they tell people I was dead? I wanted people to know I was dead, but I didn't want them to spend money on a tombstone when Eamon needed food. Where we left our ghost was not the only example of the afterlife being more important than the living. The extravagance of funerals was an example my empty stomach had resented many times, but what can you expect from people who believe the only life that matters is the next one? I didn't want my tombstone to make Eamon know that resentment. I guess it didn't really matter though. Even if they saved the funeral money, it was doubtful Eamon would get any attention until his own funeral expenses demanded it.

I heard the sound of pine hitting pine when the door slammed closed. I heard it as clearly as the day they took my Grandpa out of here for the last time. Eamon and I both sat up, and our muscles tensed even more. I pushed my head through the wall and saw Pa. His back was using the door to prop him up. He took a big gulp from the quart of moonshine he held in his right hand. As he screwed the lid back on, I pulled my head back into Eamon's room and whispered, "Lay down!"

Eamon glanced at me through wide eyes for only a second before he lay back on the mattress. I lay next to him and put my arm across him. Fear caused our breathing to accelerate, and I soon realized my breath was keeping time with Eamon's. I wondered if our heartbeats were beating in accelerated unison as well.

"Close yer eyes," I whispered, and he obeyed.

The creaking of the floor boards got louder as Pa got closer to our room. Our breathing got faster and our muscles got tighter with each step. When we saw Pa's hand pulling the curtain back, Eamon held his breath and his body began to shake. The shaking subsided a little when our Pa walked across the room and sat on my bed.

I always hated when Pa came to my bed after work. He smelled of coal dust and sweat. Sometimes, like tonight, he even smelled of alcohol. Since his presence alone made it hard for me not to vomit, those smells only made it worse. On the other hand, concentrating on not vomiting was often the only thing that helped me survive those visits. It gave me something else to think about.

He sat on the edge of my bed, rested his elbows on his muscular knees that looked like they threatened to burst through the fabric of his denim pants, and dropped his head onto his palms. His head dropped so quickly it looked like it was not attached and he had to catch it to keep it from falling to the floor.

"Sinead," he whispered before he started crying.

Eamon and I both lay still and silent as we listened to the old man say, "I nary be knowin' why things always be goin' to shit. I nary be meanin' fer ya to be dyin'. Ya be knowin' ya be my baby; my girl. I be lovin' ya more than the rest of them. I nary be believin' I cain't be holdin' ya again. I nary be knowin' how I gonna be draggin' myself through life if'n I never be havin' ya to be comin' home to." He rubbed one palm across my mattress while the other palm continued to support his head. As he rubbed the mattress, he said, "I nary be believin' I cain't be lyin' next to ya again."

I gagged. I felt like I was going to throw up, but I didn't have a body to accommodate that need. I wondered how I kept feeling these sensations when I didn't have a body anymore.

Pa cried for a long time before he said, "I ought to of stopped her." He rocked back and forth as he said the same thing several more times.

As he chanted those horrible words, I wondered who was going to stop him. All of the times he beat my brother raced through my mind. Rage rose up in my chest so strong that my ghost heart began to beat

45

faster and faster and faster. I felt like I would choke on breaths I no longer needed. I felt like my heart would jump out of the chest I didn't have anymore. I hated that old man more for hitting Eamon than I hated Ma for killing me. I flew across the room with my hands positioned to grab his throat. I just knew I could choke him to death if I thought hard enough about it. Instead, I hit him so hard that I went through his body and then the wall behind him. I was halfway to the chicken coop in the back yard before I stopped.

I thought myself back to Eamon's bed. As I sat on the bed, I realized Pa felt something when I went through him. He was no longer rocking and was looking around the room. His eyes were wide, his skin looked clammy, and his chest was rising and falling fast.

He got up and walked across the room. I jumped up and stood between him and Eamon, but he didn't come that far. He disappeared through the curtain that covered Eamon's door. Creaking – out into the main room, past the fire place, and past the curtain that covered the door to his room. Creaking – as he sat on his bed. The bed creaking, creaking, creaking. It was like this old house was an arthritic old man who was begging to be put out of his misery.

The bed kept creaking and creaking and creaking. That was the sound my bed used to make when he came to me. I thought I was holding back a tear, but then I realized it couldn't flow from my ghost body.

I looked at Eamon, and his wide eyes were staring at me from his cocoon. "Shhh," I said. "Lay back and try to sleep. H'it gonna be a'right."

When Eamon closed his eyes, I lay back and snuggled next to him. We both lay there and listened to the creak, creak, creak. When it used to happen to me, it felt like it would never end. Now, it sounded like it would never end. I lay next to Eamon and listened to the sound as I thought, 'Ya be gettin' what ya be deservin', ya ol' bitch."

CHAPTER SEVEN
WHAT'S THE PLAN?

Early the next morning I heard the steps on the front porch creak. I peeked my head through the wall. Night was trying to turn into day, and the air was crisp and clean in a way that it can only be at this hour of a late autumn to early winter morning.

MawMaw Tierney and her brother, Uncle Teagan, were walking up the porch steps. MawMaw Tierney was wrapped in her shawl, as always, but Uncle Teagan barely looked prepared for the weather in his flannel shirt and overalls. This impression of being unprepared for the weather was magnified by him not wearing the canvas cap he usually wore. Uncle Teagan knocked on the door.

While they waited for an answer, MawMaw Tierney said, "I nary be believin' the good Lord done give'd them two young'uns. They nary be takin' right care of theirselves much less young'uns. Who on God's earth be lettin' a child that small be wanderin' off to the woods alone?"

"Ya nary be knowin' with them two," Uncle Teagan said as he shook his full head of salt and pepper hair.

MawMaw Tierney began to adjust her weight from one foot to the other as she said, "I reckon they be havin' a lie in again. I reckon Eamon gonna be the next one to be wanderin' off to the woods whilst they be lyin' in the bed."

Uncle Teagan knocked again, harder.

I heard our folks bed creak and Pa say, "Who the shit that be at this hour of the mornin'?" I heard the bed creak again, and then the floor boards. When it sounded like Pa was about halfway across the front room, Uncle Teagan started beating on the door long and hard.

I heard the hinges creak as Pa opened the door. "What the shit be so important?" I heard him ask before he came through the door enough to be in my view. He leaned on the door frame and stared hard into Uncle Teagan's eyes.

"My sister here be tellin' me about what done happened yesterday," Uncle Teagan said. "We be here to be seein' how y'all be doin'."

Pa wiped his hair away from his face and said, "I reckon we be doin' about as good as we can be doin'. H'it be takin' a real toll on us. H'it be right helpful if y'all be comin' back later."

Pa started to close the door, but Uncle Teagan grabbed the door and said, "That be why we be comin' by. We done figured y'all be havin' a hard time of h'it. We reckon if'n we be takin' Eamon home with us that be givin' y'all one less thing to be worryin' about till this be over."

Pa's posture stiffened as he said, "What that be to ya? H'it ain't yers to be tellin' me how to be takin' care of my own."

MawMaw Tierney and Uncle Teagan looked at each other. Both of their eyebrows crinkled before MawMaw Tierney said, "We nary be tryin' to be tellin' ya how to be raisin' yer own. We just be tryin' to be givin' y'all a lil' help. Y'all be goin' through quite a lot these past few days."

Uncle Teagan tried to push the door open again as he said, "We just be tryin' to be neighborly, especially since y'all be family."

Pa pushed the door back with shaking hands and said, "Ya nary be takin' our child outta this here house, ya hear me? We done lost one child this week. Ya be thinkin' h'it gonna be sittin' right with Mabon if'n y'all be takin' the other one. He bein' a comfort to his Ma right now."

"We be thinkin' h'it might be good fer Eamon to be gittin' outta here fer a while," Uncle Teagan said as he placed his hand on Pa's shoulder.

Pa jumped when Uncle Teagan's hand touched him. This gave MawMaw Tierney a chance to push the door open and get in the house. As she walked through the door, she said, "With what that child done had to be seein'; the look on his face yesterday when Mabon be carryin' Sinead outta them there woods? He nary be needin' to be seein' y'all be grievin' too."

"Mabon, ya needs to be gittin' yerself on out here and be controllin' yer Ma," Pa screamed as I moved my head through the main room wall, so I could keep watching.

Ma was wrapping the gray shawl around her shoulders as she came through the curtain that separated their room from the main room. "What be goin' on out here?" she asked.

"I wanna be takin' Eamon home with me fer a few days," MawMaw Tierney said.

Ma looked at Pa with a quizzical look on her face before she said, "I think we can be takin' care of our boy just fine."

"If'n ya nary be lettin' us be takin' him with us," Uncle Teagan said, "at least be lettin' me be gittin' the Doc on over here to be takin' a look at him and be makin' sure he be a'right. My sister here be tellin' me she just about swooned when she done see'd what them animals done to poor Sinead. The boy must be feelin' mighty worrisome about now."

Ma and Pa both looked at each other, their eyes getting big. I'd seen big eyes too many times in my short life. I knew that meant they were afraid. They both spoke at the same time.

Ma said, "The last thing we be needin' right now be strangers traipsin' 'round in our business." She stopped and looked at Pa when she realized he was saying, "Mays be ya ought to be takin' the boy. I be thinkin' h'it prob'ly be a'right if he be goin' with y'all." He lay his hand on Ma's back and pushed her toward the door of Eamon's room as he said, "Mabon, I reckon ya ought to be makin' sure the boy be ready fer a few days with his MawMaw."

The house overflowed with the sound of creaking as Ma's feet walked toward Eamon's room and Pa led MawMaw Tierney and Uncle Teagan out of the house and across the creaky porch.

I pulled my head back into Eamon's room and sat next to him. Ma sat on the other side of him when she entered the room. He scooted away from her before her bottom hit the mattress.

"Ya needs to be sittin' next to me, Eamon," she said as she patted where a little bit of straw stuck out of the mattress next to her.

Eamon's eyes got full-moon big. He hesitated before he moved a little closer to her, but not as close as she wanted. There was a huge space between them, and it looked like that space was filled with the emotions both of them felt and could never express. Those emotions seemed to bounce between the two of them like they were trapped there.

I understood why those emotions were trapped between them. Eamon sat quivering in the same clothes he wore all week. He was so skinny that the belt he wore through the unbroken belt loops could barely hold his pants above his hips. The two belt loops that needed to be sewn weren't helping that matter. Ma, on the other hand, sat next to him wearing a new gown she made out of the last feed sack she got. Her gown was clean and pressed just like the dozen other gowns and dresses she made for herself. Mabon could have made a shirt for Eamon or sewn the belt loops on his pants instead of making herself yet another gown. Instead, she made more clothes for herself while she complained that she didn't have store bought dresses like Ruby had.

I suddenly realized I thought of her as Mabon. I didn't think of her as Ma anymore. She wasn't a big powerful woman. As she sat next to Eamon with her shoulders stooped and fear in her eyes, she seemed pitiful like the old mangy dogs Eamon often fed from his own sparse food. I realized I didn't think of Caelan as Pa anymore either. I thought of him as the monster who drowned one of those mangy dogs in a bucket while he made Eamon watch. I shook my head hard, but shaking my head didn't shake out the confusion or the memories.

I couldn't stand sitting this close to her, so I moved to my bed—the bed Caelan sat on and cried the night before. I didn't think about Caelan for long, because I saw Eamon jump when I materialized. When I realized he saw me, I ran my hands up and down my arms and legs to see if I was human again. I was still a ghost. I put my index finger over my lips and whispered, "Shh!".

"What do h'it be?" Mabon asked as she looked over toward my bed.

"Nary a thing," Eamon said. His voice was barely a whisper. The hoarseness of that whisper made me realize how rarely he talked. Those vocal chords weren't used to being used.

Eamon continued to stare at me when Mabon turned back to him and said, "Do ya be knowin' what done happened to Sinead?"

50

I shook my head no, and Eamon's head began to move with mine.

The fear left Mabon's eyes, and she sat up a bit straighter. I realized she had no remorse. She was only afraid of getting caught.

"She done wandered off into the woods," Mabon said. "The wild critters be gittin' to her before we be findin' her."

I nodded my head, and Eamon nodded his head with me.

"If anybody be askin', ya be makin' sure to be tellin' 'em about the wild critters. Ya be understandin'?"

I nodded, and Eamon's head moved with mine again.

"That be right good," Mabon said as she stood up. "Makes sure ya be rememberin' to be tellin' that to anybody what asks." She stopped halfway to the door and said, "If'n ya be knowin' what be good fer ya?"

I nodded, and Eamon nodded with me again.

"That be right good," Mabon said before she walked out the door.

I moved back to Eamon's side. He stared at me as I asked, "Can ya be seein' me?"

He started to say yes, but I put my fingers over his mouth. It was still odd to see my fingers go through his mouth when I didn't gauge the distance right. In spite of that shock, I said, "Nary be answerin' me, or they be hearin' ya. Just be shakin' yer head. Can ya be hearin' me?"

He nodded.

I scooted closer to him. I was surprised when I couldn't feel his shoulder touch mine like when we were alive. Instead, I felt something similar to ants crawling on my legs. I wondered if that's what MawMaw Tierney felt the day I touched her right after I died.

"I be stayin' and takin' care of ya," I said as I put my arm over his shoulder, but it didn't bring him any comfort. As soon as my arm was around him, we heard the floorboards creak again. This time it was the heavy creaking of Caelan's boots, and his feet were moving a lot faster than usual.

I learned at a young age that there are different kinds of fear. There is the low, simmering, never-ending fear that rises up when you hear the house creak and wonder who is moving and if they are going to harm you. That fear doesn't go away even when the house isn't creaking. Even in your sleep, you're listening for the creaks to start again. That fear is nothing compared to the high-pitched, panicked, heart-beating-in-your-ears fear that begins when you realize the creaks are heading in your direction. That fear is the same whether it's happening to you or someone you care about. The physical pain makes it harder when it is you, but the fear is the same. I felt that fear as I watched Caelan burst through the curtain and grab Eamon by the ear.

Caelan bent over and put his huge sneering face in front of Eamon's pint-sized face and whispered, "Sinead be dead. We be buryin' her soon." When he moved his face away from Eamon's face, he took his belt off. He bounced it off his hand like Mabon bounced a stick off her hand the night she killed me as he said, "Ya nary be sayin' nothin' whilst ya be at yer MawMaws. Do ya be understandin' me?"

Eamon nodded as he looked up at the towering tree that bounced a belt off its hand.

"If'n ya be sayin' a word, this belt be 'round yer backside when ya be gittin' home. Ya be understandin'?"

Eamon nodded again.

Caelan grabbed Eamon's arm and started to hit his backside for good measure. The only thing that saved Eamon was the sound of the porch steps creaking.

"H'it be that damn Tierney again," Caelan said as he let go of Eamon's arm and walked out of the room while he put his belt back on.

The sound of the creaking was overwhelming. The front porch was creaking in unison with Caelan's steps as he walked toward the front door.

I stood next to Eamon and said, "Nary be peein'. They be beatin' ya if'n ya pee."

He sat down on the bed, crossed his legs and held them tight together. He rocked back and forth, and I saw clammy sweat forming on his skin.

The sound of the footsteps stopped, and the creak of the front door followed.

"What ya be wantin' now?" I heard Caelan say, snapping.

"Do Eamon be ready to go?" I heard MawMaw Tierney ask.

"Mabon be right," I heard Caelan answer. "He nary be havin' no clean clothes. We done been so busy with Sinead."

"That be fine," I heard MawMaw Tierney say before she yelled, "Eamon, ya needs to be comin' on now. H'it be time to go."

As the soft creak of Eamon's tiny feet moved toward the front door, I heard MawMaw Tierney say, "I be havin' some feed sacks at the house. I be happy to be makin' the boy a shirt or two. I be believin' I be havin' some denim pants left from when my boys was lil'. If'n they nary be good or nary be fittin', we can be gittin' him a pair at the comp'ny store."

When Eamon got to the door, MawMaw Tierney grabbed his hand and said, "Ya needs to be comin' on, young'un. We needs to be gittin' ya outta here, so yer folks can be gittin' to work. They be havin' a lot to do today."

I followed MawMaw Tierney and Eamon to the hand pump where Uncle Teagan was waiting. As MawMaw Tierney approached Uncle Teagan, she said, "I nary be believin' a word of h'it. At least the boy be safe fer a while with us."

"What ya be thinkin' done happened with Sinead?" Uncle Teagan asked.

MawMaw Tierney looked down at Eamon and said, "We can be talkin' about h'it when we done got this lil' one to his MawMaw's house."

I knew Eamon would be safe with them. Since I knew he was safe, I wanted to see what our folks were going to do with my body. I wanted to see if they were going to get caught. So, I walked beside Eamon as I said, "I be goin' back to our house fer a while. Nary be a'feared without me. I be comin' over to MawMaws real soon."

He nodded, and I thought myself back to the main room.

Mabon was standing there in her new nightgown with her gray shawl wrapped tightly around her in a way that made it look like she was hugging herself. I didn't know she knew how to hug. The gray in the shawl reflected off her face and made her look old and colorless.

Caelan stood in front of her, scratching his head as he asked, "Do ya reckon that boy be knowin' what done happened?"

"I nary reckon he do," Mabon said. "He be in the house fast asleep when h'it done happened. He nary be knowin' more than the rest of 'em. He just be seein' her comin' outta the woods tore up by critters."

"Ya be sure?" Caelan asked.

"Ya needs to be stoppin' yer frettin', ol' Man. I nary be as ignorant as ya be thinkin' I be. I be knowin' that sickness story nary be holdin'

53

water. That be why I be takin' her to the woods in the first place. I be knowin' the critters be tearin' her up. Once that be done, no one cain't be holdin' nothin' over us nary more. H'it be over. Now we be havin' to be gittin' that child in the ground and be leavin' this whole nasty mess behind us."

Caelan paced back and forth as he said, "I reckon we be owin' h'it to the child to be lettin' her have a proper burial. We nary be wantin' her to be leavin' her ghost here. I be buildin' a box fer her today. Tomorrow be Sunday mornin'. We be buryin' her nice and proper after services whilst ever'body be in their Sunday best."

CHAPTER EIGHT
CAELAN'S STORY

I followed Caelan to the barn. I didn't want to stay in the house with Mabon since Eamon wasn't in there needing me to protect him. Besides, I didn't want to hear that old bitch go on and on about how horrible life was for her like she always did when Caelan wasn't around. If she knew what horrible felt like, she shouldn't be able to pass it on to others so easily. Didn't she realize she treated Eamon and me worse than she was treated? Caelan seemed like the lesser of two evils, so I chose the barn.

When I got to the barn, I was surprised by what I saw. Caelan had planks in the barn, because he was building a gun rack for himself. He felled a tree last fall and planked the wood with great care over the winter. He used the same care constructing the gun rack during the summer months. Mabon said many times that he loved that gun rack more than he loved any of us. Apparently that wasn't true. When I got to the barn, he was disassembling it. This wasn't an easy job, because he had dovetailed the wood. I watched as he measured and cut the wood to the size needed for my small coffin.

As he worked, he cried. He was already sweating so badly that it was difficult to tell which drops were tears and which drops were sweat. He was so engrossed in his work that he didn't even wipe the sweat off his brow. He just kept letting the mingling of drops flow down his face, frequently blinking his eyes when a drop of sweat rolled down his eyelid.

"I be so sorry, Sinead," he said as he cut the boards. "I ought to of stopped her. I ought to of took her to the sheriff. I ought to of told what she be doin'." He continued to cut the wood even though he stopped talking for a long time before he said, "Eamon be needin' hisself a Ma." He paused again before he said, "I reckon I be needin' myself a wife." He paused for a very long time before he said, "A part of me be wantin' to be seein' her swing from the highest tree." His next pause was very brief before he blurted out, "I nary be wantin' to be swingin' alongside her. That be what be happenin' if'n I be tellin' – unless her brothers be killin' me first."

He worked the entire time he talked. It seemed woodworking was automatic for him. He seemed to know how to put the pieces together without thinking about it.

"I be lovin' yer Ma , Sinead," he said in a tone that made me wonder if he was trying to convince me or himself. "She be the only thing I ever be lovin'. She be the only thing ever be makin' me be feelin' somethin', exceptin' ya, child. I nary be marryin' Mabon if'n her Pa nary be sportin' a shotgun on our weddin' day."

He stopped working. He looked around the barn like he'd forgotten where he was. His confusion momentarily dried his tears. Once he got his bearings, he laid the saw on the ground and knelt next to the pile of wood that would become my coffin. He laid his hand on one of the planks and stared at the pile like the coffin was already made and he was looking into it at my body.

He started crying again as he said. "Sinead, I surely do be lovin' yer Ma. Ya gotta be believin' me. I nary be meanin' her harm. Ma be tellin' me to never be marryin' no whore. She be sayin' that marryin' a whore be bringin' me to my ruin. I nary be able to be listenin' to my Ma. I be lovin' yer Ma so much I be thinkin' about her all the time. She be the only lady 'round these parts. She be wearin' store bought dresses and silk stockin's and high heels. She be the only lady 'round these parts what be keepin' her hair curled around her face instead of pullin' h'it back in a bun. Most of the buns on this here mountain be so tight they be pullin' faces right outta their smiles. Yer Ma's face be smilin' all the time. Them smiles be makin' her eyes like light. Them eyes be lookin' like they be havin' candles lit behind 'em. I nary be seein' no woman be smilin' that way before. She be puttin' red rouge on them lips of hers and I be like a spider in her web. Red rouge next to black curls and blue eyes be too temptin' fer any man. Nary a man be resistin' her. She be lookin' like heaven.

"Ma be sayin' that be a trick to be gittin' men's money, but I nary be believin' her. Ma be a whore, and she nary be lookin' a thing like my Ruby. Ma be takin' down her bun when men be comin' 'round, but her hair just be hangin' long and limp. H'it be lookin' as tired as she be lookin'. When she be smilin' fer the men, her jowls still be stiff. Her eyes still be dead. I done been raised by a whore. I be knowin' what a whore be lookin' like. I be knowin' yer Ma nary be one."

Caelan stopped crying. I saw a light in his eyes for the first time as he told a story about Ma. "Besides, no whore be fightin' to be keepin' me from kissin' her lips like yer Ma done. I be havin' to chase her 'round a tree first time I be kissin' her. I be seein' her hands feelin' that trunk while she be dancin' 'round that tree, and h'it be feelin' like them hands be on me. I about catch fire. Her curls be bouncin' each time she be peekin' 'round that trunk to be seein' if'n I still be chasin' her. Her eyes be bright like the sun. When I be a-ponderin them sun-shinin' eyes, I be comin' to realize that be the first time I ever be playin'. I be comin' to realize that be the first time I ever be laughin'. I be likin' how h'it be feelin'. I be comin' to realize a woman what be givin' me such gifts be my woman fer life.

"Ever time I be seein' other men 'round her, I be desirin' her more. I be wantin' to be takin' her away from them men and be makin' her mine. First time I be seein' her with another man, I be gittin' so hot I be beatin' him near to death. That be makin' her mad. She not be talkin' to me fer weeks. Them be the longest weeks of my life. I be knowin' I has to be gittin' her back. I nary be survivin' bein' apart from her. I be sneakin' 'round behind trees and watchin' her comin's and goin's.

"I done see'd her kissin' a man fer buyin' her a present. I be headin' straight away to the company store and puttin' a perty dress on account. I be wrappin' h'it nice in a feed sack Ma been savin' fer herself and tyin' field flowers to h'it with a length of Ma's yarn. My heart just be a-racin' when I be knockin' on her door. Her Ma be makin' me feel right ashamed when she be askin' me why I done came straight from work, because runnin' to her house done made me sweaty. When Ruby be comin' to the door, she nary be givin' h'it no never-mind. She be seein' the package and be sayin', 'Fer me!' I be forgiven. She be comin' with me to a clearin' in the woods. I be thinkin' she gonna be kissin' me in that clearin'. It nary be that easy with yer Ma.

"She be makin' me wait another week to be kissin' her. H'it be a beautiful summer day the next week. The sun be a-shinin' between branches that be makin' a roof over our heads. I be hearin' birds a-singin' in them branches. H'it be so perfect nary a bug be pesterin' us.

"I done put a bottle of toilet water on my store account. The bottle be so perty. She be holdin' her hand out fer her gift, and I be puttin' the bottle on h'it. She be stretchin' her perty neck like a struttin' rooster when she be sprayin' that toilet water on the place where ya can be seein' the heart a-beatin'. My breath be catchin' when I be seein' her heart a-beatin'. I just about be swoonin' when she be puttin' them rouge red lips on my cheek to be thankin' me."

Caelan sighed deep before he said, "When we be meetin' in that clearin' the next week, h'it be just before a rain storm. Ever thing be cold, damp and spooky lookin'. The sun be shinin' between branches in a strange yella color. I be knowin' a storm be comin' before the birds stop chirpin'. I done put a heart necklace on account fer her that week. When I be givin' h'it to her, she be givin' h'it right back. I nary know what to be thinkin' till she be turnin' her back to me and liftin' up her curls. I be touchin' her skin whilst I be puttin' that necklace on her. The softness pert near be makin' me fall to my knees. I be plum weak when she be turnin' 'round and puttin' them rouge lips on mine. She be pullin' away so fast I nary be havin' time to be puttin' my arms 'round her, but I always be rememberin' them few seconds.

"Sudden like, the sky be growin' dark. We be lookin' up and seein' clouds rollin' in fast. Rain be startin' to fall. She be grabbin' my hand and leadin' me through the woods towards home. H'it be a good thing she be leadin' me. The only thing I be knowin' be her touch.

"Fall be in the air when we be meetin' the next week. Ruby be wearin' a beautiful red sweater. H'it be lookin' so good next to her rouge lips. I done put a music box on account that week. Her eyes be lightin' up like the sun when she be openin' it. When she be puttin' her rouge lips on mine to be thankin' me, I be forgettin' to breathe. She be stayin' just long enough fer me to be puttin' my arms around her. My man part be comin' alive and makin' me pull away from her. I be feelin' my face turn red, and she be gigglin'. Her laugh be soundin' like this circus man what done come to our mountain and played music on water glasses. She be puttin' her rouge lips on mine again, and I be feelin' her tongue go in my mouth. I nary be pullin' my man parts away this time. I be pressin' them against her. I be wantin' to be throwin' her on the ground and be takin' her right there, but I be a'feared. Mays be she nary be talkin' to me like when I done beat up her suitor if'n I be doin' that. She be endin' the kiss all of the sudden and remindin' me we nary be married. She be sayin' she must be actin' like a lady.

"We be doin' this fer weeks. Each gift I be puttin' on account be gittin' me a lil' further. I be feelin' the best I ever be feelin' in my life. Ever thing be good. I nary be havin' no good in my life before, so I be doin' anything to keep this good feelin'. I be feelin' like I be floatin' on a cloud. I be feelin' so good I can even turn bad into good.

"Ruby be sittin' on a rock just a-cryin' when I be gittin' to the clearin' the next week. I be squattin' down in front of her to be askin' what be the matter. She be tellin' me a bump be formin' in her belly. Her Pa done put h'it there. Her Ma be seein' h'it and done throwed her out.

"I be offerin' to be marryin' her. She be sayin' she nary be wantin' to be livin' with Ma so long as Ma be the town whore. I be tellin' her ever' one gonna be knowin' what be goin' on over to her house if'n she not be marryin' me. She be agreein'. Maybe she be marryin' me, because she be lovin' me. Maybe she be marryin' me to be protectin' her Pa. Maybe she be marryin' me because my minin' job can git us a place of our own. I don't rightly know. All I be knowin' is she nary be wantin' to be livin' in the comp'ny housin'. She be sayin' h'it be too close to her Pa.

"Ol' Man Sitwell done worked out a deal to be lettin' us have this here place. He nary be havin' young'uns to be leavin' h'it to, so he be givin' h'it to us to be keepin' h'it from goin' to ruin. He be gettin' old and nary be able to be workin' h'it like he used to. We just have to be takin' care of him and the property until he be passin' on. I nary be rightly sure why he be makin' such a deal, because he done up and died a few days later. Maybe he be doin' h'it because he done knowed he be dying, and he be wantin' the place bein' proper cared for. Maybe

59

he done h'it, because I heared tell Ruby be some kind of relation to him. Maybe he be knowin' what her Pa be doin' to her. Maybe he be wantin' to be doin' that to her hisself. I reckon I don't rightly know what he be thinkin'. All I be knowin' is that him and Ruby be makin' me happier than I ever be. I be so happy I nary be able to be imaginin' something as awful as livin' here with a hateful creature like Mabon some day.

"We done got ourselves married. We be doin' things on our weddin' night what be makin' me feel better than I ever be feelin' before. Them things be seemin' to be makin' the light go out in Ruby's eyes. H'it be seemin' like her blue eyes done gone gray that very night. Maybe what we be doin' be makin' her think of her Pa. She be startin' to look like ever' other woman on this here mountain, exceptin' she still be havin' dark curls and rouge lips. I be lovin' her all the same. I nary be fergittin' what h'it be lookin' like when the light be in her blue eyes. I be hopin' h'it be comin' back.

"One night I be comin' home from work and findin' yer Ma sittin' in the back yard in a pool of blood. I be fallin' down beside her and wrappin' my arms 'round her. I be wishin' I nary be needin' to be askin' what be wrong. She be tellin' me she done gone and kilt the abomination what be inside her. She say my Ma done teach'ed her how to be makin' the concoction that be takin' away the babies. She be feelin' glad h'it done the job. My Ma be makin' her afeared when she be sayin' no whore be havin' young'uns if'n h'it be workin' ever time. I just be feelin' glad that she still be livin'. I be seein' whores be dyin' from the concoction all my life.

"H'it nary be matterin' how many presents I be puttin' on account. The light in her eyes done be burned out. H'it nary be comin' back. H'it be rare fer me to be feelin' pleasure with her like I done feeled the first night we be married. I nary be feelin' heat from her no more like I done feeled in the clearin'. H'it be feelin' like she nary be there when I be takin' a husband's due. Carryin' ya in her belly nary be bringin' the light back. Holdin' ya in her arms nary be bringin' the light back. Lookin' fer that light be the only thing be keepin' me lovin' her even after she be denyin' me a husband's due.

"I be comin' home one night many months after ya be born'ed, and I be seein' the light in her eyes again. I be so happy. I be thinkin' this be a sign she be comin' back to me. I be tryin' to pull her into my arms,

60

but she be pullin' away. I be hopin' she be comin' back to me even though she not be wantin' my touch. My hope be stayin' strong – til I be seein' the perty things I not be buyin' fer her. One day she be wearin' a perty dress; one day she be wearin' a new necklace; one day she be havin' new baubles hangin' from her ears. I be feelin' the heat risin' up in me. She be my wife. I be havin' certain rights.

"I be tellin' my foreman I be sick the next day, so I can be comin' home early. I be hearin' her a-gigglin' whilst I be walkin' toward the house. I be havin' a sick feelin' in my gut whilst I be walkin' toward the bedroom. I be right to be havin' a sick feelin'. I be pullin' the curtain back and findin' her rollin' around on our bed with a stout man I nary be seein' before.

"I nary be seein' red till she be pullin' the quilt up to be hidin' her body from me, her husband, when she be showin' h'it freely to this stranger. The next time I be seein' something other than red, they both be dead. I nary be knowin' what done happened, but I be knowin' I done h'it. I be the only one there. I must be the one what done h'it.

"I be sittin' on the mattress rockin' her in my arms. I be beggin' her not to be leavin' me. Whilst I be beggin', I be comin' to realize she done leaved me a long time ago. Knowin' that be givin' me the strength to be wrappin' her body up in the quilt and gittin' rid of h'it. If'n anybody be hearin' the shots way out here, they be thinkin' somebody be huntin'.

I be carryin' her body to our ol' mule and tyin' her on h'it's back. I be wrappin' the man in some burlap and draggin' him out to the mule. H'it be takin' ever thing I be havin' to hoist his fat body onto that poor stumblin' animal. I be stickin' a shovel between 'em and leadin' the mule into the forest. The moon be a sliver in the sky, so I nary be worryin' about anybody seein' me before I be gittin' 'em in the ground.

"I be burnin' any cloth with blood on h'it as soon as I be gittin' back to the house. I be scrubbin' the floor and the wall with lye. No one be any the wiser when I be goin' to the sheriff askin' him to help me be findin' my missin' wife.

"Fortune be shinin' on me. Many people be seein' her runnin' 'round with that there fat man. Ever body be thinkin' she be runnin' off with him. That be the end of that."

He stared at the wall of the barn for a long time before he said, "Nary a soul would a been the wiser, except'in one night I be lettin' my anger be gittin' the better of me. I be tellin' Mabon she better be treatin' ya nicer, or I be killin' her like I done kilt yer Ma. She be knowin', and she be the type to be tellin'. That be makin' me more afeared than them fat brothers of hers. If'n any of this be gittin' out, I be swingin' right next to Mabon."

He shook his head violently like he was trying to escape the memories. He picked up a piece of the wood and held it in his arms like he was holding a baby and said, "Don't be thinkin' this be meanin' I nary be lovin' ya. Surely ya be knowin' I be lovin' ya. I be puttin' all the love I be havin' fer yer Ma into ya after she done died. I be buyin' ya presents like I done fer her. I be buyin' ya that dress you be wearin' the night Mabon done killed ya."

Even though the tears came even heavier at that moment, he got up, picked up the saw, and began to work on my coffin again as he talked. His work remained perfect even though he began to work faster and harder the more he spoke. He worked as he told his story like he was weaving his words into the wood, so he could leave them there and not be burdened by them anymore. He worked at his increased pace for so long that his flannel shirt slowly became soaked with sweat. He stopped working long enough to take the shirt off and throw it across what was left of the gun rack. Before he went back to work, he placed his left hand over his right shoulder and rubbed it as he stretched that side of his back like a cat stretching. He shook out his arm several times before he picked up his saw again.

"This arm nary stops a-painin' me," he said as he returned to his work. "I nary be havin' a Pa to be protectin' me. Ma be havin' a lot of men comin' 'round all the time. She nary be tellin' me no lies. I be knowin' they be comin' to lie with her fer money. Most of 'em be ignorin' me. One or two of 'em be nice to me. Some be downright cruel.

I be rememberin' this one man what used to be comin' 'round to be seein' Ma . He be big as a bull. He be a foot taller than Ma and twice as wide. He be wide in the chest and narrow in the butt. He be lookin' like a bull. He be snortin' like a bull, too. I be hearin' him snortin' when he be layin' on top of Ma. He be snortin' like that all the time though. He be takin' a dislike to me straight away, and he be makin' sure I be knowin' h'it. He be startin' by sayin' mean things to me. Then, he be takin' to slappin' me. When he be seein' Ma be lettin' him be slappin' me, he be takin' to beatin' me. H'it be seemin' like he be takin' his belt off ever time he be comin' 'round. One night I be tryin' to be runnin' from him. He be chasin' me into the barn. He be too big to be catchin' me, so he be puttin' a pitchfork in my back to be stoppin' me from runnin'. I nary be rememberin' the pain at all. All I be rememberin' be the sounds of my screams and him just a-laughin'. Some folks be sayin' he be my Pa and that be why he be treatin' me so bad. I surely be hopin' h'it nary be true. I nary be wantin' to be his blood. He be givin' Ma extra money that night on the promise that she nary be tellin'. No one ever be speakin' a word about h'it. Ever time this shoulder starts a-painin' me, I be seein' his face."

He shook his arm a couple of times before he said, "I reckon I be like Ma. She be lettin' him hurt me, and I be lettin' Mabon hurt ya."

At that moment, I hated him and loved him at the same time. I floated across the barn and lay my hand on the pitchfork scar that was on his back. As I placed my hand on it, I realized I should have noticed it before. It was so big it was painful to look at. You could see where the four huge tines had not only gone into his back but had sliced down his back from just above his shoulder blade to just below it. The wounds had healed in a way that made the white scars look like they were still festering. I rubbed my hand up and down the scars even though I knew he could not feel it to get any comfort from it.

As I rubbed my hand up and down his back, he began to tell more of his story. "Not ever body be as cruel as that man be. He nary be horrible just to me. He be horrible to Ma, too. I be seein' him slap her lots of times. One time he be beatin' her so bad she nary be able to be seein' other men fer three days. He be the worst of 'em.

"Some of the men be good men. There be this man what be comin' by ever Sunday after church. His name be Ol' Todd. He nary be bad. He be bringin' eggs and a bacon slab ever week. He be havin' Ma be fryin' h'it up fer all of us and not just fer hisself like the others be doin'. I be delightin' in Sunday. That be the one day I be knowin' there be a good meal. There be eggs and thick slices of bacon cut off the slab and fried up crispy the way he be preferable to 'em. I be preferable to 'em that way, too. Ma be cuttin' off thick slabs of bread and be toastin' 'em over the fire before she be puttin' thick pats of butter on 'em. He even be bringin' jelly fer our toast at Christmas. That be the best present we ever be gittin'. After we done et, Ma be sendin' me off to play. They be goin' back to her bedroom. He always be comin' out and be playin' with me fer a spell before he be a-leavin'.

"When he be gittin' to know me right good, he be startin' to hug me like a Pa be huggin' his boy. One day when we be a-standin' in the barn, he be startin' to kiss my face like Ma be doin' when she be drunk. He be kissin' my forehead and my cheeks and my eyes. H'it be feelin' real good. The next week he be kissin' me on my lips. I be likin' him real good. After a few weeks, we be goin' straight away to the barn. He be kissin' my cheeks. He be kissin' my eyes. He be kissin' my lips. Then, he be tellin' me to be takin' off all my clothes. I be doin' like he be tellin' me to be doin'. I only be feelin' shy when he be takin' his clothes off, too. I nary be seein' another man neck'ed. I nary be feelin' shy no more when he be touchin' me more soft and tender than I ever be touched. Ever thing be feelin' good till he be pushin' me down on my knees and kneelin' behind me. I soon be feelin' a pain what be tearin' through my back side. I be tryin' to git away from him fer the first time since I be meetin' him. He be stoppin' what he be doin' and be pullin' me back to him. He be runnin' gentle fingers up and down my back and be sayin', 'H'it be a'right, boy. I just be showin' ya how much I be carin' fer ya.' H'it nary be hurtin' so bad when he be startin' again. I be lettin' him be doin' h'it. I be thinkin' about how good his gentle touches be feelin' to be gittin' me through h'it. Just before he be gittin' done, he be doin' that real hard and fast. H'it be hurtin' bad then, but h'it be over before I be havin' time to be gittin' away. Before he be puttin' his clothes on, he be pullin' me to my feet. He be kissin' my forehead and my cheeks and my eyes and my lips. He be tellin' me what a good boy I be. No one ever be tellin' me that before. I be smilin' at him. He be given' Ma more money before he be leavin'. He be givin' us enough money fer us to be eatin' ever day that week even after Ma be buyin' her whiskey.

"From then on we just be goin' straight away to the barn after we done et our breakfast. H'it be hurtin' less ever time. I be startin' to like the way h'it be feelin'. He be doin' other things what be feelin' real good. He be wrappin' his hand around my manhood and movin' h'it up and down till I be feelin' the most glorious feelin'. Sometimes he be doin' that with his mouth. That be feelin' even better. He be teachin' me how to be doin' that to him. I nary be likin' that much, but I be growin' accustomed to h'it. I be gittin' so used to h'it, I be doin' h'it before he be askin' me to. That be makin' him like me best. He be stoppin' botherin' with Ma at all. I be growin' to love him. He nary be mean like the others. I be lookin' forward to him comin'. We always be havin' bacon and eggs and bread slathered with butter when he be comin'. He always be nice to me, and we always be havin' food from Sunday to Sunday when he be comin' 'round."

When Caelan stopped talking, I realized I had stopped rubbing the scar on his back when I got interested in the story. I started rubbing again, and he said, "But that just be a-tellin' ya about the nicest and the meanest men. They be all kinds comin' 'round all the time. They be black men and white men; mean men and nice men; drunk men and sober men; preachers and heathens. It nary be matterin' to Ma so long as they be havin' coin with 'em. When the concoction nary be workin', we be gittin' us a new babe. All us young'uns be sittin' outside watchin' 'em come and dreamin' about which one we be wantin' to be our Pa." Caelan shook his head hard without stopping his work and said, "That just be how things be back then. Ya young'uns nary be gittin' how good y'all be havin' h'it."

I held the hand that rubbed his scar in front of my face and stared at it. I couldn't put it back on him, because I couldn't decide if I loved him or hated him. I couldn't decide if I felt pity for him or felt like the man who hurt his back probably was his Pa since they were so alike.

He didn't slow his work pace, but he stopped talking for a long time. He only had the floor of the coffin finished when he stopped talking, and he had all four sides secured to the floor before he started talking again. By that time, his hair was wet with sweat. Sweat and tears both covered his face and his thin, muscular chest. The hair on his chest was as wet as the hair on his head, and the legs of his jeans were starting to cling to his skin in dark spots of sweat.

When he put the last nail in to secure the sides to the floor, he stopped working, stared at the box and said, "I nary be believin' my baby be goin' to be layin' in this here box." The tears began to flow so quickly down his cheeks that they looked like the water coming out of the spigot as he said, "My baby ought to be layin' next to me. She ought not be layin' in some box. She ought to be layin' next to me."

CHAPTER NINE
WHEN THEY LAID ME TO REST

When nightfall came, I sat on Eamon's bed all alone. I wasn't sure where else to go. I had tried to go to MawMaw Tierney's house after Caelan finished my coffin, but I had a hard time passing our property line. I hadn't yet figured out how to go that far away, so I came home and sat on Eamon's bed. I sure did miss him. I imagined he was missing me in much the same way since Mabon killed me. I sure felt bad for him having to feel that grief.

I stuck my head through the wall when I heard Caelan's footsteps creak into the house and across the floorboards. I watched him lift his shotgun from the pegs above the fireplace. When he left the house, I stuck my head through the front wall and watched him walk over to where my body was laying under the porch. He grabbed the edge of the shawl my body was wrapped in and pulled it toward him. He laid the shotgun on top of my body before he picked my body up, cradled it in his arms like I was a living baby and walked to the barn.

Mabon must have heard what he was doing, because she ran out the front door and followed him. She walked a few steps behind him in a flurry like a mad hen as she asked, "What ya be doin'? Her face be half gone. Nobody gonna be wantin' to be seein' that."

"I be puttin' her in that there box and nailin' the lid shut. If'n any body be tryin' to pry that lid open to be sayin' their goodbyes, we be tellin' 'em she done had the spots. Nobody be pryin' that there lid open then. They be too afeared of the spots. I don't reckon h'it be goin' that far. I be thinkin' the smell be makin' 'em afeared to be takin' them nails out."

As I followed Caelan to the barn, I wondered if people's fear of the spots would scare them away from my body. Every few years children on this mountain got the little red spots on them that spread easily to other children. Enough children died that everyone feared the spots, so his plan would probably work. It made me sad to think no one would know how I really died.

Caelan laid my body in the coffin he prepared for me. I was happy to see my body wrapped in the shawl MawMaw Tierney made for me. Without another moment's attention to my body, he picked up the lid that was propped against the side of my coffin. My body disappeared when he laid the lid on top. He quickly and efficiently hammered nails all the way around the lid.

"What we be doin' now?" Mabon asked as he hammered in the last nail. She was still dancing around like a mad hen and wringing her hands as she did.

"We be takin' her to the family graveyard in the mornin' while ever body be at church. We be coverin' her with ground before Preacher Skaggs be slowin' down on flappin' his pie hole. We might just be gettin' done before people be sniffin' 'round. Ya be knowin' how Preacher Skaggs be lovin' to be looked at. He nary be quittin' preachin' before he be losin' the last person's notice."

"H'it be almost mornin' now," Mabon said.

"I be gittin' on over to the graveyard and startin' to dig the hole," he said. "Ya be makin' sure nobody be gittin' near that there box."

"What if'n the church folk be gittin' there before we be gittin' done?" Mabon asked.

"Stop a-worryin', woman," Caelan said as he walked over to the wall and pulled a shovel off the nail it hung from. "Ya nary be goin' to swing. I done told ya what we be goin' to do. If'n they be gittin' there before we be done, we be goin' to tell 'em she done had the spots. Stop yer frettin'. Ya nary be goin' to swing." He paused for several seconds before he said, "But ya ought to."

I watched Caelan be swallowed by the night when he exited the barn door. It was as dark out there as it was in that sealed up coffin. I hoped that didn't escape his notice as I listened to his feet tromp across the gravel and dead leaves that littered the yard. When I could no longer hear his footsteps, I turned back to Mabon.

She was lying in the hay, staring at the coffin as if she were afraid to go to sleep. I wanted to toss some things around and scare her into the plot next to where I would soon be lying, but I was afraid Eamon would be blamed for anything that was amiss when Caelan returned. It wasn't beyond them to blame him for something that happened when he wasn't even around. If that happened, they might drag him back here sooner than they otherwise would. He deserved better than that. So, I sat on the other side of the barn and watched her. She stared at the coffin the entire time Caelan was gone.

It was mid-morning before Caelan returned from digging the hole. As he walked into the barn, Mabon jumped up and said, "Church be gittin' out in a hour."

"I be knowin' that, woman," Caelan said as he walked to my coffin without even looking at her. "That be why ya be quititn' yer jawin' and start workin'." He placed his hands under the head end of the coffin and said, "Ya be liftin' her feet, woman. That end be lighter. Ya ought to be able to be carryin' h'it."

Mabon jumped and obeyed like a dog who'd been kicked too many times and kept coming back for more. Within seconds, they were loading my coffin onto the wagon, which was parked in its usual place by the wall opposite where the tools hung. On this particular day, that meant the wall opposite my coffin. Mabon lay the foot of the coffin on the back of the wagon, and Caelan gave it a firm push. It slid onto the wagon.

"Ya be gittin' the mule," Caelan snapped as he tied the coffin onto the back of the wagon.

Mabon once again jumped and obeyed like a boot-shy dog. She returned with the mule in tow before Caelan had the coffin secured. He grabbed the reins out of her hand so hard that the mule reared. He pulled the mule back to the ground and led it to the front of the wagon with the efficiency most people reserve for things that are not living.

As Caelan secured the mule, he said, "If'n we be headin' over to the graveyard lookin' like we be grave diggers, people be goin' to wonder. Ya be gittin' on in that there house and be gittin' on yer Sunday best." Mabon looked like a drop of water dancing on a hot frying pan as she ran toward the house. She didn't lose any momentum when Caelan yelled, "And be quick about h'it."

Mabon was back in her best dress and hat before Caelan finished securing the mule. She often complained that Caelan never bought for her like he did my real Ma, but she certainly didn't do without. All of the feed sack material went to her, and when she got a hankering for something, she went to the company store and put it on Caelan's account herself. That is how she got the dress she was wearing when she came out of the house.

She looked like a Hollywood starlet sauntering up behind Caelan. The V-neck of her dress was trimmed with ivory lace. The big ribbon that went around the drop waist and tied in a bow on the right side of her hip was ivory satin. The hem had a second layer of ivory lace that was dragging the ground and would be ruined by the graveyard clay, and that combination of fabrics certainly couldn't be washed on a scrub board. The ivory-colored pill box hat she wore only made her look older than she was. The netting that hung over her forehead didn't do a thing to ease that affect.

It was obvious she threw that fancy dress and hat on since her hair was still in a bun, her face was still dirty with tears, and her worn out granny boots looked like they were hanging onto her feet for dear life. Her red lipstick only emphasized the need for make-up to cover her ash-gray skin tone. That lipstick was probably my real Ma's.

If Caelan hadn't been in too much of a hurry to notice, he would have smacked the stuffing out of her for wearing it. Instead, he glanced at her while he secured the final buckles and said, "That ought to be doin' just fine."

She grimaced at him before she stopped sauntering and started walking like the mountain woman she was.

When the last buckle was secured, Caelan said, "Ya be leadin' this here mule out to the front of the house. I be gittin' my suit on whilst ya be doin' that."

As I watched Mabon struggle to get the mule moving, I heard Caelan at the spigot hurriedly splashing water. When I followed Mabon out of the barn, he was cleaning his body at a pace that explained the frenzied sound of the water. He shook water out of his hair as he ran toward the house instead of taking the time to dry himself. As soon as Mabon stopped the mule at the porch steps, he ran out of the house wearing his best funeral suit and black top hat. He hopped on the passenger seat of the wagon and yelled, "Ya be gittin' this here animal a-movin'. We be runnin' outta time."

I followed the wagon as Mabon drove it down our road. About halfway down our road, I moved to the wagon and sat on my coffin. Mabon and Caelan sat so stiff and rigid on the wagon seat that they looked like stone figures. It looked unnatural when Mabon moved her arms to direct the mule.

To my great surprise, I was able to cross the property line. Since I hadn't been able to the day before, I assumed I would fall off the wagon when we crossed it. Maybe it was being with my body. Maybe it was being with the family. Maybe it was being on the wagon. Or, maybe I was just learning more the longer I was dead.

We had to drive onto the main road to get to the other corner of our property where the family graveyard entrance was. This place was chosen because it was not good for farming. The flat areas where plots could be dug were surrounded by rocky terrain on all sides except the entrance. There was no way to get a coffin, even a small one like mine, across that terrain to come in the back way. If someone tried, they would probably get bitten by a rattlesnake. Unfortunately for them, we passed the church on the other side of the main road before we got to the family graveyard entrance.

When we passed the church, Mabon's body became less stiff as she said, "Thanks be to God. They still be a-singin'." She shook the reins and clucked, but it didn't look like the mule moved any faster.

My position on the coffin faced the church, so I saw the entire congregation turn and look out the front window as the wagon went by. The music stopped seconds later. Before it stopped, the hustle and bustle of people gathering their things started. The whole congregation was soon down the steps and walking behind the wagon. MawMaw Tierney and Uncle Teagan were leading the crowd.

Eamon was in between MawMaw Tierney and Uncle Teagan. Each of them held one of his hands. They walked so fast that Eamon was stumbling, but he managed to keep up. I was happy to see he had on a new pair of denim pants and a green gingham dress shirt for church. MawMaw Tierney must have made the shirt out of a feed sack. His

70

color was better too. He probably had a good breakfast that morning for a change. I winked at him, and he smiled.

MawMaw Tierney's land shared a property line with ours. The property line was only a short distance past the church, and the family cemetery was split down the middle by it. I heard one of MawMaw Tierney's cows moo before I saw them grazing in the graveyard as they usually were. MawMaw Tierney liked to keep the graveyard well-tended, and she believed the cows kept the weeds from over-running the place.

Mabon steered the mule to the wooden gate. Before the wagon came to a complete stop, Caelan jumped off and opened the gate. He held it open while Mabon steered the wagon in.

While Caelon closed the gate, Preacher Skaggs yelled, "Howdy, Brother Teague." Preacher Skaggs laughed before he asked, "I know ya be closin' that there gate to be keepin' them there cows in, but do ya be thinkin' ya could be lettin' Jesus' lambs in before ya be closin' h'it?"

Caelan looked at Mabon and pointed toward the hole he dug. Mabon clucked and shook the reins, and the mule pulled the wagon to the desired destination.

I knew the look on Caelan's face. If he hadn't been in the company of a preacher, he would have thrown his hat on the ground, kicked it and commenced to cussing a book. Since the preacher was present, he forced his expression into a smile and said, "I nary be sure if'n that be a good idea, Preacher Skaggs. We be tryin' to be gittin' the child to ground before another body be catchin' the spots."

As soon as the words "the spots" came out of his mouth, the congregation gasped and stopped walking. Only MawMaw Tierney and Uncle Teagan, with Eamon in between them, continued their journey toward the gate.

When they reached Caelan, Uncle Teagan asked, "Why ya be tellin' folks that there child done died of the spots."

"Mabon nary be wantin' nobody to be knowin' how bad a shape that child's body be in," he whispered as he nodded toward Eamon. "We done nailed the coffin up, and Mabon nary be wantin' nobody to be pushin' to open h'it up to be sayin' their goodbyes."

"That prob'ly be best," MawMaw Tierney whispered. "H'it be best fer the young'uns."

71

Uncle Teagan and MawMaw Tierney walked back to the crowd as Uncle Teagan said loud enough for them all to hear, "H'it be best if'n we not be exposin' the young'uns to the spots. We gonna be lettin' Caelon and Mabon be doin' what they be needin' to be doin'."

Preacher Skaggs ignored Uncle Teagan and approached the gate. As I watched him walking toward Caelan, I noticed that MawMaw Tierney and Uncle Teagan were whispering to each other. They were masking their words behind cupped hands. I moved closer to them, so I could hear what they were saying. I got there just as MawMaw Tierney whispered, "Not in front of Eamon." The conversation ended.

I moved back to the hole where my body would be laid to rest. I looked around and realized my body would forever be sandwiched between MawMaw Tierney's and Caelan's land with the church sitting just a little ways down on the other side of the main road. There didn't seem to be any escaping this mountain. There would forever be violence on one side of me, frustrated love that couldn't save us on the other side, and hypocrites singing about it just across the main road.

When Preacher Skaggs reached Caelan, he patted Caelan hard on the back before he lay his arm across Caelan's shoulders and said, "We just cain't be lettin' y'all be sendin' this here child off with nobody standin' by ya. Ya be needin' yer congregation now more than ya ever be needin' h'it." Preacher Skaggs grasped Caelan's forearm and led him through the gate.

It seemed like Caelan was momentarily mesmerized by Preacher Skaggs like rats get mesmerized by snakes, but Caelan snapped out of it when they got on the other side of the gate. He stopped walking and stiffened his body so tight that it could no longer be led. He turned toward Preacher Skaggs, which forced the preacher's arm off his shoulder. When they were looking eye to eye, Caelan said, "Ya surely do be right, Preacher. This be one of the hardest things we ever be goin' through, but h'it be our Christian duty to be makin' sure no other body be gittin' the spots. We cain't be layin' some other poor body to rest next Sunday. We cain't be makin' no other Ma and Pa be feelin' like we be feelin' about now."

"I surely do be understandin'. I surely do," Preacher Skaggs said. "That be truly righteous of ya. How about if'n the congregation just be standin' here at the gate and singin' a few to be sendin' her on."

"That be right neighborly of ya," Caelan said. He stepped away from Preacher Skaggs and said, "I reckon folks ought not be 'round us since we done prepared the body. I be goin' to git on over to the hole so as not to be gittin' close to nobody."

"That be a right fine idear," Preacher Skaggs said as he backed away from Caelan.

When Caelan turned to walk toward the hole, Preacher Skaggs hurried out of the graveyard and closed the gate behind him. Caelan quickened his pace and was at the graveside in a matter of seconds. He picked up two ropes that were lying next to my coffin in the wagon and stretched them out side by side next to the hole.

When Caelan started to pull the coffin off the wagon, Preacher Skaggs yelled, "Brother Teague! Caelan! Wait a minute, will y'all?" Caelan turned to face Preacher Skaggs. Preacher Skaggs pulled something out of his pocket and said, "I done got me a new camera, brother. I be sellin' that ol' Bellows and be buyin' me a Retina 118. H'it be the most newfangled thang. H'it be fittin' right in my jacket pocket." Preacher Skaggs patted his pocket and continued, "I be thinkin' I ought to be gittin' a picture of y'all next to the coffin. H'it be givin' yer family somethin' to be rememberin' this day by since y'all nary be gittin' to be havin' a service."

"I reckon that be why he all the time be beggin' folks to be givin' tithes," Caelan mumbled. Mabon nodded while Caelan turned back to the coffin as he yelled. "Ya be givin' me time to be gittin' her off'n the wagon."

Caelan pulled the coffin until the foot of it was at the edge of the wagon. Mabon grabbed the foot end, and they carried it to the side of the grave and sat it on the ropes.

"Be this a good time?" Preacher Skaggs yelled as he began to walk toward them.

When Preacher Skaggs got halfway to the coffin, Caelan stepped in front of it and yelled, "That be far enough, Preacher – fer yer own well bein'."

Preacher Skaggs stopped. He held the camera up to his eye and said, "I cain't be gittin' the coffin in the picture when ya be standin' in front of h'it, Brother Teague. Ya be gittin' on one side of h'it and Mabon be gittin' on the other. That be givin' y'all a real nice picture fer ya and yer family."

Mabon immediately moved to the left side of my coffin and Caelan ambled to the right side.

Preacher Skaggs was still looking through the camera when he said, "I cain't quite seem to be gittin' y'all in this here picture. Y'all needs to be kneelin' down next to the coffin?"

Caelan and Mabon obeyed in unison.

The camera stayed at his eye as Preacher Skaggs said, "I just be goin' to be comin' a couple of steps closer, so I can be gittin' y'all in the picture better. Don't ya be a-worryin' about me comin' too close. I nary be wantin' to be gittin' the spots." He was three-fourths of the distance from the gate before he stopped and said, "Ya be smilin' perty fer the camera now." When neither one of them smiled, Preacher Skaggs said, "Well, of course, y'all nary be havin' nothin' to be smilin' about at present." He pressed the button on the camera and said, "Well, now, that ought to be doin' h'it."

"H'it be about time," Caelan mumbled under his breath as he got up.

Caelan picked up the ropes on one side of the coffin. When Mabon didn't immediately pick up the ropes on the other side, Caelan gave her a look that was as mean as when he yelled at her, but a look can't be heard by the congregation.

By the time Mabon picked up her ropes, Preacher Skaggs was standing in front of his flock again, saying, "Our dear brother done said he be wantin' us to be sendin' his child on with song. Let us be singin' 'Amazing Grace.'"

The congregation stood outside the gate mumbling to each other. MawMaw Tierney broke away from another whispered conversation with Uncle Teagan. She looked around her for a few seconds before she said, loudly, "Shhh! Shhh!" When the crowd got quiet, she said, "That be my Grandbaby in there. She be deservin' to be sent on with song."

While Mabon struggled to hold the rope that supported my coffin while they lowered my body into the ground, the congregation sang. No one heard the sound of my coffin hitting the earth, because their voices were raised in song. No one heard the sound of dirt hitting the roof of my body's new home, because by that time, they were singing "The Old Rugged Cross" with everything they had. They sang while Caelan took breaks and rubbed his shoulder. They sang while Mabon took a turn throwing dirt into the hole. They sang while Caelan patted the top layer of dirt down with the shovel. They sang while Caelan and Mabon steered the wagon through the crowd. They literally sang until the cows came home.

The cows were serenaded as they walked ahead of MawMaw Tierney, Uncle Teagan, and Eamon as MawMaw Tierney took them home like she did each evening. Eamon held MawMaw Tierney's herding stick that she always left leaning against the gate when she dropped the cows off in the morning. When I saw MawMaw Tierney patiently help him herd the cows, it gave me a little peace as our wagon headed for home in the other direction.

It was over. As I watched the congregation walk across the road toward the church, some of them still singing, I wondered what Eamon's children would think when they saw the picture Preacher Skaggs took. Would they think our folks were sad and loved me just because that's the expression they wore beneath their Sunday-go-to-meetin' hats, or would Eamon do me the justice of telling them the truth?"

CHAPTER TEN
REGAN'S REIGN

After a funeral, life goes on for the living, and that was no different for my family. I wandered among them, protecting Eamon as best as I could. One day rolled into the next. If I explained every abuse, my story would outlive the readers. Let it suffice to say that they were as common as getting out of bed in the morning and going to bed at night. When you look back on your life, you don't remember every time you went to bed, but you know it was a major part of the past you are remembering. It's the same with anything that becomes mundane, even violence. You only remember the abuses that were distinctive enough to stand out from the others, whether they were happening to you or someone you love.

The creaking of Caelan's and Mabon's bed became mundane as well. It was as regular as the rising and setting of the sun. The only sound that was memorable was Mabon's screams when they announced the birth of yet another child. She never made a sound when the bed was creaking for Caelan's pleasure, but childbirth was a sensation that was too strong to separate herself from it. Maybe it was the pain. Maybe it was the knowledge that yet another child had the misfortune of being born into this family. Maybe it was the knowledge that she would have yet another mouth to feed.

Each child that emerged from her womb developed into someone whose behavior developed daily just as we get up and go to bed daily. By the time these children were formed, none of us could remember everything that happened to make them what they became. We only knew the daily activities of the family added up to the sum of each child's personality. Whether we liked those personalities or not didn't enter our minds. They became who they became, and that became recognizable to us. We relied on them being who their daily activity revealed them to be, because the devil you know is a lot less dangerous than the devil you don't know.

Before it was over, ten unfortunate souls survived after they emerged from her womb. Five were girls. Five were boys. No one will ever remember everything that happened to make them who they became. I just hope that if I describe the abuses that were distinctive enough to stand out from the others, maybe that will paint a picture of the major players.

The first child to emerge after my death was a girl. Caelan took her from the arms of the midwife minutes after she was born. He held her body on his forearm and looked into her face as he said, "I done got my lil' girl back. We be goin' to be namin' her Sinead."

Mabon's eyes looked like daggers could shoot out of them when she looked at him, but she didn't say anything. I had stood by her bed for a day and a night watching her struggle with the child who seemed smart enough not to want to come out and live here. I could easily imagine she was too tired to fight about a name.

The midwife left Mabon's side to go to Caelan. She stroked the new child's hair as she said, "Caelan, h'it nary be my place to be tellin' ya what to be namin' yer young'uns, but I always hear'ed say if'n ya be namin' a babe after a dead youngun, that babe be likely to be dyin', too."

Caelan held the baby closer to his chest and wrapped his arms around her as he said, "We cain't be havin' that."

"Ya be havin' another name?" the midwife asked as she returned to the side of Mabon's bed and pulled blankets up around the new mother.

After some hemming and hawing, he finally decided to name the child Regan, and the name stuck even though he hadn't given Mabon any say. I thought after all she went through bringing the child into the world that she should have a say in its name, but things didn't work that way in our family. So, we were stuck with a Regan. The first time I said that, I was thinking we were stuck with the name. As the years unfolded, I realized we were stuck with the person.

At first, I felt jealous, because Caelan was paying as much attention to Regan as he used to pay to me. I wasn't sure why I felt jealous, because I hated his attention when I was alive. I guess I felt like I was entitled to it, because I never saw him give it to anyone else before Regan was born.

My jealousy ended when Regan was about three months old. I stood at the end of the worn out cedar crib that was used by every baby born to our family for three generations when Caelan pulled up a chair next to it. He stroked Regan's hair as he said, "I be lovin' ya, child, better than the rest of 'em, but I nary be able to be lovin' ya like I be lovin' my Sinead. Ya be comin' from Mabon's womb. Sinead be comin' from the belly of a lady, but ya be comin' from the belly of a beast. Ya be the only lil' girl I be havin' now. Ya be havin' half of my blood runnin' through yer veins. Ya always gonna be my special one."

The jealousy began to abate when he told her he loved me more. The jealousy ended permanently when he lowered his hand to her tiny diaper. He slipped his hand inside the diaper and did things that didn't have anything to do with changing it. Just like we don't remember going to bed every night of our lives, Regan never remembered this nightly ritual that helped mold her into who she was to become. As I watched her personality unfold, I realized there were fates worse than death. Maybe I was the lucky one.

As soon as Regan was old enough to appreciate them, Caelan began to buy her gifts like he had done for Ma and me when we were alive. Eamon still didn't have any toys, but Regan soon had a box full of them. She would sit on the floor and play with them for hours. The first few times Eamon touched them, she screamed like he was trying to kill her. Since this meant he got beaten, he soon stopped touching her toys.

Eamon still didn't have extra clothes. The one pair of pants he owned was given to him by MawMaw Tierney when he stayed at her house during my funeral. MawMaw Tierney bought him two new pairs of denim pants and made him two feed sack shirts while he stayed with her. The ones he wore home quickly became too short for him and were already looking worn, because he wore them every day after Caelon and Mabon went to MawMaw Tierney's house late at night and drug him home a few days after my funeral. They drug him out so fast he didn't have time to get the other set of clothes MawMaw Tierney got for him. When MawMaw Tierney brought them to our house a few days later, Caelan screamed that he didn't need charity to take care of his own. I often visited MawMaw Tierney's house. The outfit lay on the bed Eamon used when he stayed with them. MawMaw Tierney said many times they were wrapped in the hope that he would return to their house to live.

Regan, on the other hand, had a dozen every day dresses Caelan forced Mabon to make out of the feed sacks Mabon usually used for herself. Mabon's wardrobe went down considerably after Regan became old enough to learn she could insist on the feed sacks and get them. She also had enough fancy dresses for a month of Sundays.

By the time Regan was two years old, she expected everything to go her way. Caelan forbade Mabon to involve Regan in domestic responsibilities, and Mabon knew Regan would tell Caelan if that order was violated.

Even though Eamon was only six years old, he did most of the house and yard work when Caelan wasn't home. Mabon spent more time barking orders at Eamon than doing anything herself. When something was too much for Eamon to handle alone, she repeatedly called him an idiot while she picked up the slack. She was even worse when she was large with the next child. Maybe that was because her belly got bigger with that child, but she had to squeeze that belly into the same gray gingham maternity dress she wore when she was pregnant with Regan. There weren't enough feed sacks to accommodate anyone but Regan. Even after Mabon's maternity dress wore out from daily use, it was the only dress she had to wear. I never understood why that didn't help her understand that she did the same thing to Eamon.

Shortly before the next child was born, Regan wandered around the house in one of her Sunday-go-to-meeting dresses. It was a pink jumper with red roses embroidered on the bib that Caelan bought her at the company store, and it was nicer than anything anyone else in the family had. Mabon was too large and uncomfortable to keep a close eye on Regan, so she had the run of the house.

She went into the room I once shared with Eamon and jumped up and down on the bed that was once mine. There was now a wardrobe standing next to the bed, because Caelan built it for her with the same loving care he used to build my coffin. When she got tired of jumping, she opened the wardrobe and tried to get a different Sunday-go-to-meeting dress. When jumping and stretching didn't allow her to reach the hangers, she went to the kitchen and pushed Caelan's chair toward her bed. The creaking of the floorboards joined with the squeaking of the chair legs as they slid across the floor. It sounded like people imitating ghosts.

The sound reminded me of how creepy the house was. The cobwebs that accumulated in the ceiling corners while Mabon was too large with child to knock them down made it look more like a tomb than it usually did.

When Regan got the chair to the wardrobe, she stood on it and retrieved her best Sunday-go-to-meeting dress. It was white with three huge ruffles in layers down the skirt. At the top of each ruffle was a thin strip of lace, and the same lace was around the collar and the bottom of each short sleeve. When she removed the fine dress she was already wearing, she threw it on the floor like it was a feed sack that hadn't been made into clothes yet.

After she put the white dress on, she climbed down from the chair and began to spin. Every time the full hem of the skirt flared out around her, she giggled. When she became dizzy, she stumbled into the chair. She felt her way along the seat of the chair until she found her way to sit down.

She sat for a few seconds before she jumped up and started dancing around the house again. She danced across the bedroom, grabbed the curtain that hung in the door and danced with it as she exited the room, danced across the main room and around the bench that sat in front of the fire place and finally into Caelan's and Mabon's room. Shortly after she danced into their room, she stopped dancing. She spun around very slowly one last time. As she spun, she looked at everything in the room. She stopped when she saw the closet door. She went to the closet and inspected the clothing that hung from the rod one piece at a time. When she finished looking at a piece, she pushed it to the left. Halfway across the rod of clothes, she looked down at a box that sat in the middle of the closet floor. She picked it up and carried it to the living room. She sat behind the bench that faced the fireplace and pulled the lid off the box. Inside the box were my toys.

She picked up the china doll Caelan bought for me, because he said it looked like me. She ran her fingers through its long, curly black hair before she rubbed a piece of its long dark blue skirt against her face. I remembered doing that when I played with the doll, because the fabric was very soft. She laid the doll on the dirty floor and picked up my pretty pink teapot with the dainty white flowers hand painted on the metal. She lifted the lid before she pulled out a china cup and saucer and pretended to pour a cup of tea. Soon the teapot and all four cups and saucers were lying on the floor with the doll. She then picked up the dainty necklace I used to carry in my pocket, because Mabon got mad when I wore it around my neck. I tried to grab it from her before she broke it, but my hand went through it.

Regan was holding the chain in front of her face and staring at the tiny flower pendant that hung at the end when Caelan got home. She was so mesmerized by the pendant that she didn't seem to hear his footsteps scratching across the gravel walkway, the water splashing out of the spigot, the creaking of the porch floorboards or the creak of the hinges as he opened the front door. She didn't seem to hear anything until he yelled, "Regan, what in hell ya be doin'?"

She jumped up and ran to the other side of the bench as Caelan ran across the room and fell to his knees beside my toys. He picked up the doll. As he looked at it, tears streamed down his cheeks. He looked at Regan as she peeked over the back of the bench and yelled, "Ya nary be touchin' these things. Ya be hearin' me?"

That was the first time he yelled at Regan. It was obvious she didn't know what to do. She stared at him over the back of the bench with a look on her face that reminded me of a cornered animal, and her whole body shook. No one seemed to notice the sound as her pee hit the floor.

A few seconds later, Mabon's slow lumbering footsteps and the accompanying creaking were heard outside the front door. When she walked through the still open door, she asked, "What in hell be happenin' in here?"

Caelan jumped to his feet, stared at Mabon and screamed, "How do ya be lettin' Regan be gittin' into Sinead's things?"

"I be outside," Mabon answered, stammering.

Before the words were out of her mouth, Caelan traveled the distance between them and slapped her face hard. Her head swung so hard away from the slap that it pulled her off balance and caused her to fall.

Eamon came to the open front door in time to see her fall. He jumped out of sight. I went to him and found him pushing himself against the outside wall. He was visibly trembling.

Caelan walked back to the toys and fell on his knees beside them. He picked up one of the tea cups and held it very close to his face. As he stared at it, he ran his big finger along the brim of the cup. He still had the cup in his hand when he picked up the doll and hugged it to his chest. As he rocked the doll, he looked at Mabon with tears in his eyes and yelled, "Mabon, ya done kilt her! Ya done kilt my lil' girl! Ya done take't her away from me! Ya done kilt her!"

Mabon was still lying on the floor. She curled into a ball and began to cry.

It felt like a long time passed before Caelan stopped crying, carefully placed the toys back into the box, put the lid on it and returned it to the floor of his closet. When he emerged from the bedroom, Regan was standing frozen between the bench and the fireplace. He looked down at the floor and saw the pee she was standing in.

"Eamon!" he yelled.

Eamon did not answer.

"Eamon!" he yelled again.

I stood in front of Eamon and said, "Ya best be answerin' him."

Eamon walked to the front door. When Caelan saw him standing in the door, he yelled, "Ya be cleanin' up this here piss!"

As Eamon entered the house, Caelan left it. As they passed each other, Caelan grabbed Eamon's arm and said, "That there white dress done cost me a perty penny. Ya be scrubbin' h'it out and be makin' sure h'it be shinin'. If'n there be a speck of dirt on h'it when I be gittin' home, I be takin' h'it outta yer hide."

. . . . .

When Caelan returned hours later, the sparkling clean white dress was hanging on the clothes line in front of the house. When he entered the house, the living room was also sparkling clean and smelled of lye soap. Both children were in their beds.

Caelan entered the children's room and sat on the edge of Regan's bed. She was lying flat on her back with the fresh new quilt MawMaw Tierney made to replace Eamon's worn out one pulled all the way up to her chin. She stared at Caelan through big eyes as he put his hand in his pocket and pulled out a small gold tube. He removed the lid and twisted the tube to reveal a core of bright red lipstick. As he brushed some on Regan's lips, he said, "I be hopin' ya not be afeared no more, child. Ya be goin' to be lookin' so perty in this. Ya be goin' to be lookin' just like Sinead's Ma."

Regan lay still as he colored her lips red. When he finished, he twisted the lipstick back into the tube and put the lid on. He pulled the quilt away from Regan's body, opened her small fist, and put the lipstick in her hand. "This be fer ya, child," he said before he placed his lips on the red ones he had just painted.

CHAPTER ELEVEN
THE EVIL THAT IS REGAN

Regan's red lipstick wasn't enough to keep Caelan out of Mabon's bed, because the babies kept coming. The order of the child's birth or the child's name didn't matter. Even the births were becoming as mundane as the fear and the beatings. It was assumed the children would keep appearing like clockwork and would fold into the darkness of this house like walking corpses. Whoever wrote the first story about zombies must have been my ancestor, because they understood in a way I thought only my own family understood.

Most of the children born to this family made it to adulthood. While happy smiling children were taken from their families by childhood disease all around us, the offspring of this family kept hanging on and suffering. Even the beatings didn't end in eternal peace for any of them after me. Their survival was made more surprising since Regan became a master at guiding Caelan's cruel hand against the other children after they were born.

The next baby Mabon bore was a boy named Garnett. Eamon often sat on the front porch steps holding, rocking and comforting the new arrival. Sometimes he even offered the child the only laughter it might ever know. He held the baby on his lap, looked into its eyes and made faces to make it laugh.

As more babies came, he was often seen sitting on the steps holding the most recent baby with ever growing numbers of children sitting on the steps around him. The passel of children was often seen following him and helping him with his chores. And, he was often seen foraging in the woods or fishing for food for the growing brood. A time came when I saw him clean a large bucket of fish, cook them over an open fire and feed all of the children right there on the banks of the river where the fish were caught. It was as if he were the Ma and Pa instead of Mabon and Caelan. In the end, he would receive about as much gratitude for his efforts as the functional parent in a dysfunctional family usually does, thanks mostly to Regan learning to lead the opinions of the children as expertly as she learned to guide Caelan's cruel hand.

Anyone could see that Eamon and Garnett were connected at the heart. One morning when Garnett was a baby, Eamon sat on the front steps holding Garnett on his lap. Each time Eamon held Garnett to his face and coo'd, the child laughed so hard that he made Eamon laugh.

Regan stomped out on the porch and said, "That babe be ugly!"

"Naw, he nary be ugly," Eamon said as he rubbed his nose on Garnett's nose. "Ain't nary such a thing as an ugly babe."

"He nary be as perty as I be," Regan said as she spun around in a white dress that looked like the one she wore the day she got into my toys. As she spun, the dark curls that hung down her back spun with her. She didn't smile or laugh. It seemed she was spinning for other people instead of herself now, because she seemed to get no joy out of it. That seemed odd when I remembered how much she enjoyed twirling in that dress the day she got into my toys.

Eamon didn't answer. He just rubbed his nose against Garnett's nose again.

Regan kicked him in the side of his thigh and said, "Ya better be tellin' me I be more perty than that ugly ol' babe."

Eamon rubbed his thigh as he looked at Regan and said, "Ya be cuttin' that out! Ya both be perty." He returned his hand and his gaze to Garnett. He looked in Garnett's eyes and coo'd some more.

"I be hatin' ya both," Regan said.

"I be knowin' that," Eamon said. His words were not the words some adults use to dismiss the silly remarks of children. It was apparent by the tone of his voice and the look in his eyes when he glanced at her that he knew she was telling the truth.

She kicked Eamon in the thigh again and said, "Ya better be tellin' me I be more perty than that ugly ol' babe."

Eamon put his hand on his thigh again and asked, "Why ya be kickin' me fer?"

Garnett laughed, and Eamon returned his hand and his gaze to the baby again.

As Eamon rubbed his nose on Garnett's again, Regan kicked Eamon in the small of his back and said, "I be more perty than that ugly ol' babe, and ya be knowin' h'it."

Eamon arched his back and moved his hand to it as he said, "A'right, then."

Garnett grabbed Eamon's finger as Eamon moved his hand away from his back. Garnett kept holding it with a tight grip as Eamon bounced Garnett on his thighs while making horse sounds.

"Ya done got to be sayin' the words," Regan said as she kicked him in the upper back. This time she kicked him hard enough that his torso was knocked forward onto the baby. He gasped for breath for several seconds before he picked himself up.

When he sat up, he looked at Regan and said, "Ya cain't be doin' that when I be holdin' the babe. Ya might be hurtin' him."

"I nary be carin' if'n I do," Regan said as she pulled her foot back to kick him again.

Eamon wrapped his arms around Garnett and jumped to the left just in time for Regan's foot to swing past him. When she hit air instead of Eamon's back, she flew off the porch with so much force that she didn't hit any steps on the way down. She landed on her back at the bottom of the steps and got the wind knocked out of her.

After she caught her breath, she sat up and stared hard at Eamon. Her face looked like stone, and her eyes were as hard and dry as a stone in the middle of a drought field. After several minutes of staring at him, she said, "Ya gonna be payin' fer that."

She looked at her dress and touched a place that was soiled with dry dirt that would easily dust off. She looked back at Eamon and continued to stare at him as she screamed, "Pa, Eamon done up and ruin't my dress! Pa! Pa!" She threw her face into her hands and cried fake tears into her dry palms.

Mabon was kneeling in the family garden at the side of the house. She jerked her head up when Regan started screaming. When she saw it was Regan, she rolled her eyes and went back to pulling weeds out of the tomatoes.

The sound of Caelan's footsteps stomping and creaking across the floor could be heard from the second the sound escaped Regan's lips. He burst through the front door, ran down the steps, and jerked Regan up by her arm. As he dusted off the dress, he asked, demandingly, "What in hell be happenin' out here?"

"Eamon done went and pushed me off'n the porch," Regan screamed as she cried.

Caelan let her go with so much force that she fell down again. She sat on the ground and looked up at Eamon. She was smiling.

Caelan yanked Garnett out of Eamon's arms. He held Garnett by the arm in one hand while he jerked Eamon to his feet with his other one. After he dragged Eamon to the bottom of the steps, he practically threw Garnett at Regan.

"I be holdin' the babe. I nary be able to be doin' nothin'," Eamon said, stammering.

Caelan was beating on him before he could finish the sentence. Regan lay the baby in the dirt next to her and watched Caelan beat Eamon. Each time Eamon screamed, Regan laughed.

As I watched Regan laugh, my thoughts became so dark they blocked the sun. I hadn't realized the sun was shining until everything got so dark I missed the light. The darkness of this place usually dimmed the sun, but I realized some sun always seeped through. The only thing that blocked it out completely was my hatred of Regan.

CHAPTER TWELVE
JEALOUSY

I may have been mistaken when I said the order of a child's birth or even something as important as the child's name didn't matter in our family, because the births were as mundane as the fear and the beatings. There was one exception to this rule. It mattered a great deal to Regan when the next girl child was born, because Regan seemed to see girls as competition.

After Mabon stopped screaming, Caelan carried the newest baby to the porch. He held her high in the air and yelled, "H'it be a girl!"

Eamon got a big smile on his face. He stared at the baby until Caelan carried her back in the house. He then knelt in front of Garnett and said, "We be havin' ourselves a new sister."

Garnett looked at Eamon with an expression of fear on his face and asked, "Regan?"

"Naw," Eamon said. "H'it be a new sister."

"Do she be mean like Regan be?" Garnett asked.

"I surely be hopin' she nary be," Eamon answered.

Garnett began to cry. Crying caused him to lose his balance, and he fell onto his diaper on the dirt. Eamon sat beside him and pulled him close. As Eamon rocked Garnett, he said, "H'it can be a good thing to be havin' a sister. I be havin' me a sister before. Her name be Sinead. She be teachin' me how to be walkin' like I be teachin' ya to be walkin'. She be keepin' me clean. She be findin' food fer me when there nary be enough to be goin' 'round. She be like a Ma to me."

"Sinead," the boy said as he pointed toward me. He stopped crying.

88

"Yas," Eamon said, and I was warmed by the smile on his face. "That be her name."

It was good to see Eamon think of me with such fond memories. The older he got, the harder it was for him to see me. I think he was starting to believe the times we talked after I died were just dreams. The only time I knew he saw me now was when he was scared. Even if he lost contact with me completely, I would always stay with him and keep him safe.

Regan hadn't been able to see me since the night Caelan gave her the red lipstick. She not only lost the heart of a child that night; she also lost her memories of me. I wanted to feel sorry for her, but I hadn't lost heart when the same things happened to me in life. I retained some good, so I couldn't understand how she let go of so much that could have been good about her. The only consideration I gave her was what was necessary to keep Eamon safe from her.

All of my brothers and sisters could see me when they were little, although they were much older than Regan was when they lost that ability. It was all right that they all outgrew seeing beyond the veil, because they didn't need me. Eamon was taking care of them just like I took care of him when he was a child. I focused all of my energy on Eamon, because he was the one who needed me. Without me, he didn't have anyone.

"Another ugly babe I be havin' to be lookin' at!" Regan said as she stomped down the porch steps.

Garnett started crying, so Eamon whispered, "Ya nary be ugly." He put his arm around Garnett and rocked him as he whispered, "She nary be knowin' what ugly be."

Regan stopped at the bottom of the steps and said, "That ugly girl babe gonna be takin' all my things."

Eamon kept rocking Garnett.

Regan kicked dirt at them before she stomped back up the steps, across the front porch, through the front room and into her room. She was stomping so hard that the sound drowned out the creaking that usually accompanied footsteps in that house.

She took the pillow case off her pillow, gathered her things and stuffed them inside it. When all of her prized belongings were in the pillow case, she tied the end and lay on the bed next to it. She fell asleep hugging the hard, lumpy bag.

. . . . .

It didn't really matter what they named the baby. She was just one more in a long line of children to come. By the time she was six months old, she was already long and lean like Caelan. Of course, she had the typical baby fat, but it was apparent this child was going to look more like Caelan in every way. The similarity in appearance didn't attract any of Caelan's attention. She was ignored like all the other children were. Regan was the only one who got attention, but she still hid in her room and hugged her pillow case full of stuff most of the time.

That is what Regan was doing on a bright Saturday a few weeks after Eamon's eighth birthday. The family, which was only four kids at that time, was working in the field that grew to the right of the house and barn. Caelan usually left all of the work for Mabon and the children, but even he understood this was too much for them to handle during planting and harvesting seasons. The whole family was working in the fields that day. Regan was the only exception.

Mabon gave Eamon the responsibility of the horse and plow. Due to intermittent starvation and genetics, he was small for eight. It hurt me to watch him trying to maneuver a machine that was too big for him while holding onto reins that were too big for his hands. I knew he would be joining me on this side of the veil if those horses got out of hand.

Mabon sat under a shade tree at the edge of the field and held the fussy new baby. Garnett was little more than a toddler, but she had him following Eamon and dropping seeds in the ground. Every once in a while, Garnett stopped working and stared at the clouds or studied the seeds in his palm. Each time he did, Mabon yelled at him to get back to work even though yelling only made him cry.

Mabon lost her temper when Garnett's crying made the baby cry. She held the baby in front of her face, shook it and yelled, "Ya needs to be shuttin' up!" When this made the baby cry harder, Mabon yelled, "Eamon, ya needs to be gittin' yerself on over here and takin' care of this here babe. Ya be the only one what can do anythin' with these lil' money grubbers."

Eamon pulled the reins three times before the horses felt it enough to stop. When they stopped, Eamon pulled the leather strap that secured him to the plow from one handle and let it drop to the ground. He walked over to Mabon and took the baby. He held her for only a few seconds before she stopped crying.

"Ya be needin' to be carryin' that babe whilst ya be pullin' that there plow," Mabon said. "If'n we nary be gittin' this done in time, yer Pa be goin' to be havin' hisself a fit."

"She mays be gittin' hurt if'n I be doin' that," Eamon said.

Garnett toddled toward them as he said, "Ya nary hurt my Eamon." When he was about halfway to them, he tripped on a furrow and fell. He fell so fast he didn't have time to extend his arms to brace his fall, so his face hit the ground. When he landed, his hand came open and spilled the seeds.

Mabon and Eamon ran toward him. Mabon quickly gained the lead, because she was bigger and wasn't carrying a baby. When she reached the crying toddler, she grabbed his arm, yanked him up and started yelling at him. Eamon ran faster as he screamed, "I be gatherin' up them seeds; they nary be wasted." Before he got the sentence out, she slapped Garnett's face.

Eamon lay the baby on the ground and ran to Garnett. He grabbed Mabon's wrist and tried to pull her hand off Garnett's arm as he yelled, "Let him be! Let him be!" She didn't let Garnett go until Eamon yelled, "Ya be goin' to be killin' him just like ya done kilt Sinead!"

Everything went quiet the moment the words came out of his mouth; the sounds of nature couldn't be heard over the deafening silence. Mabon released Garnett's arm and spun on Eamon. During the several seconds she stared at him, her face became increasingly red. When it looked like a tomato, she yelled, "What ya be sayin' to me?"

Eamon backed away from her.

As Garnett's diapered bottom hit the ground, he yelled, "Naw! Naw hurt Eamon!" The baby started to cry. Nature remained as silent as the moments before a bad storm.

"What ya be sayin' to me?" Mabon yelled again.

Eamon backed away a few more steps, but he wasn't fast enough. She grabbed his wrist and began to beat him mercilessly. Her body was moving so fast she looked like a tornado. You couldn't see her movements, but you could hear the smacks raining down on him. You could hear him scream in response to each one, but all you could see was a dust cloud rising around them. It wasn't until the dust cloud caused her to cough that she lost her grip on him.

The second she let go, he ran. He only out-distanced her by three plowed rows before she grabbed the back of his shirt. She yanked his shirt hard enough to make him fall. As soon as he did, she stomped three times before his screams became so primal it seemed to awaken something buried deep inside her. She stopped with her foot still in the air, lowered it to the ground and stared at the limp and torn body that lay beneath her. When blood began to color his denim pants at the hip, she whispered, "H'it be like Sinead again."

She ran across the field screaming, "Caelan! Caelan!"

Caelan was sitting under a shade tree on the other side of the field sharing a quart of moonshine with Preacher Skaggs when he heard her screaming. He looked at the preacher and asked, "What in hell done got into that there woman now?"

"Lord only be knowin'," Preacher Skaggs said. "Ya be knowin' how women be."

"I surely do be knowin' that," Caelan said as he lifted the quart to his lips again.

Caelan and Preacher Skaggs shared three more drinks before Mabon got to them. When she arrived, Caelan looked up at her and asked, "What be gittin' yer knickers in such a twist?"

"Eamon," Mabon said, panting. She leaned over and rested her palms on her knees for several seconds before she was able to say, "He be hurt. He be hurt bad."

Caelan jumped up and asked, "What done happened to him?"

"He be hurt bad!" Mabon said. "Ya gots to be comin'. He be hurt real bad."

Preacher Skaggs took another drink of moonshine as he watched Caelan and Mabon run across the field.

Caelan fell on his knees next to Eamon when they got to him. As Caelan pulled Eamon into his arms, he looked up at Mabon and said, "Tell me ya nary be doin' h'it again."

"Uh, uh, uh," Mabon said, stammering. She went on that way for several seconds before she said, "It nary be my doin', Caelan. I be swearin' h'it. H'it be them damn horses. They done runned off with him. I be findin' him like this."

Caelan looked at the horses. They were standing peacefully where Eamon left them when he came to Garnett's rescue. One of the horses was calmly picking among the freshly tilled soil for pieces of grass. Caelan stared at them for a full minute before he looked back at Mabon and said, "We gots to be gittin' this here child to that there hospital or he be goin' to be bleedin' out."

Preacher Skaggs arrived on a beautiful red stallion wearing an ornate leather saddle that matched its coat. He looked down at them and asked, "What be wrong with the boy? Do there be anythin' I can be doin' to be helpin'?"

"Yas! Ya can be ridin' on over to Teagan's farm," Caelan said. "Tell him to be bringin' his car on over here. We gots to be gittin' this here boy to the hospital."

Preacher Skaggs flicked the reins and made a clicking noise. The horse began to walk across the field, knocking flies off his haunches with his tail like he did on any leisurely summer day.

"Be quick about h'it!" Caelan yelled.

Preacher Skaggs kicked his heels into the horse's ribs as he made a clicking noise again, and the horse picked up its pace.

Caelan held Eamon as he said, "That ol' bastard done got hisself drunk. If'n he even be findin' Teagan's farm, h'it be goin' to be takin' him all day."

Mabon sat on her knees, rocking back and forth and saying, "Oh my! Oh my!" until she saw the dust of Teagan's speeding car coming at them across the field. "That be him!" Mabon said as she jumped up.

The car skidded to a stop and Teagan jumped out of it and ran to them. As he fell to his knees next to Eamon, he asked. "What done happened?"

"Um," Caelan said.

Before Caelan could articulate what he wanted to say, Mabon chimed in and said, "H'it be the horses. They done dragged him. They done hurt him bad."

Teagan grabbed his hat off his head and threw it on the ground as he asked, screaming, "Why in hell do ya'll be havin' an eight-year-ol' boy be pullin' a damn plow?"

"Ya always be havin' yer girls workin' in yer fields," Mabon said, defensive. "Nary be judgin' us fer workin' a boy."

Teagan pulled Eamon away from Caelan and lifted Eamon into his arms. As he stood, he said, "I be takin' this here boy to the hospital. If'n any of ya be wantin' to be comin' along, ya needs to be gittin' yerself into that there car now."

As Teagan walked toward the car, Caelan stood up and yelled to Mabon, "See if'n ya can be doin' a better job watchin' them other younguns whilst I be gone."

Teagan laid Eamon in the back seat and was getting in the driver's seat before Caelan got to the car. Caelan climbed into the passenger seat, and they sped off. Mabon stood where they left her and watched the dust cloud until it was too far away to see. Only then did she turn and see her baby lying in the dirt and Garnett sitting at the edge of a furrow with a black eye.

As she picked the baby up, she said, "I nary be knowin' what I goin' to be doin' with these damn young'uns if'n Eamon nary be gittin' better enough to be helpin' me with 'em." She followed Garnett across the field as she yelled, "Ya needs to be gittin' along. We done got to be gittin' on home." She yelled at him for not keeping up all the way home. She never took his hand to help him. She just kept threatening to blacken his other eye if he didn't get a move on.

When they finally got to their front yard, Garnett sat on his dirty diaper and cried. She sat the baby next to him and went in the house. The sound of creaking couldn't be heard over the crying children, so Regan was taken by surprise when Mabon entered her room.

Mabon marched over to the bed where Regan laid all day and grabbed the pillow case. Regan tightened her grip and pulled back as she yelled, "Naw!"

Mabon slapped her face and said, "Ya be givin' me one of them there toys to be takin' to Eamon at the hospital. I gots to be makin' sure he nary be tellin' no one what done happened. I gots to be makin' sure he be comin' home to be helpin' me with these young'uns."

Regan released the pillowcase and put her hand on her cheek. She looked at Mabon through tear-filled eyes and said, "I be goin' to be tellin' Pa."

"Yer Pa nary be carin' about that now," Mabon said as she untied the pillowcase. "Eamon done be on his way to the hospital. That be all yer Pa be carin' about now."

Mabon opened the pillow case and rummaged through it for several minutes before she threw it at Regan and said, "There be nary a thing in there fittin' fer a boy."

As Mabon walked out of the room, Regan yelled, "Good. I nary be wantin' Eamon to be havin' nothin' what be mine anyhow."

Regan tied the end of the pillow case before she sat on the bed and hugged it like it was a doll.

CHAPTER THIRTEEN
PREACHER'S SECRET

Fifty years later, Eamon would remember that Caelan visited him in the hospital and actually seemed to care while he was there. The only other visitors he had were Preacher Skaggs and Uncle Teagan. Only the good Lord knew what Preacher Skaggs' intentions were with anything he did. Genuine care was expected from Uncle Teagan, but Eamon was surprised to see it in Caelan. He always remembered Caelan showing concern during that hospital stay, because it was the first time he saw Caelan express concern.

Later in life, Eamon would tell people his Pa was the better of his folks because of that visit. He would remember Caelan sitting by his bed with tears in his eyes confessing his fear that Eamon might have ended up like Sinead. Eamon would never realize a visit from both folks should be a given. Even as an old man, he continued to be surprised that one of his parents had visited him while he was recovering from an injury that left him handicapped for life.

Eamon needed to hear the fears, care, and concern Caelan spoke as he sat next to Eamon's bed and cried. Eamon didn't have time to process them though, because Preacher Skaggs arrived seconds after Caelan stopped speaking. Preacher Skaggs' visit was so inappropriate that Eamon's child-mind blocked that memory for years, but I never forgot. When Preacher Skaggs entered the room, Eamon was beginning to nod off.

Caelan stopped talking when he saw Eamon's eyes close. He sat quietly on the chair next to the bed and cried. Preacher Skaggs pulled a chair next to Caelan's, sat down and put his arm over Caelan's shoulder as he said, "I be knowin' how ya be feelin', brother. This here be a hard thing to be goin' through. The doctor be sayin' he gonna be a'right though."

"The doctor be sayin' he gonna live," Caelan said and started crying again. "The doctor nary be sayin' he be a'right."

"The doctor be sayin' he gonna live," Preacher Skaggs said as he patted Caelan's back.

"I reckon I ought to be grateful fer that," Caelan said. "He could be bein' like Sinead."

"Naw," Preacher Skaggs said. "The spots done taked Sinead. This boy nary be havin' no sickness. He just be hurt."

"I reckon ya be right," Caelan said as he sat up, which caused Preacher Skaggs' hand to slide off Caelan's back.

Eamon began to lightly snore. When he did, Caelan said, "The boy cain't rightly be hearin' me now, so I reckon h'it be a'right fer me to be tellin' ya somethin'."

"Unburden yer soul," Preacher Skaggs said.

"Ya see, Preacher, I be feelin' right awful. If'n he be dyin', I be havin' to be confessin' I nary be treatin' the boy proper. I be perty good to Sinead, because she be my Ruby's girl. I be perty good to Regan, because she be a perty lil' gal. But," he lowered his voice to a whisper and said, "I be ponderin' on if'n this boy be mine. I be havin' to marry his Ma. She be in the family way. How I to know if'n she be lyin' with other men. Some be sayin' this boy be belongin' to Mabon's Pa."

Preacher Skaggs placed his elbows on his knees and clasped his hands between his legs as he leaned forward and stared at the floor. He tisked a couple of times before he said, "Let us be hopin' that nary be true, Brother Caelan. Let us be hopin' that nary be true at all."

Caelan continued to unburden his soul. He didn't seem to be aware that Preacher Skaggs stopped listening to him shortly after he started talking, but talking seemed to be making him feel better.

The faraway look on Preacher Skaggs face made me wonder what was so much more important to him than what Caelan was saying. My curiosity was so great that I learned another thing I could do as a ghost. I found myself in Preacher Skaggs mind, and he was thinking about a time when Mabon once came to his church.

When I entered his thoughts, he was remembering a dark afternoon when he arrived at the small country church later than usual. When he opened the door, he heard the faint sound of weeping. He entered the building and found Sister Mabon sitting in a middle pew weeping into a linen handkerchief that had pink and red roses embroidered on it. He wondered where she got such a fancy trinket before he closed the door and locked it. He decided by the time he locked the door that the trinket came from a man and thought he knew why she came here to cry.

When the door lock clicked, Mabon jumped and turned toward the sound while she wiped her eyes with the fancy trinket.

"Preacher Skaggs," she said as she quickly dried her eyes.

He didn't answer until he walked down the aisle and seated himself next to her. He put his arm across her shoulder and asked, "How ya be gittin' into the buildin', Sister Mabon?"

Her brow crinkled as she looked at him and said, "The door be unlocked. The door always be unlocked. Ya be knowin' nobody 'round here be lockin' nary doors."

"Yas," Preacher Skaggs said, nodding. "I reckon I be meanin' to be askin' what be bringin' ya here?"

"I be needin' to be talkin' to, the Lord – Oh, Lordy, I dunno if'n he be wantin' to be hearin' from me. I be needin' to be where he be, so I can be makin' sure he be hearin' me."

"What ya done to be makin' ya be believin' the Lord nary be wantin' to be hearin' from ya, child?"

Mabon began to cry again. She crumpled forward into the fancy trinket and sobbed so hard it caused her whole body to shake. Preacher Skaggs pulled her into his embrace. As he placed both arms around her, she hid her face in his chest and let the tears flow. She cried for so long that Preacher Skaggs was looking around the building impatiently by the time she sat up and dried her eyes. He kept his arm over her shoulder.

"What be makin' ya despair so, child?" Preacher Skaggs asked.

"Preacher, what if'n I be with child?"

"What done happened to be makin' ya be thinkin' ya be with child?"

Tears ran down her cheeks as she said, "A, a, a, I be walkin' along in them there woods."

She paused for so long that Preacher Skaggs said, "I nary be hearin' of nobody gittin' with child walkin' along in the woods."

"Naw, naw," Mabon said, stammering. "Ya nary be understandin'. Whilst I be walkin' along in them there woods, this here boy come on outta, well, first I be thinkin' he be teasin' me, then he be touchin' me." Her whole body shook as she said, "I nary be able to be gittin' away; he be knockin' me onto the ground and layin' on me."

"Now, Sister Mabon," Preacher Skaggs said as he pulled her to him again. "Ya be sure ya nary be recollectin' wrong?"

Mabon crinkled her brow and looked at Preacher Skaggs like she was looking through him. After a moment, she shook her head and said, stammering, "Naw, naw, naw, that be the way h'it be."

"What ya be a-wearin', Sister Mabon?"

"I be wearin' the white dress with the red flowers Ma done make'd fer me. I be beat somethin' fierce fer ruinin' that there dress."

"I be seein' ya in that there dress at church," Preacher Skaggs said. "Ya be lookin' right perty in h'it. Do ya be thinkin', maybe, that dress be givin' the boy the wrong idear?"

Mabon shook her head as she said, "Naw, naw, naw, Ma be makin' me that there dress fer wearin' to church. Church dresses not be makin' boys be gittin' wrong idears."

"I nary be sayin' h'it be right, Sister Mabon, but ya be a right perty lil' gal. Ya be lookin' right perty in that there dress. Men folk be havin' desires. Girl folk be havin' to be careful."

"Naw," Mabon said as she pulled away from him. "Naw, Preacher, h'it nary be that way at all."

"Ya be a right perty lil' gal whatever ya be a-wearin'. I reckon that there boy be overcome. I reckon he be feelin' real sorry fer what he done. The Good Lord be tellin' us to be forgivin'."

"Yassir," Mabon said as she looked down at the handkerchief she was ringing between her hands. "Mays be. But, what if'n I be with child." She began to sob uncontrollably again.

Preacher Skaggs pulled her into his arms. As she wet the lapel of his suit with her tears, he kissed the back of her head. She looked up at him. Her eyebrows were crinkled again.

He kissed the crinkle between her eyes and said, "Ya surely be too perty to be crinklin' up yer face that a-way." He placed his lips on hers and gave her a soft, sweet kiss.

"That nary be how Caelan be a-kissin' me," she said. "He just about be breakin' my mouth."

"This be how a man supposed to be kissin' a woman," Preacher Skaggs said as he placed his index finger and thumb on her chin and raised her lips to meet his again. This time she kissed him back. After several sweet kisses, he lay her back on the pew and began to kiss her more passionately. As the passion increased, she pushed him away and said, "Naw, we cain't be doin' this."

"Ya be enjoyin' h'it?" Preacher Skaggs asked and kissed her again.

After several more minutes of kissing, she tried to push him off her again.

"There nary be a reason to be stoppin'," Preacher Skaggs said. "Ya done lost yer maiden-head. If'n ya gonna be carryin' a child, ya ought to be havin' the pleasure of makin' one instead of the pain Caelan done gived ya."

"What about – " She groaned with pleasure instead of finishing the sentence, because the preacher lowered his mouth to her breast and started sucking on her nipple through the thin fabric. He continued to provide this pleasure as he unbuttoned the front of her dress. When he raised her bra above her breast, her pleasure increased enough to allow him to pull her skirt up and place his hand on the spot that had only known a violent touch. His touch brought enough pleasure that their passion peaked even though memories of Caelan caused her to resist at first. Their writhing caused them to fall off the pew and onto the floor. He continued to kiss her as he undid his zipper, removed his manhood from his trousers and led it into the soft wet part of her that his hands had already explored every inch of. When her hips rose to meet his, his thrusts became confident. She screamed during the last intense thrusts that brought his pleasure. When he spilled his seed, he pulled himself up to his knees, closed his trousers and sat on the pew.

As she adjusted her clothes, he said, "Sister Mabon, ya need to be tellin' me the truth about what be done to ya by Caelan."

"I done tell'ed ya ever thing," she said as she covered her exposed bosoms with her forearm while she pulled her bra down with her other hand.

"Sister Mabon, a woman what done haved her virtue be stealed from her nary gonna be enjoyin' a man like ya be enjoyin' me just now."

Mabon's eyes filled with tears and her mouth fell open for a full minute before she said, "But, Preacher – "

"Ya be thinkin' ya can be blamin' that there child in yer belly on me if'n we be together this a-way? Ya be thinkin' ya be becomin' the Preacher's wife and be gittin' the respect of the congregation despite ya bein' nothin' but a whore? What about the wife I done got? Ya be thinkin' about her?"

Mabon quickly fixed her clothes to cover herself before she got up and ran to the door. She fumbled with the lock for several seconds before she was able to get the door open and run out of the church, leaving her fancy trinket behind. When the door closed, Preacher Skaggs picked the trinket up off the floor, held it to his nose, and inhaled deeply. From the look on his face, it appeared that he liked the smell of tears.

His daydreaming mind moved to another memory. The next time he saw Mabon, her Pa brought her and Caelan to the church to be married by force. Apparently, Mabon was with child. It could have been Caelan's, and it could have been his. As far as Preacher Skaggs was concerned, it didn't really matter. The child was going to have a Pa, and that was all that mattered. He opened his Bible, and began the marriage ceremony. Mabon cried through the whole thing.

"So, what ya be thinkin', Preacher?" Caelan asked, interrupting Preacher Skagg's daydream. "Preacher? Preacher?"

Preacher Skaggs shook his head to bring himself back to the moment and said, "I be so sorry, Caelan. I be gittin' lost in my own thinkin' from time to time."

"What ya be thinkin' about?"

"Uh, uh, uh, I just be havin' a hard time shakin' from my mind what this boy done been through today. Ya be rememberin' I be there when h'it be happenin'?"

"Yas, yas, of course," Caelan said, nodding.

"What be yer question?"

"What if'n Eamon be just like Sinead? Them there horses just be standin' in the rows."

Preacher Skaggs patted Caelan on the back and said, "I done tell'ed ya, brother, nary way this be like Sinead. Ya be havin' nothin' to be worryin' about." He winked at Caelan.

I was learning that intense emotions always made it easier for me to do supernatural things. Caelan's intense fear allowed me to read his thoughts without trying. He thought Preacher Skaggs winked to assure him of a pact between them: no one will ever know. Caelan had no idea Preacher Skaggs daydreamed through his confession that Mabon killed me, so justice once again wouldn't be done.

My rage was so strong that I began to beat Pastor Skaggs with my fists, but they went through him. Apparently intense emotion was enough to make him aware of me, too. He looked around frantically through frightened eyes, but that wasn't going to bring me justice.

"What be the matter, Preacher?" Caelan asked.

"I nary be knowin'," Preacher Skaggs said as he returned his focus to Caelan. "I reckon so much done happened in these ol' hospitals that they be a bit spooky at times."

Caelan nodded his head and asked, "Do ya be havin' any wisdom fer me?"

Preacher Skaggs' answer assured me that even if he had heard Caelan's confession, it wouldn't have made any difference. The only thing it would have done is given him power over Caelan and Mabon. He didn't care what happened to any of us children.

"Caelan," Preacher Skaggs said as he sat up in his chair and crossed his legs. "He be yer eldest boy. Ya be knowin' in yer heart hi't be true. They nary be enough men 'round these here parts fer h'it to be any other way. If'n she be doin' things she ought not be doin', ya surely would be hearin' about h'it. Think about yer own Ma and what folks always be sayin' about her. Folks just rightly know what be goin' on. He be yer boy. He be yer eldest boy. He be the one what be carryin' on yer family name. Ya got to be teachin' him how to be a man."

Caelan nodded.

"One thing I be seein' in this boy is he just be too soft. He be carin' fer them young'uns like he be a woman or somethin'. That be makin' him be whinin' like a woman. Ya cain't be makin' a boy what always be whinin' about his trials into a man. Some already be sayin' Mabon done beat this boy to be makin' him like this. We nary be concernin' ourselves with what people be sayin'. H'it be the Good Lord hisself be tellin' us to spare the rod be to spoil the child. He got to be learnin' to be takin' what be comin' to him without grumblin' about h'it. He cain't be runnin' 'round tellin' yer family secrets to ever body. Folks nary be knowin' the whole story. They mays be takin' h'it the wrong way."

Caelan nodded.

Both men looked toward Eamon when his snoring stopped. Preacher Skaggs leaned forward and lay his hand on Eamon's hand. Eamon pulled his hand away as Preacher Skaggs said, "How ya be feelin', boy?"

Eamon didn't answer.

"Ya be respectin' yer elders, boy," Preacher Skaggs said in a harsh voice. "When grown folks be askin' how ya be feelin', ya be tellin' 'em."

"Yassir," Eamon said with a weak voice. "I be feelin' fine as frog's hair."

"That be right good to hear. Yer Pa be worryin' hisself sick over ya."

Eamon glanced at Caelan before he asked, "Do Ma be worryin'?"

"What ya be meanin' by that, boy?" Caelan snapped.

"Nothin'," Eamon answered.

Preacher Skaggs scooted his chair closer to the bed and said, "Ya be listenin' to me, boy. Yer Ma be doin' the best she be knowin' how to be doin'. She be a Godly woman. The Bible itself say if'n we be sparin' the rod we be spoilin' the child. Some be sayin' yer Ma be doin' this to ya. H'it nary be makin' no never mind to me. I nary be needin' to be knowin' if'n that be true. I just be needin' ya to be understandin' that yer Ma be doing what she be doin' in the name of the Lord."

I felt my rage rising again. Maybe the old bastard hadn't heard Caelan's confession about what happened to me, but he knew Mabon did this. That was obvious. I lay on the bed next to Eamon and wrapped my arms around him. His body became less stiff when I began to hold him.

"Do ya be hearin' what I be sayin' to ya, boy?" Preacher Skaggs asked.

"Yassir," Eamon said as he turned his face toward me.

"Ya be lookin' at yer elders when they be talkin' to ya, boy."

Eamon's body stiffened again before he looked back at the Preacher.

"Ya be knowin' yer Ma be tryin' to be teachin' ya to be a godly man?" Preacher Skaggs asked.

"Yassir."

"Do ya be knowin' what h'it be meanin' to be a godly man?"

"I reckon not."

"A godly man nary be goin' 'round whinin' about ever thing. He be knowin' God nary be puttin' nothin' on us what we cain't be handlin'. A godly man be loyal to his family. A godly man nary be tellin' family business. He be protectin' the Ma of his younguns. He be knowin' God done maked him to be the head of her. He also be protectin' the Ma of his brothers and sisters. Ya be gittin' what I be sayin' to ya, boy?"

"Yassir."

"I reckon we be a'right here then," Preacher Skaggs said as he stood up. He looked down at Eamon and said, "I be prayin' fer ya, boy." He shook Caelan's hand and said, "I be prayin' fer all of ya."

"Much obliged," Caelan said as he shook Preacher Skaggs' hand.

When Preacher Skaggs was halfway across the room, Uncle Teagan entered it.

"Preacher," Uncle Teagan said without looking at Preacher Skaggs. Uncle Teagan walked past him to the chair he just left. Before Uncle Teagan sat down, he nodded at Caelan and said, "Caelan."

Caelan nodded back.

Preacher Skaggs stopped at the door and watched.

Uncle Teagan grasped Eamon's hand. Eamon wrapped his little fingers as far around Uncle Teagan's hand as he could and said, "Howdy, Uncle Teagan."

"Howdy," Uncle Teagan said and smiled. "How ya be a-feelin' this day, Eamon."

Eamon glanced over at Preacher Skaggs before he said, "I be fine as frog's hair. A godly man nary be goin' 'round whinin' about his trials."

Preacher Skaggs smiled and left the room.

Uncle Teagan looked back at the door as he said, "I reckon that be true some of the time, but nary a thing be true all of the time."

"Ya be goin' to be visitin' fer a spell?" Caelan asked.

"I reckon," Uncle Teagan said as he turned back to Eamon and smiled.

Caelan leaned back in his chair and said, "I reckon I be stayin' and visitin' with ya."

No one talked. Uncle Teagan and Eamon held hands and smiled at each other while Caelan watched from his chair. When Caelan's head dropped forward and he began to snore, Uncle Teagan asked, "How do ya really be doin'?"

Eamon looked at Caelan before he asked, "Will ya be comin' and takin' me to yer house when h'it be time fer me to be goin' home?"

"I be doin' ever thing I can be doin' to be makin' that happen," Uncle Teagan said before he kissed Eamon's tiny hand. "I be watchin' out over ya whether ya be at my house or yer Pa's house. I nary be lettin' 'em be hurtin' ya anymore."

CHAPTER FOURTEEN
THE WATERMELON PATCH

Uncle Teagan picked Eamon up from the hospital, but Caelan and Mabon wouldn't allow him to take Eamon to his house. As soon as Uncle Teagan entered their house carrying Eamon, he said to Caelan, "I be goin' to be checkin' on this here boy ever day. Ya best be takin' care of him."

"We be takin' care of our own," Mabon said, defensively, as Uncle Teagan walked toward the door of the children's room.

"Yas, yas," Uncle Teagan said as he carried Eamon to the bed and gently laid him down. When he laid Eamon on the mattress, he whispered, "They be yer folks, so I be havin' to be doin' what they be tellin' me to be doin'. They be sayin' I cain't be takin' ya to my house. I be swearin' to ya that I be comin' by ever day to be checkin' on ya."

Caelan came to the door and said, "H'it be time fer ya to be leavin'. The boy be needin' his rest."

Caelan leaned against the door frame and watched while Uncle Teagan kissed Eamon on the forehead and said, "I be by to be seein' ya tomorrow."

When Uncle Teagan tried to leave the children's room, Caelan put his palm on the opposite door frame to block Uncle Teagan's exit. He stared into Uncle Teagan's eyes and said, "Ya be havin' yer selves a good talk in that there car of yers on the way back?"

Uncle Teagan put his face right in front of Caelan's face and said, "The boy be sleepin' all the way. Ya nary be havin' nothin' to be worryin' about. Leave the child be and let him get well."

. . . . .

As I watched Eamon heal, I realized all of the children who followed me into this family survived when so many happy healthy children died of childhood diseases all around us, because having life so hard made them strong of body and spirit. Fifty years later when Eamon would tell the story of how his Pa visited him in the hospital, people would whisper that he was just too stubborn to let his handicaps hold him back. I didn't see it as being stubborn. I saw it as being determined, because I watched it develop over the weeks it took him to heal. He had to be determined not only to heal but to survive.

Eamon's determination wasn't the only reason he survived "the accident." Uncle Teagan took him to the hospital for medical care and paid the hospital bill when he picked Eamon up. When Eamon was no longer receiving the good care the hospital provided, Uncle Teagan made sure he got fed. He brought a plate of food and a mason jar full of lemonade or cider every morning and every night. He sat on the edge of the bed and talked to Eamon while he ate. When Caelan and Mabon tried to discourage Uncle Teagan from coming, he threatened to bring the sheriff around the next time he came. They, of course, let him keep visiting.

During one meal, Eamon whispered to Uncle Teagan, "How come ya always be sitting on my bed whilst I be eatin'?"

"I be afeared they be takin' yer food fer their selves if'n I nary be watching ya et h'it."

"How come ya nary be bringin' the sheriff 'round like ya be tellin' Pa ya be doin'? Mays be I be comin' 'round and livin' with ya then."

"The sheriff just be tellin' me to be mindin' to my own. Yer Pa be havin' so much to be feelin' guilty about that h'it nary be hard to be scarin' him. If'n I ever be callin' the sheriff, he be findin' out that I nary be havin' a leg to be standin' on. I nary be able to be visitin' ya after that. H'it gots to be our lil' secret."

At the end of each visit, Uncle Teagan took Eamon to the outhouse, cleaned him up and dressed him in one of the clean pairs of pajamas MawMaw Tierney made out of feed sacks. Every night, Uncle Teagan took the dirty ones home for MawMaw Tierney to wash for the next night. The denim pants and feed sack shirt that had been waiting at MawMaw Tierney's were tucked under Eamon's mattress waiting for the day when he would be well enough to wear them.

Garnett was also helpful. Every time he saw a chance to get something for Eamon, he did: a half-cup of water Caelan left on the table, a biscuit that sat on the unwashed dishes all morning, or an apple that was hanging low enough on the tree for Garnett to reach it.

The baby was often left lying on the mattress under Eamon's care. Her smile was as healing as everything Uncle Teagan, MawMaw Tierney and Garnett were doing for him.

MawMaw Tierney taught Regan how to help him heal. She knelt in front of Regan, looked into Regan's eyes and said as sweet as can be, "Do ya be knowin' why a farmer be shootin' a fox fer raidin' his chickens? H'it be because them chickens be havin' no defense. The farmer be havin' to be defendin' 'em. Ya nary be wantin' to be that fox fer harmin' Eamon when he be havin' no defense now, does ya?" After that, Regan only came into the room at night, and Eamon didn't hear her until the next morning unless Caelan came into the room to visit her.

Because of the good care the family members who still had the ability to feel gave him, Eamon slowly recovered from the injuries and infections the hospital treated. Unfortunately, Eamon was left handicapped just like the doctors said would happen.

He knew that being vulnerable was sure death in this family. His survival instinct evolved in the form of determination that would later be judged as stubbornness. As soon as his legs would support him, he let Garnett watch the baby while he walked around the room holding onto things. He was walking to the outhouse by himself by the second week. My eyes were filled with tears while I made that journey with him, because I realized the sound of one heavy footstep followed by one light footstep were the sounds his feet would make for the rest of his life. I realized the way his leg twisted out from the hip, making it shorter than the other one, was a pain he would never escape. I worried about what kind of life he would have in this condition. My life had been hard as the favored girl in a healthy body, so I didn't know how he was going to survive.

Survive he did. He healed faster than your modern doctors with their modern gadgets would believe and was limping around the property doing everything he had before and more.

Caelan and Mabon only fed their kids enough to barely keep them alive, but there were times when even those meager feedings became sparser. Sometimes it was because one of them wasted money on themselves. Sometimes it was because Caelan imbibed too much on moonshine. Less often, it was due to hard times. We didn't feel the depression as bad as people in the city did, because we had the land to sustain us. We did have some harder times we could blame on the economy, but usually a moonshine bender preceded the hard times.

Although I was thin and hungry in life, Caelan usually gave me enough food to keep me going. I think he did it out of respect for my real Ma. Fortunately, by the time Eamon came along, I was old enough to forage. I supplemented what Caelan gave me and shared it with Eamon. Now that I was gone and Eamon was the oldest, he was taking over for me and foraging for the younger children during the lean times.

Eamon had only been out of the hospital for a few months when one of the lean times hit. This one was made harder by the next baby that came out of Mabon's belly while Eamon was recovering. I still remember the morning it started. Caelan was at the mines, and Mabon was sitting at his spot at the table. She was drinking a cup of coffee and staring into the kitchen as if there was something very interesting in there. When Eamon limped out of his room to go to the outhouse, her gaze was drawn to him. She watched him limp across the room in a pair of pajamas MawMaw Tierney made for him out of a brown and white gingham feed sack. When he was halfway across the room, Mabon reached for Caelan's moonshine jar that sat on the table next to the wall. That was the beginning of the next lean time.

Whenever the lean times started, Caelan and Mabon knew they had more to hide. Even Uncle Teagan's and MawMaw Tierney's threats of the sheriff didn't get them into the house to feed the children. MawMaw Tierney left a plate of baked goods on the porch early every morning, but the children only got them if they beat their folks to them and found a place to hide while they ate. It was hard for Eamon to get to the plate in time since his handicap made it difficult for him to walk

109

softly, but he never gave up. He always made an early morning trip to the outhouse and grabbed the plate if it was still there. Fortunately, Caelan and Mabon were often too drunk to remember to get the plate.

Eamon wasn't only independent and determined. He was also smart. He knew he couldn't chase down a critter without harming himself more and making all the children more vulnerable, so he found new ways to feed them. When he heard the creaking begin in his folk's room, his footsteps clomped and creaked out of the house unnoticed. He walked to the end of the porch farthest away from the steps, picked up the reins he hid under the bench earlier in the day, and whistled softly for the white and black Pinto pony Uncle Teagan loaned him after the accident. Uncle Teagan said this pony would help Eamon get around, because she was so smart she seemed to know what people were thinking. This proved to be true. She always heard the soft whistle and came right away. Eamon put the reins on her and used a spot where the rail was broken as an easy way to mount without hurting his hip. The horse seemed to understand. She stood completely still until Eamon patted the side of her neck and said, "H'it be time, Lil' Gal." Only then did she trot gingerly away from the porch.

At the end of the driveway, Eamon patted her on the neck and said, "Uncle Teagan's place be the closest, but Ma and Pa be gettin' riled if'n they be gettin' word I be over there. They be thinkin' I be tellin' Uncle Teagan what be goin' on over here. I be havin' to work ya a bit harder this night. I be awful sorry."

Lil' gal began to walk in the other direction.

"I be thinkin' ya be knowin' what I be sayin'," Eamon said as he patted the side of her neck. She carried him down the country road to the next farm a couple of miles away. When they reached the watermelon patch that was near the road, Eamon said, "This here be h'it, Lil' Gal." Lil' Gal stopped. Eamon used the reins for the first time since he mounted her to lead her close to the fence. When she was steady by the fence, Eamon patted her neck one more time and said, "Ya be still now, Lil' Gal. This here goin' to be tricky."

He wrapped his arms around Lil Gal's neck before he put the foot of his good leg on the top rung of the fence. When that leg was balanced, he threw his bad leg over and balanced it. He grabbed the fence post with one hand before he released Lil Gal's neck with the other one. Once he had both hands on the fence post, he was in a position to use his arms to climb down the three rungs of the fence. Once he did, he limped into the watermelon patch, bent over, and thumped the first watermelon he came to.

"I done found a good one," Eamon said, and Lil' Gal whinnied as if she understood. He pulled the watermelon off the vine, rolled it across the field, under the bottom rung of the fence, and stopped it by Lil' Gal's feet. "Ya nary be steppin' on h'it, Lil' Gal," he said before he crawled under the bottom rung and stood next to her.

He pulled a drawstring bag out of the waist of his pajama pants and put the watermelon in it. He hooked the drawstring to the fence post and climbed the rungs of the fence. When he got to the top rung, he flopped across Lil' Gal's back belly first. He used her neck as leverage to pull himself into a seated position.

Lil' Gal took a step before Eamon said, "Ya be waitin' a spell, Lil' Gal." He leaned over, grabbed the drawstring, and lifted the bag with ease. The strength he was building in his arms to compensate for his legs was becoming apparent. He sat the watermelon between his legs and said, "Ya can be goin' now, Lil' Gal."

She headed for home. When they got there, she went straight to the broken porch rail. Eamon grabbed the bag by the drawstring and sat it on the porch before he dismounted. "Ya be so good, Lil' Gal" Eamon said as he pulled the leather reins over her head. "I bet ya h'it be feelin' right good to be gittin' that ol' thing off," he said as he patted her neck. Lil' Gal whinied and nuzzled him before she wandered back to the front yard to graze.

Eamon hid the watermelon under the bench that extended the length of the porch. When Caelan went to work and Mabon started sipping moonshine, the children would enjoy the watermelon together. Even the baby could suck on the soft juicy insides.

The children survived for several days on MawMaw Tierney's baked goods and the watermelons Eamon retrieved each night. On the fifth night, the farmer was waiting in the watermelon patch when Eamon arrived. As Eamon maneuvered his way onto the top rung of the fence, the farmer came up behind him, put his big hands around Eamon's waist and lowered Eamon to the ground.

When Eamon's feet hit the ground, he spun around and asked, "What ya be doin' to me?"

"I could be askin' ya the same," the farmer said. "This here be my garden."

Eamon tried to run away, but his limp slowed him down so much the farmer grabbed his shoulders before he made three steps. "Don't ya be worryin'," the farmer said as he turned Eamon gently around. "Ya nary be in trouble."

Eamon stared up at him and asked, "Then what ya be doin' out here?"

The farmer knelt in front of Eamon and put a big hand on each of Eamon's upper arms before he said, "I be knowin' h'it be ya what be takin' my melons when I be seein' yer footprints. One of yer feet be goin' deeper into the ground. The print from yer bad leg nary be much more than yer toes."

Eamon looked down at the ground.

The farmer released one of Eamon's arms, put two delicate fingers under Eamon's chin and raised Eamon's gaze to his own before he said, "I nary be mindin' ya takin' a melon. I be knowin' what ya young'uns be goin' through at yer house."

"No joshin'?"

"No joshin'. I just nary be wantin' ya to be stompin' up my vines. Ya done ruin't a couple of my plants stompin' 'round on 'em."

"I be sorry."

"That be a'right just so long as h'it not be happenin' no more," the farmer answered. "I be tellin' ya what. I be leavin' a melon fer ya on the porch ever evenin'. H'it be yers. Go ahead an' be takin' h'it. Just be stayin' outta my vines."

Eamon nodded.

"Ya goin' to be hurtin' yer self if'n ya be climbin' onto that there fence anyhows. Just be leadin' yer pony up to the porch from now on. She be easier to be mountin' from there."

Eamon nodded.

The farmer stood and picked up a watermelon that was sitting next to him. "I done already picked this one fer ya. Let us be gittin' ya and this here melon onto yer pony."

When they got to the fence, the farmer sat the watermelon down. He picked Eamon up and lifted him over the fence. When Eamon was safely on the other side, the farmer put one big hand on the top rung of the fence and jumped over.

"Lemme be showin' ya somethin'," the farmer said when he landed. He walked over to Lil' Gal and lifted one of her front legs. He held it while he pulled the reins down. Without both front legs firmly on the ground, Lil' Gal's body followed the reins. When she was sitting on four bended knees, the farmer said, "Git on."

Eamon climbed on with ease, and Lil' Gal stood up. While the farmer went back to get the watermelon, Eamon pulled the drawstring bag out of the waist of his pajama pants. He held it open between his legs, and the farmer put the watermelon inside when he returned.

As Eamon pulled the string on the bag, the farmer hit Lil' Gal on the rump and said, "Y'all be gittin' home safe now, ya hear?"

Eamon nodded as Lil' Gal turned around to head for home.

The following evening, the watermelon was waiting on the porch just as the farmer promised. Eamon easily dismounted, put the watermelon in the bag, mounted, and pulled the watermelon onto his lap by the drawstring. It was even easier than using his own porch, because the railing was at least a foot away from the edge.

Early the next morning, Eamon gathered the children while Regan pouted in her room. While Regan lay on her mattress hugging her bag of possessions, Eamon and the other children sat under a tree pulling handfuls of watermelon out of the busted shell and shoving it into their mouths.

Eamon spat out a mouthful of seeds, looked at the children and said, "These here melons surely do be tastin' better when I be stealin' 'em."

The children squealed with laughter.

As Garnett stuffed another handful in his mouth, Eamon picked the seeds out of a small piece and put it in the newest baby's mouth. She smiled big when the sweet taste touched her tongue. Eamon smiled back before he shoved another handful in his own mouth. Every time he spit out the seeds from his bite, he gave the baby another bite before he filled his own mouth again.

Even the bees buzzing around the sweet watermelon didn't seem to bother them. For a few blessed minutes they were free from Caelan, Mabon and Regan, and at the same time, they had food to eat. At this moment, they genuinely looked happy.

CHAPTER FIFTEEN
CHRISTIAN LEARNIN'

Eamon looked up after giving the baby a bite of watermelon and saw Preacher Skaggs' horse walking toward them. Preacher Skaggs sat on top of his horse with his back so straight and his head held so high that he looked like he thought he was king of the world.

"That ol' preacher man be comin'," Eamon said through his sleeve as it slid across his lips. "Wipe yer mouths."

As the children wiped their mouths, Eamon placed his palms on the ground and pushed himself to his feet. He picked up the watermelon pieces and threw them into the woods as Preacher Skaggs pulled his beautiful stallion to a stop in front of them. Eamon picked up the baby as the preacher said, "Well, boy, I surely do be feelin' happy to be seein' ya up and about."

Eamon walked toward him as he said, "Much obliged."

"When I be seein' ya in that there field after that there horse done pulled ya, I be reckonin' I nary be seein' ya again," Preacher Skaggs said as he pulled his Stetson® hat off his head and wiped his brow with the sleeve of his white dress shirt.

When he was up on his fancy horse, he usually wore a white dress shirt, a black string tie, black trousers and a matching jacket. He wore the Stetson® when the heat would allow.

Eamon stopped a few yards from the horse. The children stopped and peeked around him.

"I just be comin' by to be seein' how ya be doin'," Preacher Skaggs said.

"I be a'right."

"I be seein' ya be walkin' with a limp. Do the doctor be sayin' if'n that leg be gittin' any better?"

Eamon shrugged as he said, "I nary be knowin'. The doctor only be tellin' Pa."

"Y'all be comin' on over to the house with me," Preacher Skaggs said as he kicked the horse lightly in the ribs. "We be goin' to be talkin' with yer Pa."

Eamon moved the baby to the side of his good leg and followed the horse. Taking the weight off of his bad leg allowed him to walk faster.

Halfway to the porch, Garnett grabbed the bottom of Eamon's shirt and said, "He be right scary, Eamon."

"He do be," Eamon said, "but Ma be sayin' he be a man of God."

"Do God be scary, Eamon?"

"I reckon I don't rightly be knowin'."

The children reached the porch just as Caelan opened the front door. As the preacher walked through the door, he said, "That boy of yers pert near died. I be comin' to be talkin' to him about his salvation."

Caelan looked at the children and yelled, "Git on in here, and be showin' some respect. Preacher Skaggs done come a-callin' on Eamon."

Eamon limped up the steps and into the house. When they got inside, Preacher Skaggs was already seated on the bench in front of the fireplace. Mabon was sitting to his left. Caelan almost ran to the bench and sat on his other side. Eamon limped across the room. The floorboards creaked his uneven gait and emphasized how bad his limp was. Mabon and Caelan didn't seem to notice.

As Eamon walked the last few steps to the bench, Preacher Skaggs turned, looked at him and said, "Why, boy, ya nary be havin' a place to be sittin'. Ya be needin' to be sittin' with that leg and all."

As the preacher got up, Eamon said, "That be a'right. Ya be sittin' there. They nary be room fer me and all these young'uns there anyhow."

"I be goin' to be gittin' ya the chair over at that there table. I be bringin' h'it on over fer ya. Them young'uns can be sittin' on the floor 'round ya."

Caelan looked at Mabon and rolled his eyes while the preacher walked over to get the chair. Mabon shrugged. I was angry that Caelan couldn't get a chair for his own crippled son after he acted like the Preacher, a man I knew he secretly hated, was the second coming that he just had to sit next to.

The preacher returned with the chair, sat it in front of the fireplace facing the bench and said, "Sit yerself on down. Ya be needin' to be restin' that there leg of yers."

As Eamon sat and positioned the baby on his lap, Preacher Skaggs said, "Sittin' this way be right good. Ever' one can be seein' ever' one else whilst we be talkin'."

As the preacher sat down, Caelan asked, "What be bringin' ya 'round this early on a Saturday mornin'? Don't ya be havin' tomorrow's preachin' to be preparin' fer?"

"There be more to the Lord's work than just preachin'," Preacher Skaggs said and laughed. "I be comin' by to be seein' how yer boy be a-doin'. Last I be seein' him, he be layin' up in the hospital."

"Well, of course ya did," Caelan said as he nodded his head slowly.

Preacher Skaggs looked into Eamon's eyes and asked, "How ya be a-doin' since ya done got home from that there hospital, boy?"

Eamon looked down at the baby he was bouncing on his good leg.

"Lemme be givin' ya some advice," Preacher Skaggs said. "Never be lookin' away from a man when he be talkin' to ya. Half the men be takin' h'it personal and be gittin' riled at ya. The other half be thinkin' ya be weak and be tryin' to be gittin' one over on ya. Either way, ya nary be makin' friends."

"Yassir," Eamon said as he looked at Preacher Skaggs.

"How ya be a-doin' since ya done got home from that there hospital?"

"I reckon I be doin' a'right," Eamon answered. Halfway through the sentence he looked down, but he immediately jerked his head up and looked at the preacher again.

"I be right happy to be hearin' that," Preacher Skaggs said. He looked at Caelan and asked, "Do the doctor be sayin' whether that there limp be gittin' any better?"

"He nary be sayin' nothin'," Caelan said, grunting.

117

Preacher Skaggs looked back at Eamon and said, "Well, I surely do be hopin' h'it be gittin' well and soon, but God be holdin' ya one way or the other. Truth be known, boy, that just be yer body anyhow. Yer body nary be no never mind. Ya gonna be leavin' h'it behind when ya be goin' to be livin' in paradise, if'n ya be goin' to be livin' in paradise. Do ya be right with the Lord, boy?"

"I reckon."

"I reckon nary be a proper answer fer the Lord. Ya done got to be sure, boy. Do ya be knowin' how close ya done comed to dyin'? Ya could of been called up by the Lord that very day in that there field. Would ya done been ready to be meetin' yer maker?

"I reckon."

"There nary be no I reckon," Caelan said as he scooted forward in his seat and stared hard at Eamon. "Ya be listenin' to this here man. He be a man of God. He be knowin' what he be talkin' about."

"I be knowin' that," Eamon said.

"Ya be listenin' to yer Pa," Preacher Skaggs said. "He be a good man. He be comin' to church right often. He be givin' as much in the offerin' as these hard times be allowin' him to be givin'. He done asked God to be forgivin' him like we about to be doin' here for ya. He be right with God. He be ready to be meetin' the Lord. We be wantin' to be makin' sure ya be ready to be meetin' the Lord, too."

Eamon looked at Caelon while Preacher Skaggs was talking. Caelon started to fidgit. The second Preacher Skaggs stopped talking, Caelon yelled, "Ya nary be lookin' at me that way, boy. Preacher be knowin' I be doin' the best I can be doin'. Preacher be knowin' I be workin' from sun-up to sun-down ever day."

Eamon looked at his lap and started shaking so hard the baby on his lap was shaking, too.

"H'it be a'right, Caelan." Preacher Skaggs looked at Caelan and said, "The boy just be admirin' ya fer being the good man of God I be tellin' him ya be. H'it be all right." The preacher looked at Eamon and said, "I be awful sorry about how ya be gittin' hurt and all. I be awful happy ya still be here with us. Truth be told, boy, h'it nary be matterin' how old ya be. If'n ya be leavin' this here world nary bein' right with the Lord, ya be goin' to hell. Even that there lil' babe in yer arms be goin' straight to hell if'n she be leavin' this world nary bein' right with the Lord. We nary be wantin' nobody to be goin' to hell, because h'it be sufferin' what never end if'n ya be goin' there. Ya be hearin' me. Yer sufferin' be never endin'."

Eamon and Garnett both swallowed hard.

"Ya be wantin' to be in heaven with yer Ma and Pa, don't ya, boy?"

Eamon didn't answer.

"Yer Ma and Pa be in church as many Sundays as they be able to be comin'. I be knowin' where they be a-goin' after they be dyin'. I be wantin' to be makin' sure ya be goin' with 'em. How can they be havin' joy in heaven if'n their younguns nary be with 'em? Ya do be wantin' to be gittin' right with the Lord, so ya can be with yer folks, don't ya, boy?"

Eamon didn't say anything.

The room sat quiet for several minutes before Caelan stood up and said, "Ya do be wantin' to be bein' in heaven with us, don't ya, boy?"

Eamon looked at Caelon and swallowed hard before he nodded.

Preacher Skaggs lay his hand on Caelan's arm and said, "Sit on down here, brother. The child just be afeared by knowin' how close he be comin' to goin' to hell. The fear done be gittin' his tongue. He be goin' to be a'right."

Caelan sat down, but he stayed on the edge of the bench like an animal getting ready to pounce.

Preacher Skaggs looked at Eamon and asked, "Has ya done accepted the Lord as yer personal Savior?"

"I nary be knowin'," Eamon answered as he shrugged.

"Do ya be desirin' to?"

"Do bein' in hell be worse than bein' here?" Eamon asked as a tear welled in the corner of his eye.

"H'it surely do be," Preacher Skaggs answered.

"If'n that be what I be havin' to be doin' to be gittin' into heaven, I reckon I be wantin' to be acceptin' the Lord."

"That be what ya be havin' to be doin'."

"Do Sinead be gittin' into heaven?"

Caelan jumped off the edge of the bench and said, "Now, ya be listenin' here – "

Preacher Skaggs laid his hand on Caelan's arm again and said, "Sit on down, brother. That be right common ta be worryin' about yer

119

loved ones what done gone on before ya." When Caelan sat down, Preacher Skaggs looked at Eamon and said, "Why, of course yer sister be bein' in heaven. She nary be at the age of accountability when she be goin' to be bein' with the Lord. Ever' one who be dyin' before the age of accountability be goin' straight to heaven."

"But Sinead be older than this here babe when she be leavin' us."

"Yas, she do. She be quite a bit older than that there babe."

"Ya just be sayin' even this here babe be goin' to hell if'n she not be acceptin' the Lord. How do I be knowin' if'n Sinead done be in heaven or hell?"

Caelan jumped up and yelled, "Ya nary be back talkin' a preacher man!"

Preacher Skaggs lay his hand on Caelan's arm and said, "We just be a-talkin' here, Brother Caelan. Nary need to be gettin' riled." He returned his attention to Eamon and said, "I be right sure yer sister be right with the Lord before she be leavin' us. She be a good lil' gal. She be comin' to church with yer folks right often."

Eamon stared at me as he asked, "Can ya be seein' folks what done gone to heaven?"

"Yas. We be seein' all of our loved ones again."

Eamon sighed deep as if he were relieved.

Preacher Skaggs looked in my direction as if he was trying to see what Eamon was looking at, but he looked at Eamon before he said, "If'n ya be gittin' right with the Lord, ya sure to be seein' ever' one again what went to heaven before ya."

Eamon looked at the preacher and asked, "Do my brothers and sisters be needin' to be acceptin' the Lord to be gittin' into heaven?"

Preacher Skaggs nodded.

"Then we all be wantin' to be doin' h'it."

Preacher Skaggs looked around the room as he asked, "Where do Regan be?"

"Ya nary be havin' to be worryin' about that lil' gal," Caelan said. "She be a good girl. She done be right with the Lord. She be spendin' most of her time on her bed just a-prayin'."

"That be right good," Preacher Skaggs said as he scooted to the edge of the bench. "Let us be gittin' ya'll ready to be bein' together in heaven. All ya young'uns be needin' to be bowin' yer heads."

120

When Eamon bowed his head, he wrapped one arm around the baby and pushed her head into a bowed position with his free hand. She looked up, and Eamon pushed her head forward again. He held his hand on the back of her head as Preacher Skaggs said, "I be wantin' y'all young'uns to be sayin' after me what I be sayin'. Dear God, we be horrible sinners."

Eamon and Garnett repeated the sentence.

"But ya be lovin' us anyhow."

All of the children spoke this sentence.

"Because ya be lovin' us, ya be forgivin' us fer bein' filthy sinners."

The volume of the children's voices decreased during the second part of that sentence.

"We be askin' ya to be forgivin' us fer our sins."

Eamon and Garnett said the last sentence.

"Amen," Preacher Skaggs said and looked up. All of the children still had their heads bowed, so he said, "We be done. Ya'll can stop bowin' yer heads, young'uns."

The children looked up. It took Eamon a second to realize he was still holding the baby's head in a bowed position. When he moved his hand, her head bounced up like a jack in the box. She started laughing.

"Ya be lookin' at that babe just a-laughin'," Preacher Skaggs said. "She be gittin' herself plum filled up with the joy of the spirit. That lil' babe be knowin' she be gittin' herself saved."

Eamon looked at the baby and smiled.

"Ya be lookin' at that boy," Preacher Skaggs said as he poked his elbow into Caelan's side. "He be a-smilin', too. That there boy done be filled up with the Holy Spirit."

When Eamon stopped smiling and rested his chin on top of the baby's head, I realized how rarely he smiled. The only time I saw him smile was when one of the babies pulled it out of him, and that smile always disappeared quickly.

"How do ya be a-feelin'?" Preacher Skaggs asked.

"Do we all be goin' to heaven now?" Eamon asked.

"Preacher be askin' ya how ya be feelin', boy! He nary be askin' ya to be askin' him questions," Caelan said as he wagged his finger at Eamon.

Eamon slid down in the chair so far that it looked like he shrank, and the baby's small body shrank with him.

"Ya be answerin' the man!" Caelan said, his voice raising.

"I reckon I be feelin' a'right," Eamon said.

"I reckon ya be feelin' a'right, too, boy," Preacher Skaggs said. "Ya done accepted the Lord just now, child."

Eamon nodded.

"What do ya be a-thinkin', boy?"

"Do we be goin' to heaven now?"

"That there be a good question, boy. Yas, y'all be goin' to heaven. H'it be assured once y'all be gittin' baptized."

"I be hopin' the water be warshin' some of the hateful off'n that there boy," Mabon said.

Preacher Skaggs turned his whole body when he looked at Mabon. He lay his hand on her knee and asked, "What ya be sayin', Sister Mabon?"

"He be bein' the most hateful young'un I ever did see. He nary be grateful fer nothin' ya be doin' fer him. He nary be bein' a good example fer the lil' ones comin' up under him. And, he be a thief. I cain't be keepin' food in that there kitchen fer the rest of us. He always be takin' what he nary supposed to be takin'."

Preacher Skaggs looked at Eamon and asked, "Do that be true, boy?"

Eamon wiped sticky watermelon juice off his chin and looked at it on his fingers before he lowered his head in shame.

The preacher looked at Mabon, patted her leg and said, "He done been forgiven fer all that just now, Sister Mabon. I just be needin' to be teachin' him what the Lord be expectin' of him now that he be belongin' to the Lord."

"Well, I surely do be wishin' ya luck with that," Mabon said as she lay her hand on the preacher's hand.

Preacher Skaggs moved his hand to the top of Mabon's and twined his fingers through hers as he asked, "Well, how about if'n the boy be comin' over to the church fer me to be learnin' him what God be wantin' from him now that he be a Christian."

"That there be soundin' like a mighty fine idear," Caelan said. "If'n I be ya, I be doin' that before ya be dunkin' him. We be wantin' to be makin' sure h'it all be gittin' warshed away."

"H'it be settled then." Preacher Skaggs looked at Eamon and said, "I be wantin' ya to be comin' on over to the church Monday mornin' as soon as yer mornin' chores be done. I be wishin' I could be seein' ya tomorrow, but a preacher be mighty busy on the Lord's Day."

"Praise God," Mabon said.

"Praise God," Caelan repeated.

As Preacher Skaggs stood up, he said, "H'it be settled then. I be seein' the boy on Monday mornin' fer some Christian learnin'."

The preacher shook Caelan's hand and gave Mabon a hug before he walked out the front door.

When the door closed, Caelan said, "Ya young'uns needs to be gittin' on outta here. Ya'll be havin' better things to be doin' than to be layin' 'round this here house all damn day."

Eamon herded the children out the front door. When the door closed, Mabon said, "I reckon h'it nary be hurtin' nothin' to be lettin' Eamon be goin' on over to the church fer Christian learnin' with preacher. H'it might be doin' him some good."

"H'it cain't be hurtin' nothin'," Caelan said. "Eamon nary be havin' nothin' to be tellin' that there preacher except what preacher already be knowin'." He paused before he said, "I reckon h'it be punishment enough that we be havin' to be kissin' that Preacher's arse fer the rest of our lives."

"Why in hell ya be confessin' to him about what I done did to Sinead whilst that boy be layin' up in that there hospital? I never be understandin' why ya be doin' that."

Caelan stared at her until she backed away. When her bottom hit the bench, he said, "I nary be knowin', woman. I reckon I be grievin' when I be confessin' to him. I be thinkin' Eamon be goin' to die. I reckon I be afeared fer my own soul if'n ya done kilt two babies."

"Ya bein' afeared done caused ya to be sellin' yer soul to that there Preacher instead of the Devil."

"H'it be the same thang," Caelan said as he walked out the door.

CHAPTER SIXTEEN
FOR THE LOVE OF CHRIST

On Monday morning, I followed Eamon as he limped down the long road that led from our house to the main road. This walk was so beautiful that it was hard to believe our creaky gray house sat on one end of our road and the rough country road that led to the church and its greasy preacher sat on the other end. I wondered how our people created such a harsh culture amid this natural beauty. It was like they were living in a bubble that made them completely unaware of the beauty around them.

When I was alive, I loved traveling down this road. A beautiful summer day made me wonder if this was what heaven was like. Most of this mountain was boulders and wild growth that was littered with an occasional dilapidated house desperately in need of a coat of white wash and a thorough cleaning, especially in the summer. Everyone was so busy growing, catching and preparing food for their ever growing families, and not just for today but also for the harsh mountain winter to come, that cleanliness took a back seat to survival. Spring cleaning was a foreign concept to us.

This was one of those perfect summer days. The sun was shining down from a clear, light blue sky that was spattered with wispy white clouds. On the left side of the road was a line of trees that created enough shade to keep the sun off Eamon's head as he walked. On the right side, our fields went farther than sight. They were interrupted by the boulders and rocks that were a constant reminder of the hardships of mountain life.

Most of the roads were also in the habit of reminding your bare feet of the hardships of mountain life. Small rocks jutted out of them like boulders jutted out of the fields. Our road, on the other hand, was mostly dirt. As long as you walked on the two bare strips where the wagon wheels kept the grass worn down, your feet would be all right. The trick was to stay off of the grass that grew between those strips and on the side of the road, because you couldn't see what you were stepping on. Poisonous snakes were an even greater concern than rocks. Rattlesnakes and copperheads populated these hills. You learned at an early age to be careful when you walked through high grass, not to play around the boulders or any place where they liked to sun or hide, and to remain still when a copperhead slithered across the river when you were bathing.

On this particular day, my focus was drawn away from this beauty to Eamon's crippled legs trying to carry him to the church on bare feet. Caelan forbade him to ride Lil' Gal, because Regan decided to ride her to school that day. Most people on this mountain didn't value education. They assumed the men were going to end up in the mines and the girls were going to be having babies. Besides, they needed the boys to work in the fields and the girls to do the never-ending list of chores the women always had to do. I never went to school when I was alive. None of the children went to school until the law intervened shortly after Eamon was grown. But, Caelon sent Regan whenever Regan wanted to go. She didn't appreciate it just like she didn't appreciate any of the many things he gave her. She stayed home and stared at herself in the mirror more than she went to school, but Caelon gave her Lil' Gal to go on this day when Eamon really needed that pony.

The legs of his denim pants were too short, so I noticed his injured leg was not only shorter than the other one but was also getting thinner. The weakness in his legs made him almost fall each time he stepped on the smallest gravel.

There was a short break in the trees that allowed me to see the family graveyard and the church steeple rising to heaven. It looked like a long way for Eamon to walk, especially when his unsteady legs would have to maneuver the rock-littered main road. It wasn't right to force Eamon to limp to that nasty preacher who didn't know anything about this place Mabon had sent me to. It was un-Christian to force a crippled child to walk instead of letting him ride his pony. What could such broken people teach him about Jesus?

When Eamon reached the church, I saw Preacher Skaggs' car sitting at the bottom of the porch steps. Even this dead child knew a country preacher shouldn't be able to afford a Duesenberg. He already had the best horse in the county even though he didn't need it for working the land. I guess he needed a car, so he could take pictures of it with his fancy camera. He certainly didn't need it to pick up crippled children who were coming to see him.

I followed Eamon as he limped up the porch steps and entered the church. It was dark inside and felt spooky. I could tell Eamon felt it, too, because he started fidgeting and stayed near the door. After several minutes, we heard Preacher Skaggs' footsteps coming down the aisle.

"Ya be bringin' yerself on in, Brother Eamon, ya be most welcome," Preacher Skaggs said as he grabbed Eamon's elbow and led him down the aisle. Preacher Skaggs walked so fast that Eamon stumbled all the way to the front pew. When Pastor Skaggs invited Eamon to sit next to him, Eamon froze and stared at the rattlesnakes that slithered in cages behind the pulpit.

"Ya nary be sittin' down?" Preacher Skaggs asked as he patted the seat next to him.

Eamon stared at the snakes as he asked, "Do we be havin' to be sittin' in the front? I nary be likin' the sound them there snakes be makin'."

Preacher Skaggs patted the seat next to him again and said, "Ya be sittin' yerself on down, boy. Ya be a Christian now. The Bible be sayin' them there snakes cain't be harmin' nary a man of God. Ya done got yerself saved in yer Ma and Pa's house just yesterday, so them there snakes cain't be harmin' ya nary more. Ya be sittin' yerself on down."

Eamon hesitated for several seconds before he sat next to the preacher.

"How ya be feelin' now that ya done accepted the Good Lord?" Preacher Skaggs asked as he slid onto one hip and threw his elbow over the back of the pew behind Eamon. He smiled big when Eamon looked up at him.

"I reckon I be feelin' a'right?"

Preacher Skaggs shook his head as he said, "Ya only be half the way there, child. Do ya be thinkin' about bein' baptized?"

"What do that be?"

"I be dunkin' ya into the water, and h'it be warshin' away yer sins," Preacher Skaggs answered.

Eamon looked around the church before he asked, "Where do the water be?"

Preacher Skaggs laughed and said, "Naw, Naw, son. The water nary be here in the church buildin'. We nary be bein' Catholics, after all. We be goin' on down to the river. Ya be needin' to be thinkin' about this. We be havin' to be gittin' h'it done before bad weather be comin' on."

Eamon started shaking when Preacher Skaggs said river. When the preacher finished talking, Eamon ran his palm up and down his leg as he said, "I nary be able to be swimmin', preacher. I prob'ly be swimmin' even worse now that I be hurt."

"Ya nary be havin' to be worryin'. I be holdin' onto ya the whole time. I nary be goin' to be lettin' ya be drowin'."

"Ya be knowin' fer sure?"

"I be knowin' fer sure. Ya be wantin' me to be showin' ya?"

"Ya be wantin' to be goin' down to the river now?" Eamon asked. He was shaking so bad that his voice trembled as he spoke.

"Naw. I can be showin' ya right here. I just be wantin' to be showin' ya how I gonna be hangin' onto ya whilst ya be in the water."

"What do I need to be doin'?"

Preacher Skaggs stood up and motioned for Eamon to join him as he said, "Ya needs to be standin' next to me."

Eamon obeyed, but his body became stiff when Preacher Skaggs laid his hand on Eamon's back. Preacher Skaggs had to shake out Eamon's arm to loosen it up before he raised Eamon's hand to his nose and said, "I be tellin' ya to be holdin' yer nose like this here. Then, I be lowerin' ya back into the water."

Preacher Skaggs bent Eamon backwards. Halfway back, Eamon's bad leg gave out, and he lost his footing. The muscles in Preacher Skaggs' arm went rigid when he tightened his grip on Eamon's back. With the other hand, he grabbed Eamon's crotch. When Eamon regained his footing, he jerked away and backed into the wooden pulpit.

Preacher Skaggs trapped him against the pulpit, put his face in Eamon's face and asked, "What be the matter, boy?"

"I nary be wantin' ya to be touchin' me in the secrets. If'n ya be doin' that whilst we be down at that there river, someone might be seein' h'it," Eamon stammered.

Preacher Skaggs laughed and said, "Boy, ever' one be knowin' what be goin' on over at yer house. We be knowin' how yer Ma and Pa be treatin' ya. I nary be knowin' what they might of done to be makin' ya so protectin' of yer secrets, but I be bettin' whatever they done be makin' ya hurt. H'it be seemin' to me like ever thing they be doin' to ya be makin' ya hurt. I just be tryin' to be keepin' ya from fallin' on yer arse. I be doin' right by ya, boy. Ya be tellin' me the truth now, boy. Do h'it be feelin' better when I be touchin' ya than when yer Ma and Pa be touchin' ya?"

Eamon froze. His only movement was his Adam's apple when he swallowed hard.

"God be givin' ya that there thing fer more than pissin', boy," Preacher Skaggs said as he caressed Eamon's crotch. When Eamon's penis hardened, Preacher Skaggs asked, "Do that be feelin' better than what yer Ma and Pa be doin' to ya?"

A tear rolled down Eamon's cheek.

Preacher Skaggs gently wiped the tear off Eamon's face before he said, "I be bettin' yer Ma and Pa nary be offerin' ya comforts when ya be cryin. I be tryin' to be doin' right by ya, boy."

"Run away," I screamed at Eamon. "Run away."

Eamon looked toward me before he tried to escape.

Preacher Skaggs put his hand on the pulpit to stop Eamon with his arm before he said, "Where do ya be goin', boy? Ya nary be havin' nothin' to be afeared of. I be a man of God. Besides, do ya nary be forgettin' that h'it be me what done been kind to ya at her Ma and Pa's house Saturday last. They be talkin' to ya right awful, and h'it be me what be stickin' up fer ya. I be a good man, son. Ya can be trustin' me. I always be havin' yer back."

"I reckon," Eamon stammered.

"Do ya be thinkin' I can be baptizin' ya if'n I nary be able to be touchin' ya?"

Clouds must have filled the sky, because the church suddenly became dark. Preacher Skaggs used the darkness to his advantage. He laid on Eamon and caressed Eamon's crotch more aggressively. The extra weight made the pulpit fall over, which agitated the snakes. Their hissing caught Eamon's attention long enough to allow Preacher Skaggs to push Eamon onto the dais, lay on him and force Eamon's hand onto his crotch. Preacher Skaggs held Eamon's hand there as he asked, "Would ya be feelin' better about me touchin' ya if'n ya be touchin' me?" Eamon fought to get his hand free, but the preacher kept rubbing it on his crotch. Preacher Skaggs smiled as he looked at his erect manhood and said, "Ya be seein' how h'it be happenin' to ever man."

Tears streamed down Eamon's face.

Preacher Skaggs looked into Eamon's eyes as he said, "I nary be meanin' ya no harm, boy. I just be wantin' ya to be knowin' this be happenin' to ever man." Preacher Skaggs released Eamon's hand and embraced Eamon like a lover as he said, "Boy, ya nary be nothin' but skin and bones. Ya be needin' somethin' to et, don't ya?"

Eamon nodded.

"If'n I be givin' ya somethin' to et, will ya be knowin' I nary be meanin' ya no harm?"

Eamon nodded.

Preacher Skaggs got up and returned the pulpit to its place in the middle of the dais. When he did, a silver lunch bucket fell out of the shelves that were inside the back of the pulpit. The church was so dark that the silver metal looked gray. He carried the bucket back to where Eamon was sitting on the edge of the dais and said, "This here be my lunch. I be thinkin' ya be needin' this here food more than I be needin' hi't." He pulled a muslin-wrapped sandwich out of the bucket, unwrapped it and gave it to Eamon.

Eamon slowly reached for the sandwich. When his hand got close, he grabbed it and began to devour it like a starving animal, which I guess he was.

As Eamon ate, Preacher Skaggs said, "I nary be the bad man some folks be makin' me out to be. I just be havin' yer best interest at heart. I just be tryin' to be teachin' ya how to be a Christian and a man. Ya do be wantin' me to be teachin' ya, don't ya, boy?"

Eamon nodded as he continued to devour the sandwich. After he was done eating it, Preacher Skaggs pulled another muslin-wrapped package out of the bucket. Light flickered in Eamon's eyes when Preacher Skaggs opened the package to reveal two oatmeal cookies. Eamon put one in each hand and took alternating bites from them.

As Eamon ate the cookies, Preacher Skaggs said, "This here be what h'it be meanin' to be a Christian. H'it be meanin' charity. Ya be havin' to be helpin' those what be in need."

When Eamon finished the cookies, he asked, "Do h'it be Christian when I be doin' fer my lil' brothers and sisters?"

"Yas, h'it do," Preacher Skaggs said as he put his arm across Eamon's shoulders. "I be goin' to be helpin' ya be a better Christian to yer brothers and sisters. I be goin' to be bringin' enough cookies fer ya and them other young'uns ever time ya be comin' over here fer Christian learnin'. How do that be soundin'?"

"That be soundin' right fine?" Eamon said before he smiled.

"A Christian man be needin' to be knowin' what h'it be like to be a man, too. Can I be showin' ya what h'it be meanin' to be a man?"

Eamon stopped smiling and his body tensed, but he said, "Yassir."

Preacher Skaggs unbuttoned his trousers and revealed his still erect manhood. As he moved his hand up and down it, he said, "God be givin' us this here thing between our legs to be allowin' us to be feelin' pleasure. That be our reward fer bein' men. H'it be feelin' mighty good to be runnin' yer hand up and down h'it like this. Ya ought to be tryin' h'it on yerself."

"I cain't be showin' no one my secrets," Eamon said.

"That surely do be true. Ya cain't be showin' them to just anyone, but ya can be showin' 'em to me. I be teachin' ya how to be a man."

Preacher Skaggs unzipped Eamon's denim pants and said, "Ya needs to be pulling yers out as well."

"My MawMaw gave me these pants. H'it nary be right fer me to – "

"Ya nary be thinkin' yer MawMaw be wantin' ya to be feelin' good?" Preacher Skaggs interrupted him to ask.

"I – I – I nary – "

"That do be a shame. I be thinkin' yer MawMaw be better than yer folks. I be thinkin' she be wantin' ya to be feelin' pleasures instead of pain."

"She do, but – "

"If'n she do, she be wantin' ya to be learnin' from me. Ya go ahead on now and be takin' that thing out." After Eamon hesitantly obeyed, Preacher Skaggs said, "Ya just be runnin' yer hand up and down h'it like I be doin'."

Eamon looked at his soft penis and said, "H'it nary be all stiff like yers be."

"H'it be gittin' stiff once ya start rubbin' h'it."

"A'right," Eamon said as he hesitantly placed his hand around his manhood.

After a few seconds, Preacher Skaggs asked, "Now, don't that be feelin' good?"

"Yassir," Eamon said as he stiffly and hesitantly moved his hand up and down his penis.

"The Bible be sayin' h'it be pollutin' yerself when ya be doin' h'it to yerself. That there be a sin. Ya gots to be lettin' someone else be doin' h'it fer ya so as not to be pollutin' yerself."

"Like when Pa be touchin' Regan down there?"

Preacher Skaggs stopped stroking himself and asked, "Ya be tellin' me yer ol' man be touchin' Regan down there?"

"Yassir,"

"I'll be dogged," Preacher Skaggs said as he started stroking himself. "And here I be thinkin' he just be after ya boys. I reckon I be needin' to be teachin' Regan a thing or two, too."

"Ya be teachin' Regan, too?"

"Nary before I be done teachin' ya," Preacher Skaggs said as he released his own manhood and forced Eamon's hand around it instead. "Now, just be doin' to me what ya just done to yerself."

When Eamon complied, Preacher Skaggs returned the favor. Both of them groaned several times before the loud hiss of a rattlesnake caused Eamon to jump. He stopped and turned his head to stare at the snakes' cages.

131

Preacher Skaggs placed his hand on Eamon's hand and forced it to move again as he asked, "What be botherin' ya? Ya be knowin' them there snakes nary be hurtin' a man of God."

"I nary be likin' them there snakes at all."

"Ya be a Christian now. Ya done accepted the Lord at yer Ma and Pa's house yesterday. Ya nary be havin' a reason to be fearin' them there snakes no more. I done told ya that."

"Yassir," Eamon said as he turned his head forward.

"Them there snakes be lookin' a whole lot like that thing ya be havin' in yer hand. Our manhood nary be hurtin' a person anymore than them there snakes do. Ya go ahead on and be doin' with h'it what ya be doin' with h'it before."

"Yassir," Eamon said before he started stroking Preacher Skaggs' manhood again. Eamon groaned when the favor was again returned.

After man and boy both ejaculated, Preacher Skaggs asked, "Do that be feelin' good?"

"Yassir."

"Ya be seein' now, boy, that I be here to be makin' ya be feelin' good. I nary be bringin' ya pain like yer Ma and Pa be doin'."

"Yassir."

"Ya gots to be rememberin' what yer Pa be like. If'n ya be tellin' him about this, he be sure to be beatin' ya. This here be havin' to be our lil' secret. Ya be understandin'?"

Eamon swallowed hard before he nodded.

"Ya nary be tellin' no one about this. Ya be the only one what be hurt by h'it if'n ya do."

"Yassir."

· · · · ·

Eamon went to the church every day for Christian learnin'. Preacher Skaggs fed him and sent cookies home for his brothers and sisters, and these food gifts made the visits tolerable. However, Preacher Skaggs grew more bold as Eamon grew more comfortable with their arrangement. After a couple of weeks, soft and gentle caresses allowed Preacher Skaggs to get Eamon's pants off. He leaned

Eamon over the dais and slowly slid his manhood into Eamon's backside.

Eamon struggled, but Preacher Skaggs lack of a handicap gave him the advantage. He held Eamon down as he slid his penis in and out of Eamon's bloody rectum.

Eamon cried as he begged, "Naw! Naw! Stop! Ya done said ya nary be goin' to be hurtin' me like Ma and Pa do! Stop!" After a while, he collapsed on the dais and stared at the snakes. When Preacher Skaggs finished, Eamon didn't move. He stared at the snakes until the tears stopped, and then he said, "That thing do be just like them there snakes. H'it do bite."

"What do ya be sayin' there, boy?"

"That thing do bite just like them there snakes," Eamon said as he pulled his pants up.

"I be right confused, boy," Preacher Skaggs said as he shrugged and crinkled his forehead. "I just be showin' ya how much I be lovin' ya just like we be doin' fer days now."

"That nary be feelin' like love."

"H'it be feelin' better the more we be doin' h'it," Preacher Skaggs said as he tried to put his arm across Eamon's shoulders.

Eamon pushed his arm away and said, "I nary be wantin' to be doin' that nary more."

"What ya be meanin'?"

"I nary be wantin' to do that nary more."

"Do that be meanin' ya nary be lovin' me nary more?" When Eamon didn't answer, Preacher Skaggs got in Eamon's face and said, "Let me be tellin' ya one thing, boy. I nary be carin' if'n ya be lovin' me or not so long as ya nary be lettin' bad feelin's ya be havin' toward me be leadin' ya to be doin' somethin' foolish. If'n ya be tellin' anyone what we be doin' here, yer Pa be findin' out and be beatin' ya near to death. If'n that nary be teachin' ya to be keepin' yer mouth shut, then I be havin' to be takin' h'it out on that lil' brother ya be lovin' so much. What be his name? Garnett. Don't be gittin' foolish, boy. Ya nary be havin' a safe place to be goin' to."

CHAPTER SEVENTEEN
TRIANGULATION STRANGULATION

Eamon ran out of the church and down the porch steps. He stumbled so bad on the steps that I was amazed he avoided falling. He stumbled almost as badly as he ran down the main road faster than I ever saw him move. I floated beside him, but there was nothing I could do to steady him. My fear for him made me realize why the people on this mountain so rarely saw its beauty. When you're constantly worried and scared, you lose the ability to appreciate beauty. I wasn't aware of my environment. I was only concerned for Eamon.

When Eamon arrived at our road, he stumbled around in a circle for several minutes before he figured out which way to go. Although his pace slowed, he continued to stumble as he walked toward our house. He was pale, sweaty, winded and exhausted when he fell on our bottom porch step. His hip must have pained him all the way home, because he started rubbing it as soon as he sat down. All of the children gathered around him, and the frowns they immediately developed revealed that they knew something was wrong.

Garnett sat down and grabbed Eamon's arm with both hands before he asked, "What be the matter?"

When the question was asked a second time, Eamon shook his head several times and stammered, "I be a'right."

"Naw, ya nary be a'right. What be the matter?"

Eamon jumped when he heard the front door open. All of the children turned when Regan walked out onto the creaky porch carrying the newest baby in her arms. She stomped down the steps and

134

thrust it at Eamon as she said, "Ma be sayin' fer ya to be watchin' after this here thing." When Regan got halfway back up the steps, she turned and said, "What be the matter with ya?"

"I be a'right," Eamon answered.

"Naw, ya nary be a'right," Regan said and laughed. She walked the rest of the way up the steps and sat on the porch bench before she laughed again and said, "I nary be knowin' what be goin' on with ya, but I be goin' to be watchin' ya till I be findin' out."

All of the children sat in silence until mid-afternoon when Garnett said, "I be hungry."

Eamon's head was cocked to the side, his brow was crinkled, and his mouth was halfway open when he responded to Garnett by staring at him. When Garnett said it again, Eamon stammered, "MawMaw Tierney be leavin' us some cakes in the mornin'."

They resumed sitting in silence. At twilight, Preacher Skaggs' Dusenberg drove up our road and parked in front of our house. Eamon gasped, his body stiffened, and he leaned back so far that he seemed to be trying to push himself into the steps behind him. Preacher Skaggs got out of the car and walked up the porch steps as if nothing had happened.

He didn't bother to greet Eamon, but he smiled at Regan and said, "Howdy, ya perty lil' gal. Where do yer Ma be?"

"She be in the house," Regan said. She smiled big before she stood and curtsied. "Come on with me. I be showin' ya where she be."

Preacher Skaggs followed Regan into the house. Eamon stood, gathered the baby and grabbed Garnett's hand. He led Garnett into the house, and all of the other children followed. They stopped just inside the door and watched. Mabon sat on Caelan's chair at the table, and Preacher Skaggs stood over her. Regan stood next to him.

Eamon gasped when Preacher Skaggs said, "I be feelin' right surprised, Sister Mabon, to be seein' that there money be gone. The only thing I can be figurin' is h'it be Garnett what done took h'it."

"What be makin' ya be thinkin' h'it be Garnett?" Mabon asked.

"He done helped me with things right after church on Sunday. He be 'round the offerin' plates then. I be wantin' to be comin' 'round sooner, but I be busy gittin' ready for Eamon's Christian learnin'. I nary be gittin' 'round to countin' the money till this very day. Ya can be imaginin' my surprise when I be findin' the plates empty."

Mabon shook her head and said, "I nary be knowin' what to be sayin'." She shook her head for a few more seconds before she saw Garnett standing by the door and said, "Git on over here, boy."

Garnett grasped Eamon's hand tighter.

"He nary be doin' nothin'," Eamon said more confidently than I'd ever seen him speak. "He be with me all the time. I be knowin' if'n he be doin' anythin' he ought not to be doin'."

Mabon looked at Preacher Skaggs and said, "The boy be right about that there."

Preacher Skaggs looked at Eamon and said, "Unless he be helpin' Garnett."

Eamon swallowed hard and said, "Ain't nary a-one of us be takin' a thing from ya."

Eamon went pale and started sweating when the sound of footsteps creaked across the porch. Caelan skipped his after work cleansing ritual, entered the house and asked, "Why do the preacher's car be sittin' in front of our house?"

"Ya better be gittin' on in here and be hearin' this," Preacher Skaggs said.

Caelan pushed his way through the children. As he walked toward the Preacher, he asked, "What be goin' on here?"

"I be hatin' to be breakin' h'it to ya, but I be believin' Garnett be stealin' when he be helpin' me to count the tithin' last Sunday."

Caelan ran back to the door, grabbed the front of Garnett's shirt and screamed, "What ya be doin' with that there money?"

Eamon was shaking so bad he could barely speak when he stammered, "Pa, Garnett done come'd straight home with us after church on Sunday. Don't ya be rememberin'?"

Caelan looked at him and said, "Ya be needin' to be mindin' yer own business. This here be between grown-up folk."

Preacher Skaggs looked at Eamon and said, "Ya done been at the church today, Eamon. Do ya be knowin' anythin' about that there money?"

Eamon stared at him and said, "Ya be knowin' ever thing what went on at that there church today. I nary be leavin' yer sight. I be runnin' outta there, because ya be touchin' me."

Most of the time, Mabon and Caelan were involved in a power dance. Caelan had mountain patriarchy behind him, so Mabon acted submissive in front of outsiders. Only extreme anger could provoke her to break that facade. I don't know if it was memories of Preacher Skaggs touching her, jealousy that he didn't touch her anymore, or a deeply buried maternal instinct that broke the facade that night, but she ran at Preacher Skaggs and screamed, "How do ya be touchin' the boy?"

Preacher Skaggs swallowed hard and said, "Ya be knowin' ya has to be touchin' a child to be showin' them how to be baptised. I be havin' to be touchin' that there crippled child to be makin' sure he nary be fallin'."

Preacher Skaggs smiled big and stared into Caelan's eyes as he walked toward him. When he got to Caelan, he laid his big hand on Caelan's shoulder and grasped it. He continued to look into Caelan's eyes while he said, "Ya be makin' up yer own mind, brother. I be yer Preacher, and I be an upstandin' man in our lil' community. Ya be knowin' ever' one 'round these parts be believin' anything I be tellin' them. Ya be tellin' me just last week what an ungrateful young'un that one be. Now he be back-talkin' ya right in front of comp'ny. Ya be knowin' what the Bible be sayin' about a child who be like that."

"Ya be gittin' on back to the church," Caelan said. "I be takin' care of these two boys."

"And that be yer right. They be yers to be doin' with like ya be seein' fit," Preacher Skaggs said as he walked toward the door. He stopped by Eamon and whispered, "Now ya be knowin' I be keepin' my promise if'n ya be openin' yer mouth."

As Preacher Skaggs walked out, I planned to hurt him as much as he hurt Eamon and Garnett, but my punches went right through him. He walked through my foot instead of tripping on it. He just pushed the door back open when I slammed it on him. His smile let me know he was too self-satisfied and smug to allow fear in. His time would come.

The boys' screams started when Preacher Skaggs left the house. He stood by his Duesenberg, stared at the house and laughed each time one of the boys screamed. When the screaming stopped, he got in his car and drove away.

When I returned to the house, the boys were already in bed. Garnett had pulled his worn-out blanket next to Eamon's bed and was lying on the floor holding Eamon's hand. Both of them were sniffling. All of the other children were lying on their blankets sniffling as well. I laid on the bed next to Eamon.

Eamon whispered, "I be sorry I nary be gittin' ya nothin' to et today. H'it be bad enough ya be gittin' beat, but ya be sufferin' double cuz ya be hungry."

"H'it be a'right," Garnett said as he squeezed Eamon's hand.

Regan sat up on her nice bed and whispered, "Y'all nary done nothin' wrong, did ya?"

"Naw," Garnett whispered. "We nary done nothin' wrong."

"That preacher done say'ed he nary be lookin' at the collection plates till today," Regan whispered. "Next he be goin' and sayin' Garnett done helped him count the money on Sunday. He done looked Pa straight in the eye and mesmerized him like snakes do. Y'all be makin' him afeared of somethin', so he be tryin' to be makin' ya afeared, too. What do he be afeared of?" When no one answered, she said, "Ya be havin' to be recognizin' that be right smart of him."

She waited for several minutes before she asked, "Do he be touchin' ya, you know, down there?" When no one answered, she laid down and said, "Ya'll cain't be bein' stupid. Ya nary be sayin' nothin' if'n folks be wrongin' ya in some way. If'n ya be keepin' yer mouth shut, folks be givin' gifts outta gratefulness. If'n ya be openin' yer big mouth, folks be hurtin' ya. If'n ya nary be able to be figurin' that out, ya be deservin' whatever be comin' to ya."

I snuggled next to Eamon and put my arm over him. I hoped he was still aware enough of me to receive some comfort from my touch. When he finally fell asleep, I went to look for Caelan.

I found him lying on the back of the wagon staring at the barn ceiling. I exhausted myself trying to throw things around the barn. When I successfully made the pitchfork land just above his head and he didn't notice, I realized he'd passed out on moonshine again. When

Eamon was in the hospital, I learned that I could read Caelan's mind, so I entered again and watched a story from his childhood unfold.

Caelan was a boy of around ten years old, just about the age Eamon was that night. An old preacher man came through the mountains. He visited Caelan's Ma to share the good news. Caelan was the one to answer when he knocked on the door.

"Howdy, boy," the preacher man said as he tipped his hat. "Do yer Ma and Pa be home?"

"Nary be havin' no Pa. Ma be workin'. I nary to be disturbin' her when she be workin'."

"I see. What be yer name, boy?"

"Caelan."

"Well, Caelan, do ya be thinkin' I can be waitin' on yer Ma?"

"I reckon," Caelan said as he stepped out of the way and let the short portly man in the door.

The preacher's scruffy white beard didn't match the gray and white hair that spilled out from under his fine black hat. He wore a fine black suit, too. There weren't many local folks that dressed up, so Caelan thought this man was a customer.

"Ma nary be takin' no trades," Caelan said over the sound of the box springs squeaking in the next room. "She be takin' nothin' but money. If'n ya nary be havin' money, ya may as well be movin' on. She be havin' too many mouths to be feedin' to be tradin' fer nothin'."

The preacher stared toward the bedroom for several minutes before his face turned red and he started a nervous side step. "Oh, I nary be here to be buyin' nothin'," he stammered as he stumbled toward the door. "I be here to be talkin' to yer Ma about God."

"We done be havin' us a preacher. He be tellin' us the Lord be good. Maybe he do be. We et better after Preacher be keepin' company with Ma. He be payin' real good."

"Oh my, oh my," the preacher said as his face got more red and he stumbled out the door.

Caelan followed him out the door and taunted, "What be the matter, preacher man. Ya be havin' to be knowin' folks be rollin' between the sheets. Ya nary be preachin' fer them to be stoppin' if'n ya nary be knowin' about h'it."

"Oh my, Oh my," the preacher said as he stumbled away from the house. He got halfway down the front path before he stopped, took several deep breaths, turned back to Caelan and said, "Come here, boy." When Caelan got to him, the preacher pulled some coins out of his pocket and said, "These here be fer ya."

Caelan took the coins, stuck them in his pocket, grabbed the preacher's hand and tried to lead him to the barn.

"What ya be doin', boy?" the preacher asked as he yanked his hand away.

"Ya be wantin' to be goin' to the barn fer this here coin, don't ya?" Caelan asked as he turned toward the preacher.

"Naw, oh my, naw," the preacher said as he backed away from Caelan. "Ya be needin' to be keepin' that there coin hid from yer Ma. H'it be fer gittin' ya some vittles if'n ya nary be havin' enough food."

Caelan shrugged and said, "A'righty then."

The preacher took several deep breaths before he walked back to Caelan, knelt in front of him and said, "Boy, just be rememberin' the Lord be yer rock. He be yer shield and yer sword. He be protectin' ya from yer enemies. Ya just be havin' to keep on askin' him."

Caelan shrugged again and said, "A'righty."

The preacher stood up and ran away.

The next customer was drunk when he came callin' on Caelan's Ma. He beat both of them. When Caelan defended himself, the man threw him face down on the kitchen table. This man wasn't gentle like the customers Caelan took in the barn, and he didn't pay.

After the man left, Caelan sat at the kitchen table and said, "The Lord be my rock. He be my shield and my sword. He be goin' to be protectin' me from my enemies."

Caelan looked in on his Ma. She was passed out drunk on her bed. He walked into town guided by the light of a full moon. When he got to town, he saw the man through the saloon window. He picked up a rock, threw it through the window and ran.

Several saloon customers caught him before he made it halfway down the main road. One held each arm as the fat saloon owner waddled toward him wearing a white apron. When he was in front of Caelan, he asked, "Why does ya be throwin' rocks through my window, boy?"

"The Lord be my rock," Caelan said as he looked through wild eyes from one man's face to the next.

"We be havin' us a smart arse here," the man said as he removed his belt. "Who be goin' to be payin' fer my window?"

"That be the whore's boy," the man who brutalized him earlier that night yelled. "She nary be havin' no money."

"Ya oughts to be knowin'," Caelan said. "Ya done cheated her outta her money just tonight. Just like ya done cheated me."

Several of the men laughed while one of them asked, "Ya be likin' the lil' boys, Jeb?"

Jeb stormed into the crowd screaming, "Y'all be believin' that there whore's boy before me. I be a fine upstandin' mountain man. I be workin' them mines with y'all. Ya be knowin' who I be." He grabbed the belt from the saloon owner, held it above his head and yelled, "I be showin' ya what I be doin' to anybody what be tellin' lies about me!"

He hit Caelan randomly wherever the folded belt landed. A scream followed each thwack. After several hits, the saloon owner took the belt from Jeb and hit Caelan several times in the same way. The screams continued.

When the saloon owner was finished, he pushed Caelan to the ground and yelled, "I nary be wantin' to be seein' ya 'round here no more, and I be by to be seein' yer Ma in the mornin'. She be payin' fer this here window with her arse."

The men laughed as they walked back to the bar, leaving Caelan lying in the middle of the road. It was hours before Caelan recovered enough to pick himself up and go home. Once he got home, he hid in the barn long enough for his Ma to forget about the man who came by the next day demanding that she pay for the window with her arse.

Caelan bided his time. He steered clear of those men when they visited his Ma. When enough time passed that they wouldn't suspect him, he snuck into town and loosened the latch on their saddles. The next morning, he heard one of them broke his neck.

That was the first time Caelan felt like he had power. He liked that feeling. After that, he enjoyed seeking revenge. He understood the pleasure those men felt when they took advantage of his weakness on the street outside the saloon. Seeing fear in a weaker person's eyes made you feel safe. That was a good feeling when you hadn't known what safety felt like before.

Remembering that feeling jolted him awake. He understood why that memory came to his dream. He was afraid he took it too far with Eamon that night. That's why he drank himself into oblivion. After he beat Garnett, Eamon looked at him with the same look Caelan had seen in the mirror after those men beat him. It was hatred. Caelan would be checking the latches on his saddle for a long time to come.

CHAPTER EIGHTEEN
POOR DAWG

A few things changed after Preacher Skaggs accused Garnett of stealing money. The most obvious and predictable is that more children were born. Less obvious was that Regan learned her lessons well from Preacher Skaggs' deception about the money, and she practiced enough to become a pro at manipulating situations to her advantage. Another practice opportunity presented itself on the day the family had a rare visitor.

It was a beautiful, bright, spring morning. Eamon sat on the porch steps with all the children around him. He bounced the newest baby boy, who was now a toddler, on the knee of his uninjured leg. The baby wore a hand-me-down gown that was so threadbare it was hard to see the gingham pattern. All of the children wore hand-me-downs. Since Regan always got the best, the girl's looked nice in their ribbons and lace even if the dresses were starting to wear out. The youngest girl wore the white dress Regan wore the day she had found my box of toys. The next oldest girl was squeezed into the pink jumper Regan had discarded for the white dress on that same day. The boys, on the other hand, wore tattered pants and feed sack shirts MawMaw Tierney made for Eamon. One of the younger boys wore the brown and white gingham shirt Eamon wore to my funeral. Of course, Regan wore a brand new, fancy, white, store bought dress with her signature ruffles and lace. It would one day be handed down as well.

Mabon sat on the bench behind them. Her large belly made it apparent that Eamon's knee would not be available to the toddler much longer. She was squeezed into the same gray, gingham, maternity dress she wore with the last pregnancy. It was ripped down one side and exposed part of her pregnant belly

Two of the younger siblings, a boy and a girl, played with the toddler on Eamon's knee. They were making faces that made him squeal with laughter.

Mabon put one hand on her stomach and the other hand on the arm of the bench for support while trying to stand. As she pushed herself up, she grumbled, "I cain't be standin' to be hearin' them young'uns be makin' all that racket nary more. I be goin' into the house."

The children got quiet until the front door closed. When it banged shut, the two siblings started making faces for the toddler again.

"That boy gonna be thinkin' yer two faces be the only thing in this here world," Eamon said as he placed his index finger first on the boy's nose and then on the girl's nose.

"That be a'right with me," the boy said as he made another silly face.

The toddler was laughing loud when Regan came out the front door, stomped across the porch and sat on the top step behind them. "Y'all be fussin' over that babe like a bunch of ol' Ma's," she said before she bit into a crab apple. As she chewed, she said, "Ma nary be feelin' good. Y'all be gittin' her ire up."

Garnett turned when Regan bit the apple. He looked at her until she finished talking and said, "Where do our apple be?"

"Pa be sayin' there only be enough fer me."

"H'it always be that way," Eamon whispered under his breath. He smiled at Garnett and said, "I be goin' to be pickin' y'all some crab apples soon as this here boy be gittin' to sleep, and I can be leavin' him."

Garnett smiled and started making faces with the other two children.

Regan snorted and said, "Ya be knowin' nary a-one of them young'uns be givin' a lick about ya, ol' Ma. They just be usin' ya up cuz nobody else be givin' a shit about 'em."

Garnett turned to Regan so fast it was almost impossible to see his head move. He stared at her hard and said, "I be lovin' my Eamon."

144

Regan stared back at him just as hard and said, "If'n ya be lovin' him so much then how come ya be tellin' me he nary be gettin' ya enough to et?"

"I nary be sayin' that," Garnett said. He ran toward Regan as he yelled, "Take h'it back!"

Eamon grabbed the straps of Garnett's overalls, so Garnett's swinging fists couldn't hit Regan. The overalls were so worn out that one of the straps started to tear. Eamon yanked Garnett back to the step and said, "Sit on down here. Ya be knowin' what Pa be doin' to ya if'n ya be hittin' her. Sit on down here."

Regan got up, ran into the house and yelled, "Ma, Garnett be hittin' me."

"He nary be touchin' ya," Eamon yelled.

Garnett grabbed Eamon's arm and leaned on it while he looked up into Eamon's eyes and said, "If'n ya be standin' up fer me, she be tellin' lies about ya tomorrow to be gittin' even. I be takin' whatever be comin' to me."

Regan returned to the porch, slapped Garnett on the side of the head and said, "That there be from Ma. She be sayin' she be too big to be doin' h'it herself." She sat on the far end of the top step. As usual, she was with the children but separated from them at the same time. She sat silently and stared at the barn. After a few minutes, her eyes got bigger, her mouth fell open, and she scooted away from the steps. When her back hit the bench, she hugged her knees.

Garnett looked toward the barn, jumped up and yelled, "A dawg!" He yanked Eamon's sleeve several times as he yelled, "Look, a dawg!"

All of the children turned to see a medium-sized white dog walking toward them. Its short hair was so dirty it looked yellowish brown except for the white face that made its contrasting dark eyes look black. Garnett ran to the dog. It jumped on him and licked his face while he petted it. With each stroke, dirt flew off the dog and uncovered more white spots.

"That mangy ol' dawg gonna be bitin' ya," Regan said as she hugged her knees tighter.

"That ol' dawg nary gonna be bitin' no one. That there dawg be a-smilin', and his tail be a-waggin'. Come here, boy," Eamon said and made the clicking sound people use to call dogs.

Garnett kept his arms around the dog's neck as it responded to Eamon's call. When the dog reached Eamon, Garnett let go. Eamon scratched it behind the ears until it put its front paws on his knee and took turns licking the toddler's and his faces. The toddler squealed with delight and wrapped his arms around the dog's neck.

"How ya be knowin' h'it be a boy?" Regan asked.

Garnett petted the dog's back as he said, "He be havin' to be a boy, because he nary be bein' mean like ya be, Regan."

"I be nice," the girl in the pink jumper said.

"Of course ya be," Eamon said before he smiled at her.

"I be tellin' Pa y'all be havin' a mangy ol' dawg out here," Regan said as she climbed over the railing as far away from the dog as possible and jumped off the porch. She ran to the barn screaming, "Pa, Pa."

"Reckon we be gittin' lucky enough fer this here dawg to et her?" Eamon asked, laughing. All of the children started laughing with him.

A few seconds later, Caelan stormed out of the barn and stomped across the front yard with Regan at his heels. He stopped in front of the children and yelled, "What in hell do that there mangy ol' dawg be doin' here?"

Regan stood behind him, impatiently tapping the toe of her new, black, mary jane shoe.

Garnett hugged the dog tighter and said, "He just be showin' up."

"Git h'it the hell outta here!" Caelan yelled as he tried to wave the dog away with his hand. "We nary be needin' another damn mouth to be feedin'. H'it prob'ly be sick, too. Y'all wanna be gittin' sick?"

"He nary be sick," Garnett said as he hugged the dog so tight it could barely breathe.

"Git h'it the hell outta here," Caelan yelled as he waved his whole arm at the dog, causing it to drag Garnett as it backed away. "Ya be lettin' go of that damn dawg before I beat yer arse!"

"I be wantin' him," Garnett said.

"I nary be givin' a good goddamn what ya be wantin'," Caelan yelled. Garnett and the dog both yelped when Caelan yanked Garnett away from the dog. Caelan held onto Garnett's arm as he stomped after the dog and yelled, "Git on outta here! Ya be gittin' the hell on outta here!"

The dog ran into the woods.

Caelan slapped Garnett's face and yelled, "Ya be doin' what I be tellin' ya, boy!"

Since Garnett was struggling to get away, he fell when Caelan let him go. Garnett crawled to the steps and snuggled under Eamon's waiting arm. Caelan stomped up the steps, and Regan followed him into the house. When the door slammed closed, Eamon moved the toddler to the other knee and embraced Garnett tighter. All of the children sat in silence.

Eamon gave Garnett a big squeeze and said, "Why ain't we pickin' us some crab apples when there be a whole tree just waitin' on us?"

Garnett wiped his eyes and said, "We be waitin' till the babe be goin' to sleep?"

"Naw," Eamon said. "We be bringin' him with us."

Garnett jumped up and ran toward the barn while Eamon adjusted the baby to the side of his good leg and used the handrail to pull himself up. He winced when he started walking, so I knew it was painful to carry the toddler. In spite of the pain, he managed to follow Garnett.

Garnett stopped in front of the barn door and screamed, "Crab apples!" He jumped up and down, spun in a circle and clapped his hands all at the same time.

"Yas," Eamon said, laughing, as he approached the barn. "Crab apples."

The rest of the children followed Eamon to the barn. When they walked around the corner to the side of the barn that couldn't be seen from the house, they saw the dog lying in the grass at the edge of the woods.

"Dawg!" Garnett yelled before he ran to the dog, fell down on his knees beside it, and wrapped his arms around its neck.

"Come on, dawg," Eamon said as the children and he continued their journey to the crab apple tree that stood behind the barn. "We be goin' to be pickin' us some crab apples."

The dog pulled away from Garnett and trotted behind the children. As Garnett chased the dog, he asked, "Does dawgs be eatin' crab apples?"

"I reckon we be findin' out," Eamon said as he approached the tree.

147

"I surely do be hopin' they does," Garnett said.

"I reckon they just might. Remember when Uncle Teagan be feedin' his dawg a whole mess of crab apples to be gittin' the worms outta h'its belly?"

Garnett nodded as he ran to the dog. When they got to the tree, the dog lay under its branches in the shade. Garnett sat next to the dog and wrapped his arms around its neck while the other children sat around the dog and petted it. Eamon sat the toddler with the other children, grabbed a low-hanging branch and pulled a crab apple off of it.

"Catch!" Eamon yelled as he threw the crab apple toward Garnett.

Garnett released the dog's neck just in time to catch the apple. He took a big bite, removed the bite from his mouth and gave it to the dog. The dog laid it on the ground between his paws and chewed on it. Garnett yelled, "Hey, Eamon, dawgs do be eatin' crab apples."

"I surely do be hopin' he nary be plannin' on gobblin' up our share," Eamon said as he pulled another crab apple off the branch and threw it to the next youngest child. When everyone except the toddler and Eamon had one, Eamon plucked two more from the tree and limped back to the children. He gave the toddler an apple, placed the other one in his front teeth and used his arms to lower himself to the ground.

The children sat under the tree eating apples, telling stories and laughing. Eamon took every other bite out of his mouth and fed it to the toddler. All of the children shared with the dog. Each time a child finished their apple, Eamon stood with the help of his strong arms and pulled another one off the tree. They must have eaten half a dozen apples each before Caelan rounded the corner of the barn. They all froze mid-bite when they saw him.

"I reckoned Regan must surely be lyin' when she be tellin' me that mangy ol' dawg still be out here!" Caelan yelled when he saw the dog lying with the children. "I done told y'all to be gittin' that there dawg on outta here!"

"He be my friend!" Garnett cried as he wrapped his arms around the dog's neck again.

Caelan stormed over to the dog. When he took his belt off, the children shrunk from him and cried. He wrapped the belt around the dog's neck, fastening it so tight the dog gagged. The gagging became worse when he dragged the dog across the yard.

"Naw," Garnett yelled as he fell into Eamon's arms, crying.

Eamon hugged Garnett as he asked, "Where do ya be takin' that ol' dawg to?"

"That nary be yer damn business!" Caelan yelled.

Eamon instructed Garnett to watch the toddler before he hurriedly struggled to his feet. When he was up, he limped behind Caelan as he said, "That there dawg nary be doin' nothin' wrong. He nary be bitin' a one of us. He nary even be scratchin' us. He be a real good dawg."

"I don't be givin' a damn! I done told y'all to be gittin' rid of h'it, and ya nary be listenin'!"

"That nary be the dawg's fault! We should of been runnin' h'it off. If'n ya be lettin' h'im go, I be swearin' to ya we be runnin' h'it off next time h'it come 'round."

"H'it be too late, boy," Caelan said as he dragged the dog across the yard.

The dog twisted and squirmed as he fought to get away. Eamon stopped and stared at the dog, which caused his face to go white and his body to shake. His condition remained the same as he watched Caelan drag the dog to the wagon and chain it there with a big, heavy, livestock chain that was stored on the back of the wagon. The dog stumbled under the weight when Caelan locked the chain in place. It quickly tired and laid its defeated body on the ground.

"Don't ya be darin' to be cryin', boy," Caelan said as he stomped toward Eamon. "Y'all be havin' to be learnin' that my word be law 'round here!" Caelan repeatedly poked Eamon in the chest with his index finger as he said, "If'n I be seein' any of y'all messin' with that there dawg, I be chainin' ya to that there wagon right next to him if'n I don't be beatin' ya to death first!"

The children ran to Eamon and wrapped their arms around him from all sides. Eamon rubbed Garnett's back.

When Caelan went into the house, Garnett started to walk toward the dog as he said, "We be havin' to be gittin' him outta here."

Eamon grabbed Garnett's overall straps and said, "That ol' man be killin' ya if'n ya do."

Garnett wrapped his arms around Eamon and said, "I nary be wantin' to be dyin'."

"I nary be wantin' ya to be dyin' neither," Eamon said as he rubbed Garnett's back again.

CHAPTER NINETEEN
DAWG GONE

I was lying in Eamon's room that night when the dog began to whine. I prayed the dog wouldn't wake him, but my prayer wasn't answered. Eamon's eyes popped open shortly after the whining started. He got out of bed and tiptoed cautiously to the window. It squeaked when he started to open it, so he froze. I floated to him and lay my hand on his shoulder. He was past the age where he could see me, but I think he felt my presence like MawMaw Tierney felt my presence shortly after I died. His body slowly relaxed, and he tiptoed back to bed.

Seconds after Eamon cocooned himself into his quilt, the dog began to bark. Eamon's body stiffened, and he became more stiff with each bark. By the time we heard Caelan's feet hit the floor and stomp across the living room, Eamon was like a human rock.

"Shut the hell up!" we heard Caelan scream as he stomped off the porch.

Seconds later, we heard a thump that made the dog yelp. By the time the third thump produced the third yelp, Eamon was crying. He continued to cry long after Caelan stomped back into the house. I rubbed Eamon's back and talked soothingly, but his eyes didn't close. He was still crying when the rooster crowed. Even the bright morning sun shining through the window failed to comfort him.

The sun brought the sound of kitchen wares clanging, Caelan yelling orders and Mabon's feet running across the creaky floor. When the noise began, Eamon returned to the window. He stood silently by the window and stared at Regan's bed until she released a light snore. Only then did he raise the window far enough to climb out and tiptoe across the porch. When he reached the bottom step, his eyes followed the chain to underneath the porch. He crawled to the dog, who drug itself to meet him despite the weight of the chain. He hugged it and said, "I surely do be sorry, dawg. I sure do be."

Eamon held the dog until the morning noise showed the first signs of disappearing. Before he crawled back to the sunlight, he whispered, "I be havin' to be goin' now. Ya be stayin' quiet." The dog whined, so Eamon stuck his head back under the porch and said, "Shush!" The dog seemed to understand.

MawMaw Tierney's cakes were waiting on the porch when Eamon emerged. He threw one to the dog before he carried them back to his window and returned to his bedroom unnoticed.

Mabon enjoyed working in the family garden, so she did that chore herself. Later that morning, she was in the garden at the same time Regan took the pony to the company store. This gave Eamon an opportunity to safely sneak away from the children who always surrounded him. He stole an old Mason jar from under the sink and a leftover biscuit from Caelan's breakfast plate and hid them under his pillow before taking the children outside for the day.

When Caelan's snoring became loud that night, Eamon again sneaked out the window and tiptoed across the creaky porch. When his feet touched the quiet earth, he limped quickly to the spigot and filled the Mason jar before he crawled under the porch and gave the dog the biscuit. The sound of his own stomach growling was drowned out by the dog's loud munching. When the biscuit was gone, Eamon held the Mason jar at an angle to allow the dog to drink. The dog drank most of the water even though its head was drooping more today from the weight of the chain than it had the day before.

"Ya needs to be bein' quiet, now, ya be hearin' me," Eamon whispered before he crawled out from under the porch. The dog whined, so Eamon whispered in his sternest voice, "Quiet!" The dog again seemed to understand.

Eamon scurried across the porch and back into his room. He gasped and swallowed hard when he saw that Regan's bed was empty. He quickly cocooned himself into his quilt. His nightly fidgeting and moaning revealed his pain to me, but he would not let anyone else see it. The only time he got sleep was when his exhaustion became greater than his pain, but he got up every morning and did what was expected of him without complaint. This morning was no different.

He crawled out of his cocoon and limped across the creaky floorboards. I knew he was going to pick up MawMaw Tierney's baked goods on the way to the outhouse just like he did every morning. As I walked to the front door with him, I was amazed by how quietly he trained his crippled legs to carry him. The quiet made the sudden gasp he released when he opened the front door sound louder. I looked out the door and saw Caelan and Regan coming out of the barn. Regan's clothes and hair were a mess, and her red lipstick was smeared around her mouth.

When Regan saw Eamon standing in the open doorway, she ran up the steps, put her face near his face and said, "I be waitin' fer Pa by the barn last night. I be seein' ya feedin' that ol' dawg." Eamon swallowed hard before she said, "I nary were gonna be tellin' Pa, but h'it be better to be havin' him trustin' me than ya and yer passel of brats. Ya be in a whole heap of trouble." She almost pushed him down when she entered the house.

When Eamon left the house, Caelan was standing next to the dog holding its chain so tight the dog was almost being hung. Eamon swallowed so hard that I heard it before Caelan yelled, "Which one of y'all lil' bastards be thinkin' h'it be a good idear to be givin' this here dawg food and water when y'all be thinkin' I nary be lookin'!" He released the dog's chain and yelled, "I bet h'it be that damn soft-hearted Garnett." The dog ran under the porch, and Caelan stomped toward the house as he yelled, "I be teachin' him a thing or two."

"Naw!" Eamon yelled. He grabbed Caelan's arm as Caelan stomped past him and said, "Garnett nary be doin' a thing wrong! H'it be me."

Caelan grabbed Eamon's arm, drug Eamon to the wagon and threw Eamon's crippled body to the ground. He pulled the chain until the struggling dog was forced to emerge from under the porch before he began to wrap the chain around Eamon.

"W-W-W-What do ya be d-d-d-doin'?" Eamon asked, stammering.

"Ya be lovin' this here damn dawg so much, ya can be livin' with h'it!" Caelan yelled. "I be goin' to be teachin' ya how to be bein' a man. I be goin' to be lettin' ya be sittin' here and be watchin' h'it die fer want of food and water whilst ya nary be able to be doin' nothin' about h'it. That be learnin' ya to be actin' like a man the next time ya can be doin' somethin' about h'it."

Tears fell from Eamon's eyes, but he didn't say a word.

Caelan secured Eamon's chains before he pulled the dog to the other side of a tree stump and secured it out of Eamon's reach. "Don't ya be tryin' to be touchin' that there damn dawg!" Caelan screamed as he walked away. "I be killin' ya both if'n ya do!"

Eamon and the dog stared at each other. After several minutes, the dog lay down and put his head on his paws, but they continued to stare at each other until Caelan came out of the house several minutes later. He was carrying a biscuit and bacon sandwich and a mason jar of water. When he gave them to Eamon, the dog stood and stared at the sandwich while it wagged its tail.

Eamon stared at the food and asked, "Why ya be givin' me these here vittles?"

"Ya be goin' to be eatin' ever bite of them there vittles. If'n ya be givin' that damn dawg one lil' bite, I be goin' to be killin' ya both."

Eamon swallowed hard and said, "I nary be hungry."

"Et them damn vittles, ya lil' bastard!" Caelan yelled.

Eamon accepted the biscuit, took a small bite and chewed for a long time. He stared at the begging dog while he chewed.

"Ya be hurryin' h'it up, or I be pushin' the damn thing down yer throat myself!" Caelan yelled. "I be havin' things to be doin'!"

Eamon gagged several times while he ate the sandwich.

When he finished it, Caelan said, "Drank this here jar of water." When Eamon took a small sip, Caelan yelled, "Drank h'it all!"

Eamon looked over the jar at the drooling dog as he drank all of the water.

When the jar was empty, Caelan jerked it out of Eamon's hands and said, "Poor dawg." He laughed as he walked back to the house.

Eamon looked at the dog and said, "I be awful sorry."

The dog wagged its tail, laid down, placed its head on its paws and stared at Eamon.

Less than an hour later, Caelan left the house wearing his work clothes but carrying a shot gun. When Eamon saw the gun, he scooted away, but Caelan left for work without harming him. Eamon and the dog sat in the hot sun, staring at each other for the rest of the day. Both of them were licking their dry mouths by noon. Even Eamon's thirst didn't get quenched until after sundown, because Caelan came home from work late that night. He laid a huge turkey next to the spigot before he started his nightly cleansing ritual. The dog stood, stared at the turkey and wagged its tail. When Caelan finished cleaning himself, he slung the turkey over his shoulder. As he carried it to the house, he laughed and said, "Poor dawg!"

Twilight came and left, leaving Eamon and the dog blanketed in a dark, star-studded sky. Eamon laid back and stared at the stars, and the dog crawled as close to Eamon as he could get. Soon, they were both snoring lightly.

Eamon jumped into a seated position when Caelan kicked him in the ribs and said, "Ya be gittin' yerself up, ya lazy good fer nothin'!" Caelan reached him a plate that had several large pieces of turkey on it. "Ya be eatin' this, and don't ya be darin' to be givin' that damn dawg one bite," Caelan said as he gave Eamon a Mason jar of water.

"I nary be hungry."

Caelan slapped the back of Eamon's head and yelled, "Et h'it!"

The dog lifted its head from its paws and growled at Caelan.

Eamon turned away from the dog as he ate, but the dog pulled at the chain trying to see the food. The dog's belly was growling loudly, and its ribs were steadily becoming more visible. This new position allowed Eamon to drop some turkey and cover it with his leg without Caelan seeing it. When the sandwich was gone and Eamon drank the water, Caelan returned to the house. Eamon threw the dropped turkey to the dog, and it pounced on the meat like it was captured prey.

Only half of the meat was eaten when Caelan stormed out of the house and started hitting Eamon. The dog left the remaining meat and barked ferociously as it fought the heavy chain trying to come to Eamon's rescue. Caelan kicked the dog, kicked the meat out of its reach and stomped back to the house mumbling curse words as he walked. A few minutes later, he returned with Garnett in tow. He stood just out of Eamon's reach and started hitting Garnett.

"Naw," Eamon yelled.

Caelan held Garnett's collar and said, "Hittin' ya nary seem to be helpin'. Hittin' the dawg nary seem to be helpin'. Besides, I nary be wantin' to be killin' the dawg. I be wantin' ya to be seein' h'it starvin' to death. If'n h'it be dying any other way, I be learnin' ya that ya can be changin' my mind by makin' a fuss. I done told ya that there dawg is gonna be starvin' to death, and that be how he be goin'. I be wantin' ya to be knowin' that ever time I be catchin' ya givin' that dawg anythin', I be goin' to be takin' h'it outta this here boy's hide."

Eamon dropped his head and said, "I nary be givin' that there dawg nary another thing."

Caelan started hitting Garnett again. As he did, Eamon threw himself at the end of the chain and begged him to stop hitting the screaming child. After a few minutes, Caelan shoved Garnett. When Garnett fell next to Eamon, Caelan said, "Ya be needin' to be makin' yer apologies to yer brother. Ya be the one what be doin' this to him. H'it nary be bein' my fault." He laughed as he walked away from them.

While Eamon and Garnett lay next to each other, MawMaw Tierney tied her pony to a tree at the end of our road. When she walked halfway across the yard, she dropped her cakes and ran to the boys. She fell on her knees next to Garnett, pulled his head onto her lap and asked, "What in hell be goin' on over here?"

Eamon looked up at her and said, "Pa be keepin' me tied here till I be seein' that there dawg starve to death."

"Oh my word," MawMaw Tierney said as she lay Garnett's head on the ground, got up and ran back to her pony. She mounted and rode away faster than she had ever rode before.

Less than half an hour later, Uncle Teagan's car parked in front of the house. He jumped out of the car and ran to the boys as he yelled, "Oh, my God! What be goin' on over here?"

"Help the dawg!" Eamon begged.

Uncle Teagan knelt next to Eamon and asked "What's that ya be sayin?"

"He be wantin' ya to be helpin' that there dawg," Garnett said as he pointed at the dog.

"Who be doin' this to ya?" Uncle Teagan asked as he unwrapped the chain.

"Pa," Eamon answered.

Caelan stomped across the creaking porch as Uncle Teagan finished unwrapping Eamon and began to work on the dog. Caelan grabbed the back of Uncle Teagan's shirt and pulled him backwards as he yelled, "Ya be gittin' the hell off'n that there dawg!"

Unce Teagan jumped up and yelled, "What in hell do ya be thinkin' ya be doin' here?"

"I can be lookin' after my own any way I be seein' fit," Caelan answered.

Eamon finished removing the dog's chains as Uncle Teagan said, "Caelan, ya done gone too far this time. I be takin' these here boys and this here dawg over to my place. Ya can be callin' the law if'n ya be havin' to, but I nary be backin' down this time. If'n I be tellin' the law ever thing my family be knowin' about y'all, I nary be reckonin' the sheriff be on yer side fer long. Ya be sendin' the law on over. Mabon's brothers be visitin' their Ma tonight anyhow. I reckon they be havin' a thing or two to be talkin' to the law about."

The dog was free and sitting on Eamon's lap when Uncle Teagan finished talking. He picked up Eamon and the dog and and carried them to the car as he said, "Come on, Garnett." Caelan picked Garnett up and held the struggling child while Uncle Teagan put Eamon and the dog in the passenger seat of his car. Uncle Teagan walked over to Caelan, looked right in his eyes and said, "Ya be lettin' the boy be goin'."

"Ya can be takin' Eamon if'n ya be wantin' to," he said as he fought to make Garnett stop struggling. "A damn crippled young'un nary be doin' us no good anyhow. We be needin' this here boy to be tendin' the fields. Ya nary be takin' him with ya."

Uncle Teagan tried to pull Garnett out of Caelan's arms, but he stopped when Garnett cried out in pain. Uncle Teagan let go and said, "He nary be bein' here fer long. I be the one what be goin' to the law. I be gittin' ever' one of them kids away from yer sorry arses." Uncle Teagan walked back to his car. Before he got in, he turned to Caelan and said, "Tierney's boys be stoppin' by later tonight to be gittin' my pony. Ya nary be goin' to be seein' that pony again now that I be knowin' how ya be takin' care of animals over here."

CHAPTER TWENTY
WITHOUT EAMON

The children were lost without Eamon. The night started with all of them on his bed, but Garnett reminded them of what would happen if Caelan and Mabon caught them there together. They all moved to their own blankets that were scattered around the floor, and everyone's hands except Regans remained linked all night. Their crying kept everyone awake for several hours, but that stopped when Regan threatened to get Caelan if they didn't shut up. The following morning, they all held hands as they walked to the porch and sat on the steps where they usually sat with Eamon. They stared straight ahead, and all of their eyes had a sunken appearance. It was obvious they didn't know what to do.

After Regan finished her breakfast, she sat on the other end of the steps and pushed her straight back so hard into the handrail that it looked like she thought she would catch something from the other children if she got too close. It wasn't just her mannerisms and her fancy, white, store bought dress that revealed her attitude about the other children; it was the way her face scrunched up when she talked to them.

Every time Regan outgrew one of her signature, white, store-bought dresses, Caelan made sure she had another one to accentuate her blossoming figure. The more her figure blossomed, the more attention, which included dresses, she got. Her tube of red lipstick never ran dry, and beautiful necklaces began to adorn her cleavage.

She was barely a teenager, but her appearance revealed that she was an experienced woman.

The other children were dressed in rags. The boy's overalls had holes in them, and they didn't have shirts or shoes. The youngest boy's overalls were worn out by four boys before him, so they looked like the holes were the only things holding them together, and the quilt he hugged was so worn and dirty that I couldn't tell what color it was anymore. The girls wore nice clothes, because they got Regan's hand-me-downs. The youngest girl's clothes were as worn out as the youngest boy's clothes were. That morning, their faces looked as tattered as their clothes.

"What y'all be doin' sittin' out here all by yer lonesome?" Regan asked as she scrunched her dark curls in her palm. Before the children could answer, she laughed and said, "Aw, yas, yer precious Eamon done gone and be leavin' y'all alone." When tears welled in the toddler's eyes, Regan said, "Aw, nary be no point to be cryin' over Eamon. I bet ya he nary be cryin' over y'all. If'n he be carin' about any of ya, he nary be leavin' ya here with nobody to be takin' care of ya."

"Ya be shuttin' yer self up," the girl who was born after Regan said as she pulled the hem of her skirt down. She was tall and thin like Caelan, so Regan's hand-me-downs were too short for her. As if ill-fitting hand-me-downs weren't insult enough, her increasing height caused Caelan to start calling her Legs. I think it was because he couldn't remember her name.

"I be seein' why ya be wantin' me to be shuttin' up," Regan said. "The truth be hurtin' ya."

"Eamon be comin' back," Garnett snapped before he spit at Regan, barely missing her.

Regan laughed and said, "I reckon I be wantin' to be spittin' on folks if'n I done been spit on like Eamon be spittin' on y'all. Y'all be needin' to be acceptin' h'it. Eamon nary be comin' back. He done been wantin' to be gittin' outta here fer a long time. He done told me he be needin' to be gittin' away from y'all. He be feelin' real sick and tired of takin' care of y'all." When some of the younger children started crying, Regan smiled and said, "I be cryin' too. H'it nary be bein' fair to be trustin' someone like y'all be trustin' Eamon only to be findin' out he be wantin' to be gittin' shet of y'all. Well, h'it be lookin' like he finally be gittin' what he be wantin'."

Regan stopped talking when the sheriff's car parked in front of the house. The children started whispering amongst themselves while Regan ran in the house yelling, "Pa! Pa!"

The sheriff approached the children and asked, "How ya young'uns be doin' today?"

The children huddled together.

"Y'all nary be needin' to be worryin' yerselves. This here uniform just be what my job be makin' me be wearin'. I nary be different than yer own Pa."

The children huddled closer together and shivered.

Caelan emerged from the house and asked, "What can I be doin' fer ya?"

Regan followed Caelan to the top of the porch steps and hid behind him.

"I be hearin' yer eldest boy be livin' at his uncle's house cuz he nary be safe 'round ya."

When Caelan walked down the steps and extended his hand to the sheriff, Regan sat on the bench and pressed her back into it like she'd done with the porch railing earlier that day.

When the sheriff shook Caelan's hand, Caelan looked into his eyes and said, "I nary be knowin' what ya be talkin' about. We done had us a fam'ly squabble last evenin', but h'it nary be nothin' to be worryin' yerself about. Their uncle be too protectin' of that crippled boy of mine. That be causin' him to be makin' a fuss and stickin' his nose where h'it nary be his business."

"They do be yers to be doin' with as ya be seein' fit," the sheriff said before he took off the tan hat that matched his tan and brown uniform and placed it under his arm. "Within reason anyhow. How were h'it yer oldest boy found hisself bein' crippled?"

Preacher Skaggs drove his Deusenberg into the yard and parked it next to the sheriff's car. While the sheriff watched him park, Regan pulled a tube of red lipstick out of her skirt pocket and applied a liberal amount to her lips.

As Preacher Skaggs walked toward the sheriff, he said, "Howdy, y'all. Good to be seein' ya. I be at the church and be seein' the sheriff drivin' onto yer road. I be thinkin' I ought to be stoppin' over to be makin' sure ever thing be a'right."

"I nary be sure just yet," Caelan answered.

Preacher Skaggs extended his hand to the sheriff and asked, "Do ever thing be a'right?"

The sheriff shook his hand and answered, "I be hearin' there be some goin's on over here yesterday. I just be checkin' things out."

"I nary be wantin' to be pressin' charges or nothin' like that there. I just be wantin' to be lettin' the boy's Pa be knowin' about h'it, so he can be correctin' them."

The sheriff crunched his eyebrows together as he asked, "Pressin' charges fer what?"

Preacher Skaggs chortled before he said, "Them there boys of his done stealed money from the church collection plate. I be thinkin' their Pa ought to be knowin' about h'it, but there nary be need fer the law. I be trustin' Caelan here to be handlin' h'it."

"This be the first I be hearin' about stolen money," the sheriff said.

Caelan looked at Preacher Skaggs and said, "Ol' Teagan be over here last night makin' a fuss about the way I be raisin' my young'uns. I reckon he be thinkin' ya ought not punish a boy no matter what he be doin'. H'it be lookin' to me like he done gone and called the law on me."

Preacher Skaggs shook his head slowly and tisked several times before he said, "That ol' man all the time be stickin' his nose in other folk's business. They be yers to be raisin' the way ya be seein' fit."

The sheriff looked at Caelan and said, "I be awful sorry to be botherin' y'all like this. Do ya be wantin' me to be bringin' that there crippled boy on back to ya?"

"Naw," Caelan said as he pulled a handkerchief out of his back pocket and wiped his brow. "Until that ol' man be calmin' down, h'it be hard to be sayin' what he might say or do." He sighed deeply before he continued, "H'it be hard to be sayin' what he might be havin' that young'un say or do. That crippled boy nary be much use to me anyhow. If'n Teagan be wantin' to be takin' on the care of him, let him go on ahead and be doin' h'it. He just be needin' to be leavin' the rest of us be whilst he does."

161

"I be tellin' him that," the sheriff said as he put his hat back on. Before he walked to his car, he tipped his hat and said, "Y'all be havin' yer selves a nice day now, ya hear."

As Preacher Skaggs watched the sheriff pull away, he said, "I nary be meanin' to be causin' y'all trouble when I be tellin' y'all about that there money."

"H'it nary be yer fault," Caelan answered.

"Yas, h'it do be," Garnett whispered. "Ya done lied about me, and ya be knowin' hi't."

The girl who was born after Regan hit him in the side with her elbow. This caused the hem of her dress to pull up, so she yanked it back down.

When Preacher Skaggs got within hearing distance, Regan said to the children, "I reckon now that Eamon be gone, y'all be havin' to be relyin' on me. I be yer sister, so I be goin' to be here fer ya."

"Ya nary be before," Legs whispered as she yanked her hem down again.

Regan smiled and said, "I be wantin' to be there fer y'all, but Eamon done keeped me away. Now that he be gone, he nary be keepin' us apart."

"Why, Regan," Preacher Skaggs said as he walked up the steps. "Ya be a right kind lil' gal. I be so proud of ya. I be sure Jesus be proud of ya, too." He tipped his expensive fedora in her direction and asked, "How ya be a-doin' today?"

"I be right fine," she said as she batted her eyelashes.

"Ya be lookin' right perty today."

"Much obliged, sir."

"Ya be as perty as a peach. I reckon I could just be reachin' up and pluckin' ya off'n – "

"I bet ya cain't," Caelan interrupted, snarling. He stomped up the porch steps, stared hard at Preacher Skaggs and yelled, "Regan, ya be gittin' yer arse in that there house!"

Regan ran past Caelan and into the house without saying a word. The only time Regan received negative attention was when a man paid attention to her. All of the children got equal attention, but Regan was the only one who got the positive kind. She kept the negative attention flowing by tattling, not always honestly, on the other children. Her smile revealed how much she enjoyed watching them being punished, but she ran like a scared rabbit when it was her turn.

"Ya be sniffin' after my girl," Caelan said, his voice steadily getting louder.

Preacher Skaggs smiled and said, "I nary be believin' ya be thinkin' that what I be comin' 'round here fer. I be a married man, Brother Caelan, and yer girl be lil' more than a child. I nary be thinkin' about disrespectin' ya. I be comin' 'round to be helpin' ya with the law."

Caelan took a deep breath, sighed and said, "Ya be right, Preacher Skaggs. I nary be knowin' why I be talkin' to ya like I be. I reckon hi't just be the trouble ol' Teagan be tryin' to be bringin' down on me this mornin'."

"I nary be surprised. No, sirree, nary lil' bit do I be surprised. Eamon done been trouble since the day he be borned, and Garnett be followin' in his footsteps of late. H'it prob'ly be best ya be gittin' shet of him."

Caelan shook his head slowly as he said, "Ya mays be right about that. Ya mays be right."

"Ya be knowin' I nary be meanin' no disrespect. I be on yer side, Brother Caelan. If'n I nary be on yer side, I be the one what be callin' the law about that collection plate money. But, I nary be doin' that. I done right by ya. I be knowin' when to be mindin' my own business, and I be knowin' when to be coverin' somebody's back. I be knowin' ya be knowin' that, too."

"Yassir, I surely do," Caelan said as he walked to the front door.

After Preacher Skaggs left the porch, Legs looked at Garnett and asked, "Do ya reckon any of that stuff Regan be sayin' about Eamon be true?

"I nary be knowin'," Garnett said as he shook his head.

Before Preacher Skaggs drove away, Regan approached his car. The window was down, so she leaned on the car door. He stared at her cleavage as he smiled, tipped his fedora and asked, "How ya be gittin' out here? I done see'd yer Pa be sendin' ya into the house."

After a coy laugh, Regan said, "Why, Preacher, we do be havin' a back door."

"Yer Pa just might be tannin' yer hide fer disobeyin' him," Preacher Skaggs said and winked at her. "He just might be paddlin' that behind of yers real good. H'it be shameful to be seein' such a perty lil' behind used in such a sad way."

"He nary be knowin' I be out here."

After several minutes of watching her run her finger along the edge of the window, Preacher Skaggs asked, "Do ya be likin' fine things like this here car, lil' gal?"

"Yassir," she said, exaggerating her drawl. "Yassir, I surely does."

"Yer Pa be workin' tomorrow afternoon. Ya be bringin' yer self on by the church on yer way home from school. I be takin' ya fer a ride in this here machine."

Regan batted her eyelashes before her pouty lips said, "Yassir, I surely will be there."

CHAPTER TWENTY-ONE
INDESCRETION

Regan arrived at the church the next day just as she promised she would. She removed her red lipstick tube from the pocket of her white dress and swept it across her lips before she ascended the steps. Although her adult demeanor made her small, perky breasts look larger than they were, she pushed them up and accentuated her cleavage before she knocked on the door. While she waited for a response, she squished her short black curls in her palms and revived their bounce.

Preacher Skaggs opened the door, smiled and said, "I be a-waitin' fer ya."

Regan batted her eyelashes as she said, "I figured ya be waitin' fer me."

He placed his hand on the small of her back and led her through the door as he said, "Ya be comin' on in. By all means, be comin' on in."

When she crossed the threshold, Preacher Skaggs pulled her into his embrace. He held his hand in front of her face and let a gold chain fall from between his fingers. A heart shaped pendant swung at the end of the chain. Regan smiled as she watched it swing.

"Do ya be likin' h'it?" Preacher Skaggs asked.

She nodded.

"I be hopin' ya be likin' h'it," he said as he stepped behind her, put the necklace around her neck and secured the latch. She placed her palm over the pendant when it touched her skin.

"Much obliged," she said as she turned and snuggled her bosom into his chest.

"Plenty more presents be a-comin'," he said as he thrust his hard manhood against her.

Regan giggled and said, "Pa be killin' ya if'n he be findin' out."

"He nary be findin' out," Preacher Skaggs said before he kissed her.

"Ya be sayin' ya be takin' me fer a ride in that there car of yers."

"Yas'm, I be wantin' to be doin' just that, but ya be havin' me burnin' with passion. Ya nary be wantin' to be puttin' out my flame before h'it be quenched, does ya?"

"I nary be wantin' that," she said as she lowered her hand to his crotch.

"Ya nary be nothin' like that brother of yers," he stammered between moans.

She jerked her hand away and asked, "What in hell do that be meanin'?"

"I just be meanin' ya be the best of the lot. Ya nary be a cold fish. Ya nary be actin' like the good Lord be puttin' somethin' awful between a man's legs."

Regan pulled away from him, stopped his approach by placing her palm on his chest and asked, "Ya be bein' with my brother? That nary be natural."

Preacher Skaggs caressed the back of the hand she had on his chest as he said, "Now, child, I nary be wantin' to be bein' with anybody but ya. Ya be knowin' ya be the pertiest lil' gal ever to be borned on this here mountain." He winked, and she giggled and let him hold her again as he said, "Them mean creatures ya be callin' brothers and sisters ought to be more like ya. How can ya be standin' them?"

"H'it be mighty hard at times."

"Yas'm, h'it do be mighty hard," he said as he placed her hand on his erect manhood. "I do be believin' I done hear'ed ya be sayin' ya be wantin' to be puttin' out my fire?"

She locked the door with her free hand before she pulled Preacher Skaggs to the floor. They quickly removed the clothes that prevented copulation, and their passion was so great he spilled his seed after a few strokes.

166

Regan pushed him away and said, "I nary be believin' I be wastin' my time fer that."

"H'it be gittin' better the more we be doin' h'it," Preacher Skaggs said as he forced her to accept his embrace. "I be wantin' ya fer so long. Ya be havin' me so heated up. H'it nary be that way next time."

"H'it better not be," Regan said as she curled into his kisses like a cat curls into being petted. "Ya be owin' me a ride in that there Duesenberg."

"Oh, child, cain't we be bein' together in the flesh?"

Regan pushed him away again and said, "Ya be listenin' to me, preacher man, I nary be some lil' whore ya can be fuckin' and throwin' away. When ya be promisin' me somethin', ya be givin' h'it to me."

"What ya be doin' about h'it if'n I don't," Preacher Skaggs asked as he kissed her neck.

"Ya nary be seein' any more of my pleasures."

"I can be gittin' them pleasures any place," he said as he moved his lips to her breasts.

"I be tellin' Pa if'n ya be mis-usin' me," she said as she pulled his head off her breasts. "Ya nary be stupid. Ya be knowin' what be goin' on in my house. Ever' one be knowin'. If'n Pa be knowin' ya be touchin' me, ya be findin' yerself swingin' from a tree. I be tellin' him the second ya nary be treatin' me like a lady. H'it nary matter if'n what I be sayin' be true or not. Ever' one be believin' me. They all be knowin' what ya really be like, and I just be a child."

Preacher Skaggs swallowed hard before he said, "Ya nary be mean like that?"

Regan pulled herself to her feet, straightened her dress and said, "If'n ya be takin' me fer that there ride ya be promisin', ya nary be findin' out."

He stood and secured his pants before he grabbed her behind to pull her closer to him. As he nuzzled her neck, he said, "Ya be killin' me, woman. Ya be wantin' to be takin' a ride in that there car when ya be havin' me burnin' fer ya."

"I be wantin' to be bein' treated like a lady."

"A'righty," he said as he wrapped her hand around his arm and led her out of the church and to the car. Before he opened the passenger door, he fondled her thoroughly while they kissed.

Regan pushed him away after several minutes and said, "I be wantin' my ride now."

As he opened the car door, the sound of mooing cows filled the air. Eamon was using MawMaw Tierney's herding stick as both a cane and a way to herd the cows out of the family graveyard across the street to take them back home.

Preacher Skaggs quickly opened the car door, and Regan jumped in. Once he was behind the wheel, he raced away from the cows as he asked, "Do that boy still be stayin' at yer MawMaw Tierney's house?"

"Yassir. I be thinkin' he nary be comin' home."

"Why that be?"

Regan looked over her shoulder and said, "Ya done passed my road."

Preacher Skaggs laughed and said, "When a lady be tellin' me she be wantin' a ride, I be givin' her a ride; sometimes h'it be in my car." She laughed as Preacher Skaggs said, "Ya nary be answerin' my question."

"Pa be sayin' Uncle Teagan done spoiled that boy so bad he nary be good fer nothin', so he may as well be keepin' him now."

Do ya be thinkin' he done see'd us back at the church?"

Regan laughed and said, "Nary need to be worryin'. I be knowin' how to be coverin' my arse."

"What ya be meanin'?"

"Ya just be leavin' h'it to me. There nary be a thing to be worryin' about."

· · · · ·

When Regan got home, she put on her newest white ruffled dress. It was similar to the ones she wore as a child, except it was low cut and accentuated what cleavage she had. She was sitting on the porch bench when Caelan got home from the mines. She leaned on the porch rail and watched his cleansing ritual, but she did not greet him until he returned to the porch.

"Howdy, lil' gal," Caelan responded to her greeting as he mounted the porch steps.

"I be wonderin' if'n we can be goin' to visit MawMaw Tierney?" she asked as he walked up the steps.

Caelan stopped at the top of the steps, looked at her and asked, "What be bringin' that on? Ya nary be wantin' to be visitin' yer MawMaw."

"I be hopin' to be seein' my brother. He be gone fer a while now. I be hopin' to be showin' him my new dress."

Caelan sighed and rolled his eyes before he said, "I reckon we can be goin' over fer a lil' while after supper. Let me be gittin' my clothes changed and et some vittles first."

"Much obliged," Regan said as she sat on the bench. "If'n ya nary be mindin', Pa, I be waitin' till we be gittin' back ta et. I nary be wantin' to be gittin' nothin' on my new dress."

"Suit yerself," Caelan said before he went into the house.

Regan sat on the porch while Caelan changed and ate.

The other children came out of the house and sat on the porch steps. As they ate the biscuit each of them was given for dinner, Garnett asked Regan, "Why ya be puttin' yer new dress on before goin' to bed?"

"I be goin' to be seein' Eamon. I nary be wantin' him to be fergittin' me. If'n he be thinkin' about us at all, he be comin' over here to be visitin' us. He nary be visitin' us. I be goin' to be remindin' him that we be here."

"Do he really be fergittin' us?"

"Mays be he done forgot all about us."

"Can we be goin' with ya?"

"Naw. I nary be wantin' y'all to be feelin' hurt if'n he nary be rememberin' ya. I be takin' that pain on myself. I be remindin' him about y'all. Don't ya be worryin'."

The kids ate their biscuits in silence. After they were done, they snuggled on the steps and watched as Caelan came out of the house and told an obedient Regan to follow him. While he went inside the barn and strapped the horses to the wagon, Regan stood outside and pressed her curls in her palm.

As the children watched, Garnett asked, "Do y'all be believin' Eamon done forgot us?"

The children shrugged and continued to watch Regan until the wagon pulled out of the barn, stopped for Regan to get on and drove past them onto the family road. Their heads followed the sound of the wagon as it traveled the short distance from their road to MawMaw Tierney's road.

When Caelan and Regan arrived, Uncle Teagan was working the fields, his three daughters were in the house canning with their Ma and MawMaw Tierney, and Eamon was working the family garden that was located to the left of the porch steps. When Eamon saw the wagon, he ran toward the house, but his bad leg kept him from making it farther than the bottom porch step before Caelan stopped the wagon inches away from him.

The difference in the two families was apparent by their property. This house wasn't gray and creaky. The road that connected their property to the main road had well-tended Rose of Sharon bushes lining the last bend that led to the house. The white-washed house was sparkling and pristine, and all of the boards were present. The porch and steps, including the railing and the handrail, were painted emerald green. There were no missing boards or balusters. There wasn't even a piece of peeling paint on any of the wood. The family garden was well tended and full of healthy producing plants, as were the marigolds that grew around the edge. Jump ropes and dolls littered the play area to the right of the porch. The barn that sat across from the house had no places where its red paint was peeling. A tire swing hung from the branches of the huge tree that grew to the right of the barn. A clean chicken coop stood on the other side of the tree, and the cow field was behind it. Several small goats wandered around the yard.

The crop fields extended from the other side of the family road to Caelan and Mabon's property line. Everyone worked to alternate the wheat and tobacco crops. Uncle Teagan saved a little money from each crop even though Caelan and Mabon made fun of him for planning for the future. His dream was for each of his girls to be accepted into Berea College, because he wanted them to have more options in life than marrying a mountain man who might treat them like Tierney's man had treated her. Although it was tuition free, Uncle Teagan knew the girls would need money for board, books and expenses. The money he had saved was what enabled him to pay Eamon's hospital bill.

"Wait there, boy," Caelan said as he climbed off the wagon. "I nary be here to be draggin' ya back. Yer sister be wantin' to be visitin'. She be wantin' to be showin' ya her new dress."

Eamon watched Caelan and Regan get off the wagon. Even though he was a teenager, their presence still made him pale and start shaking like he had always done around them. Since he was no longer able to see me, I was unable to comfort him.

Regan slinked toward her brother like she did with Preacher Skaggs earlier that day. When she got close to him, she twirled and asked, "How ya be likin' my new dress?"

"H'it be right perty," Eamon said as he backed up one step.

"Where ya be goin'?" Caelan asked.

"I be goin' to be gittin' MawMaw Tierney," Eamon stammered before he ran up the steps.

MawMaw Tierney stomped to the top of the porch steps seconds after Eamon went into the house. "Ya nary be takin' that child with ya," she said as she wiped her hands on her apron.

"We nary be comin' to be takin' him," Caelan said. "Regan be wantin' to be visitin' him."

MawMaw Tierney squinted as she looked Regan up and down and said, "I reckon that be a'right." She continued to stare at Regan as she yelled, "Girls, ya be comin' on out here. We be havin' comp'ny."

Uncle Teagan's three daughters and his wife came out of the house. They all had dark hair and wore clean and pressed feed-sack dresses and saddle shoes. All of them were sturdy from farm work. Since Uncle Teagan didn't have a son, his girls often helped with farm work. In spite of being sturdy, they were surprisingly thin and petite. They filed onto the porch and stood in a line from shortest to tallest at the top of the steps. They ranged in height from about five feet to about five feet four inches tall. It was easy to see where their petite stature came from. Their mother was the height of the shortest girl and was barely visible as she stood behind them sporting the same dark hair and a similar feed-sack dress. The girl's Ma often stood behind them, because she was the shy type. Everyone talked about how well it went when MawMaw Tierney moved in with Uncle Teagan after her husband died. There was no squabbling about which woman made the decisions, because it was a role the girl's Ma was very happy to surrender to MawMaw Tierney, especially since MawMaw Tierney treated her well.

"I reckon ya may as well be comin' on up and sittin' a spell, Caelan," MawMaw Tierney said. "The young'uns done been workin' hard all day. They can be takin' a break fer a while."

Caelan walked up the steps and sat on one of the half dozen white-washed rocking chairs that sat along the length of the porch.

MawMaw Tierney sat on the chair next to Caelan before she looked at the girls' Ma and asked, "Could ya be bringin' us all some lemonade?"

The girls' Ma nodded and disappeared into the house. While Caelan and MawMaw Tierney waited for the lemonade, they rocked in silent unison and watched the children play on the tire swing.

When Regan got on the swing, Caelan yelled, "Regan, ya be bein' careful not to be gittin' that there dress dirty. I done paid a perty penny fer h'it."

Regan smiled at him before she got off the swing.

The girls' Ma emerged from the house a few minutes later and gave each of the adults a glass of lemonade. Before she went back into the house, she said, "Can ya be tellin' them there young'uns there be a pitcher of lemonade in the kitchen when they be gittin' ready fer h'it."

"I surely will," MawMaw Tierney said as she held the cool glass to her forehead.

Caelan drank his in one drink and sat the glass on the porch floor. MawMaw Tierney took small sips between holding the glass to her forehead and cheeks. Even though they continued to watch the children play, Caelan seemed ignorant to what caused the ruckus that was starting.

Regan was playing with the spigot that was located at the corner of the family garden nearest the porch steps. She splashed water on every child that got near her, but none of them could get close enough to splash her back. Even Eamon was laughing and having fun. All of the children were soaking wet by the time Eamon limped directly into the spray and got close enough to splash Regan. When the water hit her, Regan started screaming and wouldn't stop.

Caelan ran down the porch steps as he asked, "What in hell be goin' on?"

Regan held out the skirt of her dress like she was about to curtsy and said, "Eamon done went and ruined my new dress!"

Caelan yanked his belt out of his belt loops and started hitting Eamon with it. By the third hit, Eamon was crouched on all fours with his hands over the back of his head. MawMaw Tierney ran down the steps and grabbed Caelan's arm. When he pushed MawMaw Tierney down, Teagan's youngest girl ran to her aid while the other two girls ran toward the field screaming, "Pa! Pa! Come help Eamon! Pa, help!" Regan stood by the spigot and laughed through all of it.

Fortunately, it was near dusk, so Uncle Teagan was on his way home from the fields. When he heard the girls, he started running. By the time he reached them, he saw what they were yelling about. He ran past them, grabbed the belt out of Caelan's hand and punched Caelan in the face. Caelan fell next to Eamon, and Uncle Teagan stood over him and yelled, "Ya son of a whore. Ya be comin' over here and beatin' this boy again. What in hell be the matter with ya?"

The oldest girl said, "He knocked MawMaw Tierney down."

Uncle Teagan kicked Caelan in the ass and yelled, "Ya be takin' yer whore daughter and be gittin' the hell outta here. Ya be leavin' that there boy alone!"

Caelan crawled a few feet before he got up and walked to the wagon. When he was on it, Regan ran to join him. As the wagon pulled out, Uncle Teagan picked Eamon up and carried him into the house while the girl's helped MawMaw Tierney stand and walk up the steps.

After the wagon passed the Rose of Sharon bushes, Regan said, "I always be fergettin' what them folks be like. Just be rememberin', Pa, ya cain't be believin' a word any of them folks be sayin'. They be likely to be sayin' anything to be gittin' even with us now."

Caelan tousled Regan's hair as he said, "Ya nary be havin' to be worryin' about that child. I be knowin' what them folks be like."

Regan smiled the rest of the way home. For her it was over, but Eamon would tell his daughter fifty years later that he could still feel that beating when he closed his eyes. The saddest part is that Regan's cover-up wasn't necessary. Eamon was so focused on herding the cows that morning that he hadn't noticed Regan across the street with the preacher. Regan and Preacher Skaggs never had anything to fear.

When Caelan and Regan arrived home, all of the children ran to meet the wagon. They circled Regan and asked questions so fast it was impossible to know which child asked which question: "How do Eamon be?" "Do Eamon be askin' about us?" "Do Eamon be a'right?" "When do Eamon be comin' home?"

"He just be feelin' glad to be shet of y'all. All ya ever done was be buggin' him fer stuff. He nary be yer Pa, ya know," Regan said as she plowed through them as if she were tilling soil.

CHAPTER TWENTY-TWO
EAMON RECEIVES PRAISE

The only thing Eamon knew was work. The one time he experienced fun, he was beaten for getting Regan's dress wet even though she soaked his clothes, which made play even less understandable to him. Therefore, he surrendered himself to the only thing he understood.

Before his body, and more importantly his hip, recovered from the beating, Eamon returned to the fields. His dog had been recovering in the house since Uncle Tilmon rescued it, and it also ventured from its sick bed that day. It danced around Eamon's feet as he walked toward the door, and it scratched the inside of the door when Eamon left the house.

MawMaw Tierney opened the door and said, "Ya better be takin' him with ya, Eamon, or he be wearin' my doors plum out."

"Come on, boy." The dog was beside him before he finished that short sentence. As they walked toward the barn, Eamon said, "I just be goin' to be gittin' me a sickle off'n the barn wall. The hay on the far side of the field be gittin' ready fer threshin', and Uncle Teagan be workin' too hard in them there mines to be doin' h'it all by hisself."

When they got to the barn, the dog stuck his head inside. He immediately tucked his tail between his legs, backed a few yards away, sat and waited until Eamon returned. As they walked toward the field, Eamon said, "Ya nary be likin' dark places, do ya, boy? I cain't be sayin' I be blamin' ya one bit. H'it must be remindin' ya of that ol'

175

porch ya had to be hidin' under. I be knowin' what h'it be like to nary be able to be fergittin'."

When they got to the field, Eamon demonstrated several sickle strikes to show the dog he must stay out of the way. The dog seemed to understand, because he went to the edge of the field and lay down. When the dog was a safe distance away, Eamon began to cut the hay. He had half a hay stack done when Teagan's daughters ran across the field. He stopped and wiped the sweat off his brow with his sleeve while he waited for them.

The oldest girl gave him a sealed Mason jar full of lemonade and said, 'We nary be knowin' ya be out here. We be thinkin' ya be off a-playin' with yer dawg. Ya ought not be workin'. Ya still be a-healin'."

Eamon unscrewed the lid, took a big drink and held the cold jar to his forehead before he said, "I be healin' a'right, because Uncle Teagan done taked care of me right away. I be wantin' to be doin' this fer him to be makin' his life a lil' easier, too."

"We be helpin' ya," the middle girl said as she held up a sickle.

Eamon took another drink, put the lid on the jar and sat it at the edge of the field before the oldest girl and he resumed cutting the hay while the two younger girls stacked it. When Uncle Teagan drove down the family road that night, he drove very slowly and stared at the hay stacks. When he reached the Rose of Sharon bushes, he stopped the car and got out.

The car was a Ford Model B Coupe he purchased in 1934, which was the last year Ford manufactured that model. That model was on the market for two years, and it took him that long to save the $490 required to buy it. Saving for it taught him the value of the car. It was over ten years old, and it still looked brand new. He changed the oil and washed it regularly, and every night he wiped the coal dust off his seat. Fortunately, the car and the interior were both black, so coal dust wasn't apparent between washings.

He was halfway across the field when he met four sweaty children and Eamon's dog coming from the other direction. They had so much hay stuck to them that they resembled scarecrows, but they looked happy and proud.

"Lordy," Uncle Teagan said as he took his dirty mining hat off and left a streak of coal dust across his forehead while he wiped it with his dirty sleeve, "What ya young'uns been up to? I surely do be feelin' blessed that the winter wheat nary be in yet, because h'it would of kept me from seein' them beautiful hay stacks."

"Eamon done did most of h'it," the oldest girl said. "We be seein' him workin' on the hay about mid-day, so we done decided to be helpin' him."

Uncle Teagan put his arm across Eamon's shoulders and said, "I be feelin' awful proud of ya, son. Ya be savin' me a whole heap of work. Let us be goin' on in the house and be havin' us a nice supper. Y'all done earned h'it."

Eamon's dog barked and looked up at Eamon like he was proud of him, too.

As the girls walked toward the house, Uncle Teagan said, "Eamon and me be goin' to be parkin' the car and wipin' h'it off. Tell yer Ma to be startin' a cake or a pie. Y'all done earned h'it today."

As Uncle Teagan walked to the car with his arm across Eamon's shoulders, he said, "Thank ya, boy. Thank ya so much."

Eamon smiled bigger than I had ever seen him smile.

CHAPTER TWENTY-THREE
DAWG

Every day that Eamon lived at Uncle Teagan's house was as good or better than the day the girls and he harvested the hay. This was partly due to his dog. They went every place together. They shared Eamon's breakfast each morning before they went to work the field. The dog kept Eamon company while he worked the field. They shared lunch when the girls brought it to them. When the girls stayed and worked with Eamon in the afternoon, the dog was company for them, too.

One evening when Eamon and the dog were coming home from the field, they stopped at a porch rocker to rest before they went in the house. As they rocked, Eamon said, "If'n ya gonna be livin' with us, ya be needin' a name. I be goin' to be namin' ya Dawg, because that be what ya be. I nary be wantin' to be makin' some name up. I nary be wantin' to be treatin' ya like Pa done treated me. I be wantin' ya to be just who ya be. Do that be a'right with ya?" Dog looked pleased as he licked Eamon's nose, so that sealed his name.

When Eamon worked in the field, his limp became worse as the day wore on, but other than the occasional wince, the look on his face made me believe he was happy. I could understand why. He had enough to eat, he had Dog, he worked in sunshine and fresh air, it was quiet, he didn't have to fear being hit, and he was doing something that he seemed to enjoy. He often said he enjoyed doing the work, because it expressed his gratitude to Uncle Teagan. This was the first time his world made sense, so it followed that he would be happy.

Supper was family time at Uncle Teagan's house, and the women made a fine meal for them each night, including dessert. If there wasn't cake or pie, the girls sat on the top porch step and made homemade ice cream. The rest of the family, including Dog, sat on the rocking chairs and waited while the girls took turns cranking the ice cream maker.

One night while they waited, Uncle Teagan looked at Eamon and said, "I surely do be obliged fer all the work ya be doin' 'round here. I nary be havin' to be goin' back to the field after supper no more. Thanks be to ya, I can be sittin' on this here porch after supper."

"I be happy to be doin' h'it."

The oldest girl removed the lid from the ice cream maker and said, "H'it be done."

While the girls served the ice cream, Eamon said, "I be obliged to ya, Uncle Teagan. Before I be stayin' here, I nary be believin' life could be good. Now, I be eatin' ice cream."

"I be mighty glad to be hearin that, son. I be mighty glad to be hearin' h'it."

After several weeks of enjoying family bliss, Eamon noticed Caelan clearing brush along the property line. He didn't return Caelan's wave when Caelan sat down for an early lunch. Trying to ignore Caelan proved futile, because he started throwing pieces of his sandwich to Dog. The sandwich pieces landed closer to Caelan each time. By the time the girls brought Eamon's lunch, Dog was getting close enough that Caelan was trying to pet him when he crawled slowly toward the food, grabbed it and ran away before Caelan could touch him. Eamon called Dog for lunch, and he transformed from a hunkering, frightened animal to a bouncy pup as he followed Eamon across the field. They sat under a tree far away from Caelan and ate together. Caelan continued to work at the property line, so Eamon took Dog home the next day and left him at home for the rest of the week.

On Friday, Uncle Teagan got home early enough to help Eamon in the field. Caelan crossed the property line and approached Uncle Teagan, smiling big as he did. Uncle Teagan and Eamon stopped working and stared at Caelan as he approached them. When Caelan reached Uncle Teagan, he extended his hand and said, "Howdy."

Uncle Teagan ignored Caelan's hand, leaned on the handle of his hoe and asked, "What ya be wantin'?"

"I be wonderin', tomorrow bein' Saturday and all, if'n ya might be helpin' me fell a couple of them there trees. I be needin' fire wood fer the family."

"Why on God's green earth would I be doin' that fer ya?"

Caelan lowered his extended hand and said, "I be knowin' ya nary be havin' love fer me. I reckon I can be figurin' why. My young'uns nary be doin' nothin' to ya though. Them young'uns be needin' firewood this winter comin'. I reckoned, ya bein' their Uncle and all."

Uncle Teagan stared at Caelan for a full minute before he returned to covering the winter wheat seeds. As he worked, he said, "I reckon we can be helpin', just be knowin' we nary be doin' h'it fer ya. We be doin' h'it fer them young'uns of yers."

"Much obliged," Caelan said before he returned to his own property.

"Let us be gittin' on home," Uncle Teagan said as he walked across the field with Eamon close at his heels. "H'it be gittin' too crowded out here."

When they got home, Eamon sat on the porch and held Dog all evening. MawMaw Tierney brought their dinner to the porch, because Eamon refused to come in. An hour after sunset, Uncle Teagan finally told Eamon to go to bed, and he slept with Dog in his arms all night. The next morning, he locked Dog in the house before they left for the field.

An hour after they left, Eamon turned toward the sound of Dog barking. He laid his saw down, knelt and let Dog run into his embrace as he asked, "How ya be gittin' outta the house?"

Uncle Teagan continued sawing on the recently felled tree as he said, "Ya be knowin' how my sister be on a perty day. She prob'ly done propped the door open to be lettin' in the fresh air."

Eamon crinkled his brow as he said, "I surely be hopin' Dog gonna be a'right."

He sat Dog down and petted him vigorously before returning to work. Dog stayed near Eamon and watched him saw the tree into lumber. After the lumber was stacked on the back of Caelan's wagon, they felled another tree. This one was huge, so Eamon stood far away and held Dog until the tree was on the ground.

After the tree was de-branched, Caelan said, "I reckon this one be makin' some mighty good boards. I still be needin' boards to be finishin' up my gun rack. I done gived all of my boards to Sinead's coffin, and I cain't be believin' I nary be replacin' them yet." He ran his hands up and down the trunk and said, "Let us be cuttin' this here piece at about six feet. That ought to be givin' me a good start fer makin' boards." He set up the two man saw at the six foot mark, and Eamon grabbed the other side of it. Caelan stared at Eamon. After a few seconds of eye contact, Eamon looked down. When the six foot section was cut, Caelan said, "Ya be helpin' me to be gittin' this on that there wagon, boy."

"Ya be waitin' just a minute," Uncle Teagan said as he dropped his axe by the cord he was splitting and walked over to Caelan. "That there boy can be doin' a whole lot more than most folks be thinkin' he be able to be doin', but he ought not be liftin' nothin' that heavy on that hip of his. I be helpin' ya with that."

"Whatever ya be thinkin' be best," Caelan said as he smiled at Eamon.

Uncle Teagan picked up one end of the log, and Caelan picked up the other end. When they walked past Dog, Caelan side-stepped to position his end of the log over the unsuspecting animal before he dropped it. The log hit Dog with a thump that was accompanied by one yelp.

"Naw," Eamon screamed as he ran to Dog and fell on his knees beside his injured friend. "He be dead! He be dead! Naw! Naw!"

Uncle Teagan laid his end of the log down, ran to the bed of Caelan's truck, grabbed the rifle and ran back to Dog. With one swift motion, he shot Dog in the head.

"Naw!" Eamon screamed as he threw himself on Dog's head. "Naw! What ya be doin' that fer? What fer?"

Uncle Teagan knelt next to Eamon and rubbed his back as he said, "Dawg be sufferin', son. I be needin' to be gittin' him outta his misery."

Eamon continued to hold Dog's head and scream while Uncle Teagan got up, grabbed Caelan by the collar, backed him into the nearest tree and yelled, "What ya be doin' that fer?"

Caelan swallowed hard and said, "I done told that there boy he be goin' to be watchin' that dawg die, so I just be keepin' my word. Maybe that be learnin' ya to be keepin' yer nose in yer own business."

Uncle Teagan punched Caelan in the face and screamed, "Ya stupid bastard. How much ya gonna be hurtin' that there child before ya be done?"

At that moment, I saw Dog's spirit rise out of his body. As it did, Eamon sat up, stopped crying and looked into the sky like he saw it, too. When Dog's spirit reached the tree limbs, Eamon threw himself back on the body and wailed.

I looked up at Dog and said, "Come here, boy." He stopped elevating and looked at me, so I said it again.

Dog jumped to the ground and ran into my embrace. I was surprised when my arms didn't go through him. I could touch him like I had touched people when I was alive, but our spirits merged in a way that allowed us to know each other, really know each other, instantly.

A few minutes later, the Angel descended. As she took Dog from my embrace, she looked into my eyes and said, "It's never too late for you to come with me."

"I gots to be watchin' out over Eamon."

"We're watching him," she assured me.

"I cain't be leavin' him as long as he be with folks the likes of him," I said as I nodded toward Caelan.

"Okay," she said as she slowly ascended. "Dog will be waiting for Eamon when he crosses over. You can come and wait with him."

I looked at Eamon wailing over Dog's body, and I knew he needed me here. I shook my head no. When I did, Dog squirmed out of the Angel's arms and ran to Eamon. I looked at the Angel and assured her I would be watching out for both of them, and she disappeared.

CHAPTER TWENTY-FOUR
THE MAN OF GOD

I called for Dog several times after the Angel left, but he didn't come to me until Caelan fell so close to Eamon that it scared Dog into my arms. Eamon screamed and ran across the field. Even though he was limping, he was running almost as fast as a healthy boy. He was halfway across the field before Uncle Teagan broke away from the fight and ran after him. Dog jumped out of my arms and followed Uncle Teagan.

I watched Eamon run to the front yard, pull Lil' Gal's reins like the watermelon man taught him to do and mount her. They barreled around the Rose of Sharon bushes and onto the family road just as Uncle Teagan and Dog reached the edge of the field. I thought myself onto Lil' Gal's back and tried to put my arms around Eamon, but my inability to hold onto him only reminded me that I couldn't do anything to help him if he fell.

Fortunately, nobody was on the main road, because Lil' Gal didn't stop before making a right turn onto it. I thought Eamon was going to his family's house to seek revenge. Instead, she ran to the church and knelt at the bottom of the porch steps without Eamon having to ask her to.

Eamon dismounted and ran up the steps so fast that I don't think he realized how bad he was stumbling. I stayed behind him, but I knew there was nothing I could do if he fell. I felt my ghost heart skip a beat when he fell halfway up the steps, but he was able to get up and run to the top. He ran into the church door as if he expected it to be open. When it didn't, he grabbed the doorknob and wrestled with it as he screamed, "Preacher Skaggs!"

Several minutes later, Preacher Skaggs opened the door just enough to slip out. He was buckling his belt as he stood in front of Eamon and asked, "Why in hell do ya be makin' all that ruckus?"

"He kilt my dawg!"

"Who kilt yer dawg?" he asked as he grabbed Eamon's arm and led him to the steps.

As Preacher Skaggs sat on the steps, Eamon yelled, "Pa! He done kilt my dawg!"

Preacher Skaggs tried to grab Eamon's arm, but Eamon moved out of his reach three times before he yelled, "Set yer arse down here, boy, so I can be lookin' at ya whilst we be talkin'. I cain't be listenin' to ya when ya be jumpin' 'round like a hen on a hot griddle." When Eamon sat down, Preacher Skaggs asked, "What done happened?"

"Pa done kilt my dawg. He done dropped a tree on him."

Eamon was crying so hard it was difficult to understand what he was saying. I realized that I still saw him as a child even though he was close to being a man. I had taken care of him since he was a small child, so in my mind, he remained that way. As I watched him cry, I realized this was the first time something hurt him bad enough to let him release the emotions children should naturally release. He had always been forced to conduct himself like an adult. It is unfair how abuse twists the emotions of a child.

"That do be soundin' right awful, but what ya be wantin' me to be doin' about h'it?"

This was also the first time Eamon was hurt enough to speak what we all knew should never be spoken. He looked into Preacher Skaggs eyes and said, "I nary be fergittin' what ya done to me, but ya be the only preacher man 'round these here parts what can be tellin' me if'n dawgs be goin' to heaven?"

"I reckon I don't rightly be knowin'," Preacher Skaggs said, and Eamon started crying harder. The preacher pulled a handkerchief out of his jacket pocket and gave it to Eamon as he said, "Do be tryin' to be calmin' down, boy."

Eamon didn't seem to notice the red lipstick on the handkerchief as he wiped his face with it, took a couple of deep breaths and said, "Ya done said ya got to be gittin' saved and baptized before ya can be goin' to heaven, but Dawg never done them things."

"What ya be worryin' so much about an ol' dawg fer anyway?"

"He be my only friend," Eamon said before he started crying again.

Preacher Skaggs tried to put his arm over Eamon's shoulder, but Eamon scooted away. As the preacher lowered his arm, he said, "I reckon ya nary be havin' many friends, boy, has ya? I been tellin' ya I be yer friend. If'n ya be lettin' me be yer friend, I nary reckon ya be havin' to put so much stock in that there dawg."

"I nary be wantin' to be yer friend! I just be wantin' to be knowin' if'n dawgs be goin' to heaven."

Preacher Skaggs turned so fast when the church door creaked that he was rubbing the side of his injured neck before Regan peeked out. His sudden movement caused Eamon to look at him, so he slapped his neck where he was rubbing it and blamed it on a bee. When Eamon turned away, the preacher tried to wave Regan back inside, but she didn't obey until Uncle Teagan's car pulled into the churchyard.

Uncle Teagan parked at the bottom of the steps. As he got out of the car, he said, "I be seein' Lil' Gal grazin', so I be knowin' to be stoppin' here."

"He be mighty upset," Preacher Skaggs said as he patted Eamon's back.

Eamon scooted away from the preacher as Uncle Teagan walked up the steps, knelt in front of Eamon and asked, "What ya be comin' here fer?"

"I be wantin' to be knowin' if'n Dawg done gone to heaven?"

"What ya be tellin' him?" Uncle Teagan looked at Preacher Skaggs and asked.

"I done told him I don't rightly be knowin'."

Uncle Teagan grasped Eamon's hands and said, "I be thinkin' critters must surely be goin' to heaven."

Eamon's crying slowed down and his eyes got brighter as he asked, "Even if'n they nary be saved and baptized like Preacher be sayin' we all be havin' to be?"

"Jesus nary be tellin' critters they be havin' to be saved and baptized. I reckon there nary be one place in that there Good Book where Jesus be baptizin' no donkeys nor dawgs nor nothin'. Jesus, he be a right smart man. If'n them critters be needin' to be saved and baptized, don't ya be thinkin' he be dunkin' 'em in the water right there besides the people?"

Eamon wiped his eyes on Preacher Skaggs' handkerchief and said, "I reckon that be so."

When Uncle Teagan saw the smear of red lipstick, he grabbed Eamon's hand, looked at the handkerchief and asked, "Ya be bleedin', boy?"

"Naw, I nary be thinkin' I be."

Preacher Skaggs took the handkerchief out of their hands as he said, "My wife done gone and left lipstick all over my cheek this mornin'. I done used this to be gittin' h'it off before anyone be seein' h'it."

Uncle Teagan glared at Preacher Skaggs for several seconds before he looked back at Eamon and said, "Remember that there story about how Jesus be ridin' a donkey into Jerusalem? Don't ya reckon Jesus be feelin' right grateful to that donkey? Don't ya reckon he be baptizin' that donkey right there if'n h'it be needin' h'it, with him bein' grateful to h'it and all?"

"Yassir."

"Jesus be a right smart man. He be knowin' them critters nary be needin' no baptizin' to be gittin' into heaven, or he be a-dunkin' animals all along. I bet Dawg be up there playin' with Jesus right now."

"Really?" Eamon asked before he stopped crying and smiled.

"Remember how bad Dawg done suffered before ya be gittin' him? Just be thinkin', there nary gonna be no more sufferin' fer that lil' critter."

"That be good," Eamon said as he wiped his nose on his sleeve.

"This nary gonna be the last time ya be seein' Dawg neither. When yer day be comin', that lil' fella gonna be waitin' at the pearly gates fer ya with his tail just a waggin'."

Eamon smiled and asked, "Ya be promisin'?"

"I be promisin'. Hows about if'n ya be comin' on home with me. I be tellin' the girls to be makin' somethin' extra special fer dessert fer ya."

"Okay," Eamon said as he started to get up.

Before he got to his feet, Preacher Skaggs grabbed his arm. When Eamon was seated again, the preacher said, "I nary be hearin' h'it be explained like that before. I just be knowin' yer Uncle be right about that dawg. I just be sure that dawg be up in heaven a-waitin' fer ya, but ya be wantin' to be makin' sure ya be gittin' there to be meetin' him. Ya nary be baptized yet. We be havin' the last baptism of the summer on Sunday, and ya be needin' to be there."

"Do that be true, son?" Uncle Teagan asked.

"Yassir," Eamon answered as he nodded.

"I reckon Preacher Skaggs be right. I reckon ya ought to be gittin' yerself baptized."

"I reckon I ought to. I surely do be wantin' to be seein' Dawg again."

While Uncle Teagan helped Eamon stand, he said, "He gonna be there on Sunday."

"That be right good news," Preacher Skaggs said as he followed them down the steps and across the churchyard. "The boy ought to be comin' 'round this week to be gittin' some Christian learnin' before Sunday."

Uncle Teagan led Eamon to Lil' Gal as he said, "My sister be knowin' that there Bible about better than anyone 'round these here parts. She be happy to be learnin' the boy anything he be needin' to be knowin'." After he lifted Eamon onto Lil' Gal, he looked at Preacher Skaggs and whispered, "I be thinkin' the boy done been through enough this week. He nary be needin' to be learnin' from the likes of ya." He continued to look at Preacher Skaggs as he patted Eamon's leg and said, "Ya nary be tearin' outta here like ya done before. H'it nary be safe. I be seein' ya back at the house in just a few minutes."

"Yassir," Eamon said as he gently guided Lil' Gal onto the main road.

Uncle Teagan pushed past Preacher Skaggs and returned to his car. When he drove out of the churchyard, he followed Lil' Gal as she slowly meandered home. Preacher Skaggs watched until they turned onto Uncle Teagan's road before he returned to the church.

When Preacher Skaggs started to open the church door, Regan stormed out so fast she almost knocked him down the steps. As he grabbed the handrail, she slapped his face and yelled, "Ya be right friendly with Eamon! What ya be doin' to him that he nary be fergittin'? Why he nary be wantin' to be yer friend? Why he be scootin' away from ya when ya be touchin' him?"

"Ya nary be needin' to be worryin about yer brother," he said as he regained his balance. "Ya be knowin' ya be havin' my heart."

"I nary be worryin' about the likes of him. I be knowin' what ever' one 'round these parts be sayin' about ya, and I nary be givin' myself to someone what be havin' unnatural affections."

He forcibly embraced her until she stopped struggling before he said, "Ya ought to be knowin' ya cain't be listenin' to gossipy ol' biddies what be havin' nothin' better to do than be talkin' about folks. Ya be thinkin' folks 'round here be lettin' me preach if'n them stories be true?"

"I reckon not."

"If'n I be havin' unnatural affections, do ya be thinkin' I be showin' ya, a gal, my affections? Ya cain't be likin' men folk and women folk both, don't ya be knowin' that? I done proved to ya many a time that h'it be women folk I be likin'."

She smiled and lay her head onto his chest as she said, "I reckon that be true."

He kissed the top of her head and said, "I just be doin' my job as a preacher. I be havin' to be there fer folks when they be havin' trials. Now, ya be gittin' yerself on home. Eamon be tellin' me there be some ruckus over yer house about his ol' dawg. Ya nary be needin' to be gittin' yer Pa riled about now. Ya be goin' on home and be doin' what he be tellin' ya. Ya be hearin' me?"

"Yassir," she said as she pulled out of his embrace. "Ya be drivin' me to my road. I be a lady, and I nary be walkin' that far when I be havin' a man to be servin' me."

He sighed before he obediently walked down the steps and opened the passenger door.

CHAPTER TWENTY-FIVE
THE BAPTISM

After Sunday services, the church members walked to the river even though it was almost a mile away. The white robe Eamon wore was the nicest thing I'd ever seen him wear. A woman with short, curly, blonde hair walked to the right of him, and a young girl who wore a white scarf tied tightly around her head walked on the other side. Both wore white robes.

I remembered the two women from when I was alive. The blonde woman was Sister Madge, and the young girl was her little sister, Melanie. I barely knew Melanie, because she was a baby when my mother killed me. Madge, on the other hand, was one of the few people in the congregation who played with me.

Most of the members avoided me when I was alive. They knew what my family was like. As young as I was, I knew their smiles were faked. Even if I'd never heard them talking about us behind our backs, their distance made it quite clear. I guess it was easier for them to gossip than to relieve the suffering of children. It was definitely easier for them to gossip than to confront Caelan. Not only was he mean and impossible to reason with, but he had a special bond with Preacher Skaggs that was cemented by mutual blackmail.

Apparently, becoming a Christian turned Madge into one of them, and she was willing to wash away childhood innocence in the river today. Neither she nor Melanie spoke to Eamon during the long walk to the river, nor did they get unnecessarily close to him. I guess it wore off on you if you stayed on this mountain long enough. Maybe conforming is why they were still alive with bodies that were still intact.

Eamon's limp got a little worse with each step. I couldn't believe these people wanted to baptize him into a religion of love when they didn't possess enough love to put him on Lil' Gal or the preacher's fine horse. I don't think Jesus asked anyone to suffer just for suffering's sake. Regan, on the other hand, arrived in the Duesenberg, because she was willing to spread her legs for that snake of a preacher. No wonder he was so popular; folks around here thought it was godly to handle snakes. When we arrived, the congregation gathered along the riverbank and sang.

Madge was the first to enter the river. She smiled at Preacher Skaggs before he raised her hand to her nose and dunked her. Melanie looked down as if she were in pious prayer while he did the same thing to her. Both baptisms went smoothly. Eamon's was another story. He kept slipping on the slimy river bottom as he limped to Preacher Skaggs, and his leg buckled when the preacher dunked him in the water. As Eamon splashed frantically, Preacher Skaggs grabbed the back of his neck and his crotch to stand him up again.

When they got to shore, Preacher Skaggs put his arm over Eamon's shoulder and said, "I done told ya I nary be lettin' nothin' be happening' to ya, didn't I? Just be rememberin' that anything I be doin' be done to be keepin' ya safe. I be wantin' to be yer friend, and ya be needin' a friend now that Dawg be gone."

Eamon was shivering too bad to answer, so Preacher Skaggs rolled his eyes and left Eamon's side to mingle with the crowd. The only time the preacher stopped watching Eamon was when Regan demanded his attention. When Eamon limped toward the main road, Preacher Skaggs grasped the hands of the old woman he was talking to, a woman he had known all of his life but couldn't remember her name, and said, "Excuse me, ma'am. I be needin' to be checkin' on that there crippled boy. He be havin' hisself a mighty hard time in that there water, and I be wantin' to be makin' sure he be a'right."

The old woman nodded, and Preacher Skaggs ran to Eamon. He called Eamon's name several times as he ran. When he got to Eamon, he said, "I be thinkin' we done got off on the wrong foot. Now that I done baptized ya, I be thinkin' ya be seein' how I just be tryin' to be doin' what be best fer ya."

Eamon stammered as he said, "But, after ya done showed me, ah, well, ya be knowin' what done happened."

"Sometimes when we be misunderstandin' somethin', we just be keepin' on misunderstandin' till we be givin' the sitch-e-ation a chance to be provin' h'itself different. Can ya be givin' me a chance now, boy, to be provin' h'it be different?"

"I don't rightly know," Eamon stammered. "I just don't rightly know."

"Ya be a Christian now, boy. H'it be the right thing to be doin'. Jesus be tellin' us to be forgivin'. If'n we nary be able to be forgivin', we nary be makin' h'it into heaven. Ya nary be able to be seein' Dawg again if'n ya don't make h'it. I be wantin' ya to be seein' Dawg again. Won't ya be forgivin' me and be comin' to the church tomorrow?

"I don't rightly be knowin'," Eamon said, hesitantly.

"Ya be comin' on down to the church tomorrow. I be expectin' ya. I be thinkin' I be havin' an ol' ball glove my boy be too old fer now. Surely there be some vittles left from today we can be sharin'. Just be stoppin' on by to be havin' a meal with me."

"I don't rightly, I not, I not be sure."

Preacher Skaggs angrily said, "Now that ya be gittin' fed regular, ya be fergittin' how I done fed ya when ya nary be havin' nothin'."

"I reckon not," Eamon said as he looked down.

"Good; I be seein' ya tomorrow then."

When Preacher Skaggs started to walk away, Eamon asked as he took his robe off, "Can ya be takin' this here robe back to the church fer me? I surely be hatin' to be gittin' h'it dirty. I nary be seein' nothin' so nice in all my days."

Preacher Skaggs looked Eamon up and down while Eamon took off the robe. When Eamon reached it to him, he smiled coyly and said, "I surely will be doin' that fer ya."

While Eamon walked to the main road to begin his journey home, Preacher Skaggs carried the robe to the Deusenberg and threw it in the back seat of the parked car before returning to the party. There was no reason why he couldn't offer Eamon a ride home.

CHAPTER TWENTY-SIX
BUSINESS AS USUAL

I didn't mention Eamon's brothers and sisters at the baptism, because they didn't come. When Regan went home the day Dog died, I followed her. I knew Eamon was safe with Uncle Teagan, so I chose to take care of him by learning how Regan's jealousy would lead her to avenge him.

When she got home, she sat on the porch bench behind where the other children were sitting on the steps. She removed a compact from her purse and looked in the mirror while she pressed her curls in her palm. She did this for several minutes before she said, "Eamon's dawg done up and died today."

The children gasped and turned to her as Garnett asked, "What done happened to h'it?"

"I nary be knowin'," Regan answered. "All I be knowin' is Eamon done been down at the church just a bawlin' his eyes out like a lil' babe. I nary be seein' him be cryin' that hard before. He nary be cryin' a tear when he done got taked away from y'all. H'it must be feelin' right awful to be knowin' an ol' mangy dawg be meanin' more to him than y'all do."

The children looked down at their laps while Garnett glared at Regan and said, "Naw, h'it nary be so."

Regan closed her compact and put it back in her purse as she said, "I be sorry h'it be hurtin' so bad to be hearin', but h'it do be so. Ask Uncle Teagan. He be seein' Eamon bawlin' over that ol' mangy dawg.

Whilst ya be at h'it, ask Uncle Teagan if'n Eamon ever be cryin' over y'all like that."

Garnett joined the other children in looking down at their laps.

Regan chuckled and said, "Y'all be sittin' on this here porch day after day just waitin' fer him to be comin' back. He nary be comin' back. He just be feelin' glad to be shet of y'all. He done taked care of y'all fer so long he just plain be gittin' tired of h'it."

When none of the children responded, Regan said, "I hear'ed tell Eamon be gittin' baptized this Sunday. I reckon y'all be runnin' down to that there river to be seein' him like he nary be doin' a thing against ya. H'it be sad how y'all be lettin' him be treatin' ya."

Garnett whispered, "Mays be she be right. Mays be we nary be needin' to be goin' to be seein' him be gittin' baptized. He nary be comin' to be seein' us since he done left."

"Mays be he be afeared Pa be beatin' him if'n he be comin' 'round," Legs whispered as she tugged the hem of her too-short skirt.

"He nary be worryin' about if'n Pa be over here beatin' y'all," Regan said.

The children sat silently for several minutes before Legs said, "I reckon we nary be needin' to be goin' to that there baptism. Folks at that there church just be lookin' at us like we be a bunch of thieves any ways after what Garnett done did."

"I nary be doin' nothing wrong," Garnett snapped. "I done been wrongful accused and y'all be knowin' h'it."

"That nary be meanin' the folks at that there church be knowin' h'it," Regan said. "Ya be wantin' them all to be whisperin' about ya whilst ya be there?"

Garnett shook his head as he said, "I reckon there nary be no need for us to be goin'."

Regan picked up her purse and went into the house. When she was inside, she laughed and said out loud, "I reckon my work here be done."

I followed her into her room. Eamon's side of the room was still sparse even though it accommodated all of the children while Regan's side of the room was more extravagant than the last time I'd seen it. She had several blankets and pillows. The chifforobe was so full of dresses she couldn't close the door. There was an oak vanity table and chair at the foot of her bed, and the vanity top was covered with creams, make-up, and jewelry. I was angry about all this new stuff until I heard what she had to say to her reflection in the vanity mirror when she sat in front of it.

I sat on the foot of her bed and was surprised that I didn't see my own reflection in the mirror as I watched her brush her hair. While the brushing straightened the curls she so valued, she said, "I cain't be believin' that ol' preacher done sat on them there steps tryin' to be holdin' a boy. I be knowin' he nary be meanin' nothin' innocent by h'it. What people be sayin' 'round here, h'it must surely be true. I be knowin' he be havin' intentions in that direction. I be knowin' he do." Her strokes became harder and more damaging to her hair as she said, "I be damned if'n I be goin' to be lettin' that ol' preacher be treatin' me this way. I be tellin' Pa. That what I be doin'. I be tellin' Pa that preacher done forced his-self on me. That be the end of that ol' varmint. He nary be treatin' me this way nary more."

She stopped brushing and said, "Oh, my, just be lookin' at what I be doin' to my perty hair." She gently touched the side of her eye and said, "It nary be just my hair; just be lookin' at what be happenin' to my face. I only be fourteen year old, and I be gittin' them lines 'round my eyes. I gonna be all wrinkled up like Ma be at a young age. I nary be havin' nothin' then."

She stared at her reflection for a long time before she said, "I still be perty." She grabbed her lipstick from the vanity and rubbed it slowly and sensually across her lips before she said, "Besides, Eamon be older than I be. He be nearly three year old before I be borned. He always gonna be older than me. That ol' preacher man gots to be seein' that."

She quietly stared at her reflection for so long that I got bored and returned to the porch. Mabon put the children to work, so I sat on the steps alone and waited for Caelan. I wanted to see if he had plans to harm Eamon before I returned to Uncle Teagan's house. Several hours later, Caelan stomped across the yard and started his familiar after-work cleansing ritual. When he was done, I followed him into the house and watched him sit at the table, open the Mason jar and take a drink of moonshine.

Regan approached him before he finished the first drink and said, "Pa."

He sat the Mason jar on the table and asked, "What?"

"Do ya still be thinkin' I be perty?"

"Of course ya be perty," he said as looked her up and down.

"Ya nary be thinkin' I be gittin' too old lookin'?"

"Naw, ya nary be old lookin' at all." He laughed and said, "Yer Ma be old lookin'."

"I be lookin' like her one day."

"What that be matterin' to me? I done be in the grave by then."

"Who be goin' to be lovin' me then?"

"Ya be gittin' on outta here, girl," he said as he waved his hand in a gesture of dismissal. "What ya be botherin' me with all this nonsense fer anyhow?"

Tears welled in her eyes before she walked away.

"Come here, lil' gal," he said as he motioned her back. When she got to him, he looked around the house quickly before he kissed her and said, "Ya be comin' on out to the barn after ever' one done gone to bed. I be showin' ya how perty ya be then."

She left the house and went immediately to the barn. She sat on the edge of the wagon until she fell asleep. Several hours later, Caelan woke her by putting his hand up her dress.

I saw their encounters many times when I was lying in bed with Eamon. She always lay quietly under him as stiff as a board with tears streaming down the side of her face and making a puddle on the mattress. This time, she met his lips and body with passion. He seemed to enjoy their union until a few seconds after his climax. He stood on his knees, pulled his pants up and buckled his belt. When she sat up, he slapped her face so hard that it knocked her back onto the wagon bed.

She covered her cheek with her palm and looked up at him as he said, "Ya be whorin' just like yer Ma done. Ya nary be movin' like that before. Who be learnin' ya that?" When she didn't answer, he covered her like a dog on all fours, put his face right in her face and asked, "Who be learnin' ya that?"

Tears streamed down her cheeks as she said, "No one, Pa! I nary be lyin' to ya."

He grabbed her hair and pulled her head back as he asked, snarling, "Who h'it be? I nary be askin' ya again!"

"H'it nary be no one. I just be wantin' to be knowin' ya still be thinkin' I be perty."

He let go of her hair and calmly said, "Ya do be askin' me about bein' perty before. Ya be wantin' to be perty fer me?"

"Yassir."

"Ya be so perty, child, that I be wantin' ya just fer me and no other man. Ya gots to be knowin' what be happenin' to ya if'n I ever be catchin' ya with another man," he said as he flipped her over and lifted her bottom into the air. He swatted her bare bottom with the palm of his hand. He must have enjoyed her cries of pain, because each one fueled the intensity of his punishment. When he was finished, he stared at her red bottom as he licked his lips, knelt behind her and unbuckled his belt.

When Caelan was finished with Regan, he left her on the back of the wagon. She curled up in a ball and cried for the rest of the night. When he left for work in the morning, she got dressed and returned to her room. She couldn't sit in front of the mirror until she put a pillow on the chair. When she saw her straw-filled hair and bruised face in the reflection, she cried. She tried to brush her hair, but the brush got caught in a tangle. She threw it onto the vanity and stormed out of the room.

Mabon sat on Caelan's chair eating his leftovers. Regan stomped across the room, grabbed Mabon's hair and pulled Mabon's head back like Caelan did to her the night before.

"What in hell ya be doin' girl?," Mabon asked as she struggled to get free. "Ya be knowin' I be tannin' yer hide fer this!"

Regan laughed and said, "This nary be yer hide to be tannin', ol' woman. My hide be belongin' to Pa, and ya be knowin' what he be doin' to ya if'n ya be puttin' any marks on h'it." Regan pulled Mabon's hair harder and said, "Ya be walkin' to the comp'ny store today. Ya be buyin' me that there make-up kit I be wantin'."

Mabon winced as she said, "I nary be havin' no daughter of mine prancin' 'round lookin' like a whore. H'it be bad enough yer Pa done bought ya that red lipstick."

Regan pulled harder and said, "Ya be knowin' why Pa be buyin' me that there lipstick, ol' woman. Ya cain't be actin' like ya nary be knowin'. Ya cain't be actin' like ya nary be knowin' a whole mess of

196

stuff what be happenin' 'round here. I reckon I be havin' a whole mess of stuff to be tellin' if'n ya nary be walkin' to that there store."

"What ya be thinkin' I be payin' fer h'it with?"

"Ya be puttin' h'it on Pa's account."

"H'it be two mile to that there store. I nary be able to be walkin' that far."

Regan pulled harder and said, "Ya be knowin' I can be gittin' Pa to be hurtin' ya bad, ol' woman. Ya be knowin' I can be tellin' all manner of things that be hurtin' ya bad. Ya best be doin' what I be tellin' ya."

"A'right," Mabon said as she massaged her neck. "A'right. I be goin' fer ya."

"That be a right smart move, ol' woman," Regan said as she released Mabon's hair. "Ya be gittin' on outta here."

Regan followed Mabon to the porch and watched her walk past the children sitting on the steps. When she was out of sight, Regan said, "There be biscuits and gravy on the stove. If'n y'all be goin' in there and be eatin' 'em while Ma be gone, I nary be tellin' on ya."

Regan followed them to the kitchen. While they ate the leftovers, she said, "I be bettin' Eamon nary be doin' nothin' this kind fer ya. He be makin' ya be thinkin' I be bad, but I nary be bad."

"We be knowin' ya nary be bad," Legs said. Her mouth was so full it was hard to understand her, but Regan must have understood, because she smiled and walked away.

CHAPTER TWENTY-SEVEN
HONKY-TONKIN'

It was early afternoon before Mabon returned with the make-up kit. She was sweating and obviously exhausted as she walked up the stairs, but Regan didn't seem to notice when they met on the porch. Regan grabbed the make-up kit and ran to her room, leaving Mabon to sit on the porch bench trying to catch her breath.

I followed Regan to her room. She sat in front of the mirror and placed the small red box on top of the vanity, gingerly lifted the little gold latch before lifting the lid, and gasped at the treasures inside. After opening a drawer on her vanity, she pulled out one of her copies of Screen Romance Magazine, opened it to a picture of Greta Garbo and leaned the picture against the bottom of the mirror. She picked up a container of light pink eye shadow and swiped her finger across it, but she stared at it on her finger for several minutes before she applied it. She stared at her reflection in the same way before she applied it to the other eye. After she laid the eye shadow on the vanity, she picked up a container of rouge, put some on her fingers, and swiped a bold red streak across each cheek in a manner reminiscent of war paint. She stared at her reflection for a long time before she blended the rouge with such harsh rubbing that she winced when she got near her bruises. When her cheeks were bright red from a combination of rouge and rubbing, she picked up the compact. After her face was covered with pressed powder, she tried to cover the bruises with extra powder.

Tears welled in her eyes when the bruises remained slightly visible, but she continued. Mascara was applied to its brush and her eyelashes with movements that were so rapid and angry it seemed unsafe that close to her eyes. Her movements became quicker with each product she applied. It looked like she was becoming anxious to get to the box's greatest treasure: the gold lipstick case. She held it in front of her like it was an object to be worshiped. Her smile grew as she removed the lid, twisted the tube and revealed the red lipstick hidden inside. Her smile was so big by the time she pressed the red to her lips that she had a hard time applying it. When she was finished, she carefully placed all of the items back in the red box, closed the lid and secured the latch.

She stared at her reflection and crimped her curls in her hand as she said, "I do be perty. I be perty enough to be gittin' Pa back fer what he done to me last night, and I will, too, if'n h'it be the last thing I be doin'."

She walked to the porch and yelled for one of her younger sisters, Clea, for several minutes before a tiny girl about eleven years old ran to the porch, stood at the bottom of the steps and looked up at Regan. The girl looked like Regan except malnutrition had prevented her from developing in height and figure like Regan had, and her clothes were tattered and dirty.

"What be takin' ya so long?" Regan asked, yelling.

"I nary be sure ya be callin' me. I nary be hearin' ya be sayin' my name before."

Regan crinkled her brow and said, "I nary be sayin' yer name before. Well, that about to be changin'. Ya be wantin' to be goin' fer a walk with me?"

"Ma be havin' me warshin' clothes," Clea said as she pointed to a metal bucket and washboard in front of the barn.

"Ya nary be havin' to be worryin' about Ma," Regan said before she turned toward the house and yelled for Mabon. When Mabon came to the porch, Regan said, "Clea be goin' fer a walk with me. Ya nary be wantin' me to bein' tellin' Pa, or maybe other folks, what might be bringin' ya to be sayin' no, does ya?"

When Mabon shook her head and returned to the house, Clea smiled. The smile grew as the girls walked down the family road even though the close proximity emphasized Clea's neglect. Regan wore a well-kept white dress, make-up, and Shirley Temple curls while Clea wore Regan's hand-me-down rags, pig tails, and a dirty face.

When they turned onto the main road and began the two-mile walk to the mining town, Clea asked, "Where we be goin'?"

"We be goin' to town. I be wantin' to be seein' what that there honky-tonk be like."

Clea shrugged and said, "A'right."

They walked the rest of the way without talking. When they arrived, the honky-tonk was already jumping even though there was still light in the sky. Regan grabbed Clea's shoulders, backed her up against the wall next to the front door and said, "Ya be needin' to be stayin' right here. Ya be lettin' me be knowin' if'n ya be seein' Pa or Preacher Skaggs comin'."

"Cain't I be goin' in with ya?"

"Ya be too young. Ya just be waitin' right here. Ya be lettin' me be knowin' if'n ya be seein' 'em. A'right?"

"A'right."

Regan entered the honky-tonk. She smiled when most of the men turned to look at her. She flirted with all of the miners who approached her, but she quickly set her sights on a man who was wearing a suit and drinking alone at a corner table. She approached him and allowed him to buy her a drink, and he laughed when she spit her first drink of Kentucky bourbon back into the glass and said, "This be awful!"

"Is this the first time you've been in a honky-tonk?"

"Yassir," Regan answered and batted her eyes at the man.

"How old are you, child?"

"I be twenty-one."

"You don't look twenty-one," he said as he looked her up and down. "But, that's all right with me. Younger is sweeter as far as I'm concerned. Why don't we leave and find something to do that tastes better than alcohol."

She ran her fingers up and down his lapel as she asked, "Do ya be a boss man fer that there minin' company? Ya be lookin' like ya be a big man."

He looked at his crotch and said, "I'm a big man every place. Let's get out of here."

Before Regan could answer, Clea ran into the room and looked around frantically before she ran to Regan's table and said, "Regan! Pa be comin'!"

Regan grabbed her purse off the table and ran out the back door with Clea. The sky turned pitch dark while Regan was in the honky-tonk, so it was hard to believe they knew where they were going. They ran until they were so out of breath they were forced to start walking, which made it quiet enough for them to hear a noise that frightened them into each other's embrace.

Clea whispered, "We needs to be hidin' in the woods!"

"Ya ninny! What if'n h'it be a bear."

The sound stopped when a dark horse was reigned in beside them. Regan's suitor from the honky-tonk tipped his hat and said, "Hello, ladies."

Regan smiled and asked, "What ya doin' out here?"

"I couldn't let a pretty lady like you get away," he said as he put his hat back on and extended his hand to Regan. "Why don't you get on and let me give you a ride?"

Regan grasped his hand, and he pulled her onto the horse behind him before he extended his hand to Clea and pulled her onto the horse in front of him. While they road, Regan snuggled her breasts into his back while Clea looked around like an excited child on a carnival ride. The girls had no way of knowing that the clearing he took them to was the same one where Caelan had courted my Ma. The man dismounted after he helped Regan off the horse. He then placed his big hands under Clea's arms and lowered her to the ground beside him.

He put his arm over Regan's shoulders and said, "I couldn't take a chance on losing a pretty lady like you. How about if we take a walk while your sister watches my horse?"

"A'right," Clea said as she grabbed the horse's reins and petted its muzzle.

Clea petted the horse until the man returned from the dark woods over an hour later with Regan stumbling behind him trying to regain his attention. Just before they got to Clea, the man turned to Regan and said, "Hey, listen girlie, I had fun with you tonight, but that doesn't mean I owe you anything. I don't care what your father did to you. I'm not going to ruin my future avenging a girl I don't even know."

"Ya cain't be sayin' ya nary be knowin' me after what we just done," Regan said as she grabbed his arm to keep him from walking away. "I be thinkin' ya be knowin' me perty good."

The man yanked his arm away from Regan. When he got to Clea and took the reins from her, she said, "Awww. I be havin' fun pettin' him. Cain't I be pettin' him fer a while longer?"

The man smiled and rubbed Clea's cheek as he said, "Well, maybe you can."

Clea reached for the horse's reins, but the man placed his hands under her arms, lifted her until her face was in front of his, and tried to kiss her.

Clea started squirming as she screamed, "What ya be doin'? Ya be lettin' me down!"

She fought the man's attempts to kiss her until she accidentally kicked him in the crotch. He dropped her as he fell to his knees, and Clea ran onto the main road.

Regan tried to help him up, but he pushed her away and yelled, "Get off of me, you fucking whore!" After several minutes lying on his side and groaning, he got up and mounted his horse, leaving Regan standing in the middle of the field crying.

Clea ran all the way home. She only stopped once to duck into the woods when the man rode past her. When she got home, she sat on the porch steps and waited for Regan, who didn't get home until almost an hour later.

"Ya be a'right?" Clea asked as Regan walked up the steps.

"I be just fine," Regan said as she stormed past Clea and went to her room. She sat at her vanity, opened her new make-up kit, removed the compact and stared at herself in its mirror for several minutes before she yelled, "Clea!"

Clea ran into the room and said, "Shush! Ya be goin' to be wakin' Ma up."

"I nary be afeared of that ol' woman," Regan said as she reached the compact to Clea. "Ya be holdin' this here mirror whilst I be combin' my hair." Clea took the compact and held it in front of Regan's face. Regan ran the comb through her hair once and said, "Ya be movin' h'it."

"I nary be movin' h'it."

Regan ran the comb through her hair one more time before she grabbed Clea's arm, held it still and said, "Ya be holdin' h'it still like this here!"

"I be gittin' tired. I nary be wantin' to be doin' this no more."

Regan jerked Clea's arm and hissed, "Ya be holdin' the mirror, and ya be holdin' h'it still!"

A tear ran down Clea's cheek as she steadied her arm. Regan ran the comb through her hair several times before she grabbed Clea's arm and started scratching it with the comb's teeth.

"Owww!" Clea yelled as she tried to pull her arm free. "Ya be lettin' me be goin'!"

Regan continued to scratch Clea's arm as she said, "Ya nary be goin' after what be mine."

"I nary did," Clea said as she struggled to get her arm free.

"Ya done tried to be takin' that there comp'ny man from me," Regan said as she grabbed the compact out of Clea's hand. "Mays be he could of been gittin' me off'n this here mountain, but ya done ruin't h'it fer me." Regan threw the comb at Clea and screamed, "Ya be gittin' on outta here! Now!"

Clea's feet moved so fast that they slipped as she tried to get out of the room before Regan had time to change her mind.

Regan stared at her reflection in the vanity mirror for several minutes before she said, "I reckon Pa be the only man nary be leavin' me. I reckon he be all I be havin'."

CHAPTER TWENTY-EIGHT
TESTING THE WATER

Preacher Skaggs parked his Duesenberg in front of Uncle Teagan's house soon after the rooster crowed. He got out of the car, walked to the passenger door and picked up a covered plate and a baseball glove off the passenger seat before he went to the front door and knocked.

Uncle Teagan answered and asked, "What do ya be doin' here at this hour? Some of the family nary be dressed."

"I be bringin' these here things by fer Eamon. He done told me that he be comin' by the church yesterday to be gittin' them, but he nary did."

Uncle Teagan walked onto the porch and said, "Eamon be mighty busy in the fields yesterday. I reckon he nary be havin' time to be comin' over to the church."

"I see," Preacher Skaggs said as he shifted his weight from one foot to the other.

Uncle Teagan grasped both items and said, "That be right neighborly of ya. I be right happy to be givin' these here things to Eamon fer ya."

Preacher Skaggs tried to pull them away from Uncle Teagan as he said, "I be preferrin' to be givin' them to the boy myself."

"The boy be havin' a name," Uncle Teagan said as he cocked an eyebrow. "Eamon be gittin' dressed. If'n ya just be wantin' the boy to be havin' these here things, there nary be a reason why I cain't be givin' them to him."

Preacher Skaggs released his grip on the gifts and let Uncle Teagan take them as he said, "I be thinkin' h'it be right proper fer the boy to be stoppin' by the church later today to be thankin' me fer these things. H'it be good to be teachin' a boy manners."

"I be makin' sure the boy be gittin' a thank ya to ya one way or the other."

Preacher Skaggs stared at him for so long that Uncle Teagan said, "Do that be h'it?"

"Yassir," Preacher Skaggs said before he walked toward his car.

· · · · ·

Later that day, Uncle Teagan parked his car at the bottom of the church steps. When Eamon started to get out, Uncle Teagan laid his palm on Eamon's shoulder and asked, "Do ya be wantin' me to be comin' in with ya?"

"Naw. I be thinkin' I be needin' to be returnin' these here things myself."

Uncle Teagan nodded, and Eamon got out of the car. He was shaking as he walked up the church steps, but he composed himself before he knocked assertively on the slightly open door. The door opened enough for him to enter. He was halfway down the aisle before he saw Preacher Skaggs sitting next to Regan and playing with one of her dark curls as they talked.

When Eamon cleared his throat, Preacher Skaggs hopped up, ran down the aisle and asked, "What ya be doin' here, boy?"

"I be thinkin' h'it be right fer me to be givin' these here things back to ya," Eamon stammered as he looked at Regan.

"Ya be comin' on back tomorrow, and we can be talkin' about h'it then," Preacher Skaggs said as he grabbed Eamon's arm and led him toward the door. When they got to the door, Preacher Skaggs said, "I be a preacher man, boy. We be doin' more than just preachin' on Sunday. We be havin' to be here fer our members who be havin' trials."

"Why do my sister be here?" Eamon asked as he looked at Regan.

"She be wantin' to be talkin' about some trials she be havin'."

Eamon looked down at the ball glove as he asked, "Do she be talkin' to ya about Pa?"

205

"Naw," Preacher Skaggs said as he laid his hand on the small of Eamon's back and tried to push him out the door.

Eamon stood firm and asked, "Do she be talkin' to ya about Ma?"

"Naw. She be talkin' to me about God. Yer baptism done moved her, so she be wantin' to be knowin' more about God."

"She nary comed to my baptism," Eamon said as he pushed the ball glove and cookies at Preacher Skaggs. "I be leavin' these here things with ya. I nary be havin' no use fer 'em."

When Preacher Skaggs took them, Eamon stepped out of the darkness of the church and into the light of day without needing to be pushed. Preacher Skaggs closed the door so fast that he spoke from the other side of it when he said, "Ya be comin' back 'round here when I nary be busy, so we can be talkin' about this here ball glove." It seemed like Preacher Skaggs was afraid of the light that only caused Eamon to squint as he walked confidently into its brightness.

"Do ya be a'right?" Uncle Teagan asked.

"Yassir, I be just fine. The sun just be a-blindin' me a bit."

"Do h'it be dark in there?" Uncle Teagan crinkled his brow and asked as Eamon walked down the steps. "Why do h'it be dark in there?"

"I don't rightly be knowin'. He be havin' all the shades drawn. He be sayin' he be givin' Regan Christian learnin'."

"Oh, my Lord," Uncle Teagan said as Eamon got in the car.

"Do ya reckon Regan be a'right?"

"I be more worried about that there Preacher. Ya done gived them things back to him?"

"Yassir."

"I reckon all we can be doin' now is just be goin' on home," Uncle Teagan said as he drove away from the church.

When they got home, MawMaw Tierney had supper ready. The family enjoyed the meal and a few hours together on the porch before they went to bed. Eamon was almost asleep when someone knocked on the window. He jumped up so fast that he almost fell off the bed before he scooted against the far wall. His room was long and thin. Even though his bed was on the opposite wall, there were only about five steps between it and the window. He grabbed the new quilt MawMaw Tierney made for him in various shades of brown sack cloth and pulled it up under his chin as he stared at the darkness outside. A few seconds later, Clea pressed her face against the window.

Eamon got out of bed, took the five steps to the window, opened it and asked. "What ya be doin' here?" Clea climbed in the window and was sitting on the edge of his bed before he had time to close it. He walked back to the bed, sat next to her and asked, "Do ya be a'right?"

Clea hugged him as she said, "I be a'right."

He returned a rigid hug as he said, "If'n Pa be findin' ya out and about like this, he be beatin' ya."

"He nary be knowin' I be out and about."

"What ya be doin' over here this time of night?"

Clea pulled out of their hug, looked at him and said, "This time of night be the only time I can be sneakin' out, because Pa done be down at the honky-tonk." She pulled on the front of his pajama shirt and said, "They be takin' right good care of ya. Ya be havin' new pajamas."

He looked down at his pajamas and said, "Yas, they do be takin' right good care of me. Do ya be a'right over at the house?"

"H'it be the same hi't always be. Why ya nary be comin' to be visitin' us?"

Eamon swallowed hard and tears welled in his eyes before he answered, "Pa done told me he be takin' h'it out of yer hides if'n I be comin' over to be seein' y'all. I nary be wantin' y'all to be gittin' beat, so I be stayin' away. I surely do be missin' y'all."

"We be missin' ya, too."

"I be mighty happy to be seein' ya now, but I be worryin' about what Pa be goin' to be doin' to ya."

"I be makin' sure to be gittin' home before he be missin' me. Besides, I nary just be comin' fer a visit."

Eamon crinkled his eyebrows as he asked, "What do ya be comin' fer?"

"That horse nary busted up yer leg, did h'it?"

Eamon picked at the quilt for a long time before he answered, "Naw."

"I nary be thinkin' so."

"How ya be knowin'?"

"I nary be stupid. I be knowin' things. Besides, now that ya be gone, Regan be treatin' me the same way she used to be treatin' ya. I be knowin' how much danger ya was livin' in."

Eamon wiped a tear from his cheek as he said, "I surely do be sorry to be hearin' that."

Clea held her arm out and pointed to the scratches Regan put on it with the comb as she said, "She done got this mad at me over some ol' man what be payin' me some attention."

"I be so sorry, Clea. Do h'it be hurtin'?"

"Nary no more. Ya be knowin' what? I nary even be wantin' that man to be payin' no attention to me. I runned from him." Clea looked into Eamon's eyes for several seconds before she took both of his hands in hers and said, "I be knowin' what Regan be like. I be comin' to be warnin' ya to be watchin' yer back. She be tellin' all the other young'uns stories to be makin' them be thinkin' ya nary be carin' nothin' about them no more. I be tryin' to be tellin' them the truth, but she be better at lyin' than I be at tellin' the truth. She be awful mad at ya about somethin' be happenin' over at the church today, so she really be tellin' stories now. Ya be havin' to be careful."

Eamon held Clea's gaze the entire time she talked. He blinked a couple of times when she finished and said, "I surely do be obliged fer ya warnin' me. I be swearin' to ya that I be careful."

Clea stood up and asked, "Ya be goin' down in them there mines soon, won't ya?"

"Yas," Eamon said as he stood up next to her.

"Ya be bein' careful down there with that leg of yers and all."

"I surely will be."

Clea gave him a big hug. She held him so tight for so long that I thought she might break his back. When she released him, she scurried out the window without saying another word.

After Eamon closed the window, he pressed his face against it and watched her until she was out of sight. When he returned to his bed, he sat on the edge of it, placed his face in his palms, and cried.

CHAPTER TWENTY-NINE
TESTING THE WATER FAILS

Uncle Teagan did get Eamon a job in the mines. His shift started at midnight. He worked down in those dark tunnels all night and then rode his pony home in the morning light. After months of offering Eamon gifts he wouldn't accept, Preacher Skaggs sent a message to the mine foreman asking him to tell Eamon his Pa passed away, and he needed to come immediately to the church. Even though the mine owners were usually too heartless to consider the needs of their employees, the foremen were usually mountain men who knew how seriously the people of this mountain took burial customs. They allowed Eamon to leave in the middle of the night.

Eamon rode his pony under the dark sky of a waning crescent moon. His eyes remained dry and his face was like stone throughout the ride. Shortly after he arrived at the church and sat on a pew, Preacher Skaggs pounced on Eamon like a mountain lion pouncing on its prey.

Eamon lay on the pew underneath him and yelled, "What ya be doin', Preacher? What ya be doin'? When Preacher Skaggs kissed Eamon, he pushed the preacher away, spat and yelled, "I nary be no queer!"

Eamon's legs were weak, but his arms and shoulders gained a lot of strength working in the mines. Since he was crippled, they often tied a coal cart to his back and had him crawl into narrow tunnels on all fours. This made his shoulders and chest muscular and strong when compared to his otherwise thin body and legs. He threw Preacher

Skaggs off and yelled, "Pa nary be dead, do he? Ya just be makin' that up to be gittin' me over here."

"H'it done got ya here, didn't h'it?" Preacher Skaggs yelled as he ran at Eamon, tackled him, and pinned him to a pew.

Eamon fought, but Preacher Skaggs was ready for him this time. They wrestled so hard that they fell off the pew and onto the floor. Preacher Skaggs rolled on top of Eamon, placed his knees on Eamon's arms and held Eamon down with the weight of a pampered preacher who didn't get enough exercise to burn off the excess calories that were paid for by the tithes of his undernourished parishioners. Eamon's legs were so weak they were unable to give him the leverage he needed to knock the preacher off of him.

Preacher Skaggs looked into Eamon's eyes and said, "I nary be tryin' to be harmin' ya, boy. I just be tryin' to be showin' ya how much I be lovin' ya. There nary be a person on this here mountain what been nicer to ya than I has."

"Uncle Teagan and MawMaw Tierney be the ones what been nice to me," Eamon said as he struggled to get his arms free.

"Teagan just be workin' ya like an ol' horse to be makin' ya be payin' him back fer ever thing he ever done fer ya. I nary be askin' a thing of ya. Ya be owin' me, boy, after all I be doin' fer ya this past winter."

Tears ran down Eamon's cheeks as he yelled, "I nary be askin' ya fer nothin' ya be doin' fer me. I be tryin' to be gittin' ya to be quittin' doin' h'it." Eamon struggled harder as he yelled, "Git off'n me! I nary be no queer!"

I kicked Preacher Skaggs several times, but he didn't even look toward me like he sensed me. I sat on the pew behind them and cried.

The preacher didn't notice me, but he noticed when someone knocked on the door. After several knocks, that person beat harder as they screamed, "What in hell be goin' on in there."

"H'it be Regan!" Preacher Skaggs said, panicked, as he jumped off of Eamon and ran down the aisle.

When he unlocked the door, she pushed him out of the way and stormed down the aisle like a rampaging bull. Eamon was heading for the door, so she met him halfway down the aisle and yelled, "I done seen Lil' Gal out front. What in hell be goin' on in here?"

"Nothin', sweetheart," Preacher Skaggs said as he grabbed her arm.

She jerked her arm away from him and yelled, "Look at ya both! Yer clothes be a mess, and ya be havin' sweat in yer hair and on yer skin! Yer manhood be standin' up like h'it nary be havin' no shame. H'it be true what people be sayin' 'round here about ya!"

"Naw, sweetheart, h'it nary be nothin' like that. We just be wrestlin'."

"Fuck you!" Regan screamed and slapped his face. She looked at Eamon and screamed, "He be Mine! Mine! Do ya be hearin' me?"

"We nary be doin' nothin' like what ya be talkin' about! I be tryin' to be gittin' away from this ol' bastard. He done had my arms pinned down with the weight of his legs."

"If'n ya nary be doin' nothin', h'it only be because I be gittin' here before ya did!" Regan screamed as she picked up a Bible from a nearby pew and threw it at Eamon.

Eamon jumped out of the Bible's way, and Regan ran down the aisle. Preacher Skaggs ran after her. When she was almost to the door, he grabbed for her arm but got her dress sleeve instead. The beautiful white sleeve tore and was hanging off her shoulder when she ran out the door.

When Eamon followed her, Preacher Skaggs grabbed Eamon's arm when he was halfway out the door and said, "Ya be gittin' on back in here, or I be tellin' yer Pa all about ya."

"Regan be headin' home to be tellin' him right now," Eamon said as he walked out the door into the twilight of early morning. He walked down the steps faster than was safe for his legs and ran as good as his legs would allow him to across the front yard to Lil' Gal. She knelt to allow him to mount and then galloped away without any prompting. She ran down the main road so fast that the wind was causing Eamon's tears to be sprayed behind them.

They ran until Lil' Gal was so winded that Eamon clicked his tongue and yelled, "Stop, Lil' Gal! Don't ya be a-doin' this to yerself."

She stopped and knelt for him to dismount. He walked across a field they were near, and Lil' Gal followed him. They found a creek on the other side. While Lil' Gal drank, Eamon sat on a rock, hugged his knees and cried. When Lil' Gal drank her fill, she nuzzled him.

He patted her muzzle and said, "Ya be so good to me. Let us be gittin' on home."

Lil' Gal knelt for him to mount, and they headed for home. They passed Uncle Teagan's car on the family road as he left for his shift at the mines. Lil' Gal went to the barn and knelt for Eamon to dismount. After he did, he gave her some hay and brushed her while she ate. Seconds after he started brushing, Caelan emerged from behind the wagon. He held a rope taut between his hands, and he quickly pulled it down the front of Eamon's body from behind. Eamon dropped the brush when his arms were pushed down to his sides, and it hit his foot as Caelan tied the rope behind his back, securing his arms.

"What in hell!" Eamon screamed as Caelan led him to the back door of the barn.

Lil' Gal followed them and tried to push Caelan away from Eamon with her muzzle. When Caelan pushed Eamon out the back door, he held the rope with one hand and closed the door with the other. I walked through the closed door at the same time Lil' Gal started beating on it with her front hooves.

"What in hell ya be doin?" Eamon yelled as Caelan led him, stumbling, toward the side of the barn farthest away from Uncle Teagan's house.

"Regan done told me what ya and Garnett be doin' to her last night. Her dress done be about tore off. What kind of animals be goin' after they own sister."

"I nary be seein' Garnett since I done left that hell hole ya be callin' a home."

"Ya about to be seein' him," Caelan said as they rounded the corner of the barn.

"Naw," Eamon screamed when he saw Garnett tied to the side of the barn. Garnett was naked, and the rope around his wrists was secured to a hook above his head.

Garnett's tear-stained cheek leaning against the barn wall reminded me of how I saw my own cheek pressed into the barn floor when I had floated above my body right after I died. I felt like the stomach I no longer had a body to sustain was going to empty its contents.

Eamon screamed and started fighting harder. Caelan threw him into the barn wall and punched him in the face. When he fell half-conscious to the ground, Caelan removed the rope from around his body and tied his wrists with it before pulling him to his feet and securing the rope to a hook in the same way Garnett was tethered. He ripped Eamon's shirt down the back and tore it off him before he stepped a few feet away and picked up a bullwhip he had in the grass.

I ran to the front of the barn and fell on my knees. I was being controlled by dry heaves that my lack of a body would not allow me to vomit and find relief from. The dry heaves became worse when I heard the first crack of the whip and the first scream.

The sound of Lil' Gal's hooves on the back door stopped at the same time I heard the first scream. I looked up and saw her through the open front door of the barn. The scream released her from her frenzy to get out the back door. When she looked toward the sound of the scream, she saw the front door was open and ran through it. She ran to the house and stomped the porch steps with her front hooves as she screamed wildly.

When MawMaw Tierney ran out of the house to see why Lil' Gal was so upset, I heard the second crack of the whip and the second scream. She returned to the house and was back on the porch with a double-barrel shotgun before I heard the third crack of the whip and the third scream. She was rounding the corner of the barn when I heard the fourth crack of the whip and the fourth scream. She stopped at the edge of the barn, so I could see her point the shotgun at Caelan and yell, "Ya be hittin' them there boys one more time, and I be endin' ya, ol' man!"

Lil' Gal came up behind MawMaw Tierney and whinnied as if she were expressing a threat of her own. I suppressed my dry heaves and stood by them to create a united front, but Caelan lifted his arm to crack the whip again anyway. Instead of hearing the whip crack, I heard MawMaw Tierney cock the shotgun and say, "Nary be testin' me, ol' man. I be takin' no greater pleasure in this here life than to be endin' yers."

"Fuck ya, ol' woman," Caelan said as he rushed her.

MawMaw Tierney fired a shot that grazed his cheek, leaving a long burn just under his cheekbone and a nick chopped out of his ear. She

213

moved her finger to the second trigger before she said "I mays be a woman, but I be bein' one of the best shots in this here county. Ya be takin' one more step, ol' man, and I be endin' ya."

When Caelan stopped, she yelled, "Drop that there whip!" When he stared defiantly at her, she screamed it again so loud that it startled the whip out of his hand. "Now, ya be gittin' the hell outta here. I nary be wantin' to be seein' ya on this here property again."

When Caelan ran away, she pulled a knife out of her granny boot and cut Garnett's rope. When he fell to his knees, she knelt next to him and said, "Ya be gittin' yer self on over to the house, son. I be bein' over shortly to be tendin' to them there wounds. Eamon be livin' in the long room. Ya be takin' yer self on in there and be lyin' down."

Garnett was staggering, but he made it to the porch by the time MawMaw Tierney got Eamon cut down. She led Eamon to Lil' Gal, who knelt to allow him to fall belly first over her back. When Lil' Gal got to the front porch, she knelt in front of the steps, and MawMaw Tierney helped Eamon dismount and limp into the house and to his room. When he got to his room, she helped him lay face down on the bed next to Garnett before she yelled for Uncle Teagan's oldest daughter.

When the girl appeared in the doorway, MawMaw Tierney said, "Ya be needin' to be gittin' me some warm soapy water and some of that there salve I done made up last fall."

The girl's eyes grew wide and her mouth dropped open when she looked at the boys. "Yas'm," she said as she scurried from the room.

When the girl returned with the requested supplies, MawMaw Tierney washed Eamon's wounds. He winced and hollered several times while she cleaned them, but he quickly calmed down when she started applying the salve.

As she applied the salve, she said, "That there ol' man done had h'it out fer ya since ya be born'd. He nary be believin' he be yer rightful Pa. He done had to be marryin' that girl of mine cuz she done had ya in her belly. H'it nary be gittin' no better fer ya 'round here. H'it nary be gittin' no better fer Garnett whilst ya be 'round here. He be knowin' ya be lovin' Garnett the best. He be goin' to be usin' Garnett to be hurtin' ya."

214

"I be knowin' that," Eamon said as he turned his head and looked at MawMaw Tierney.

She removed five dollars from her apron pocket, laid it on the bed in front of Eamon's face and said, "This here be emergency money I be savin'. I be knowin' that there minin' comp'ny be puttin' yer paycheck toward yer Pa's comp'ny store bill til ya be turnin' twenty-one. I be wantin' ya to be takin' this here five dollars and be beatin' h'it on outta here in the mornin'."

"Where do I be goin' to?"

"Ya be gittin' yer self into the city no matter what ya be havin' to be doin' to be gittin' there."

"What be happenin' to Garnett?"

"He only be pickin' on Garnett to be hurtin' ya. Once ya be gone, he be leavin' Garnett alone. Besides, now that we be havin' Garnett over here, he can be stayin' with us. I reckon Caelan nary be makin' a fuss about h'it. Once you be gone, he nary be havin' no need of Garnett."

"I nary be wantin' to be leavin' y'all."

"I be knowin' that, son," MawMaw Tierney said as she covered the last bit of wound with salve. "I nary be wantin' ya to be leavin' neither. Ya be doin' right fine in the city though. Ya be rememberin' that there car ya be wantin' to be buyin' so ya can be givin' yer legs some rest? Nary folks be takin' yer check in the city. Ya can be gittin' yer self that there car one day."

"Yas'm" Eamon said as a tear slid from his eye, across the bridge of his nose and fell onto the quilt he was laying on.

"When ya be gittin' to that there city, there nary be no comp'ny store. Ya be havin' yer self a fresh start. Ya be usin' yer money fer what be good fer ya. Ya be livin' a better life. Once ya done gots yer self that there car, ya be drivin' h'it back down here to be visitin'. Ya nary be goin' to yer Pa's house when ya be visitin'. Ya be comin' to our house where ya be safe. When yer Pa be findin' out ya be drivin' a car to be visitin' us, h'it be eatin' his insides out. That be yer revenge, son. Ya be livin' a good life, and that be yer revenge. The Bible be sayin' h'it be the same as droppin' hot coals on his head. Nary be forgettin' that. Nary be throwin' yer future nor yer soul away tryin' to avenge what yer folks done did to ya. Ya just be livin' yer self a good life and be lettin' the

215

good Lord be droppin' them there hot coals on they head when they be seein' ya be havin' a good life. Ya be promisin' me that?"

"Yas'm."

She sat in silence for a few minutes before she started washing Garnett's back. As she rubbed salve on his motionless body, she said, "This poor child done gone and passed out."

When she finished Garnett's back, she said, "H'it be more than just yer Pa why ya be needin' to be gittin' outta here. Ya nary be wantin' to be owin' yer life to that there comp'ny store like too many folks 'round here be doin'. Ya be lil' more than a slave when ya be owin' them."

"Yas'm" Eamon said as MawMaw Tierney stood up.

"Ya be takin' that there five dollars. Ya be eatin' yer self a good breakfast in the mornin', and then ya be gittin' on Lil' Gal and be ridin' her to the highway. She be knowin' her way back once ya be gittin' there. Ya be sendin' her on home before ya be stickin' out yer thumb to be askin' a car what be passin' by fer a ride. That be how ya be askin' fer a ride; ya be stickin' out yer thumb when a car be passin' by. Some folks might be keepin' on goin' without stoppin' fer ya, but someone be pickin' ya up some time. When they does, ya be tellin' them ya be needin' a ride into the city.

"When ya be gittin' to the city, ya be needin' to be findin' yer self a church first thing. Ya nary be believin' that all preachers be like Preacher Skaggs. I hear tell there be some right fine preachers in that there city. Church folks likely to be helpin' ya out till ya be findin' yer self a job. Ya be keepin' on attendin' that there church, so them church folks be knowin' who ya be. Church folks be real good about helpin' out their own. Once ya be gittin' settled, then ya be askin' the preacher to be writin' fer ya. Them city preachers be right educated men. They be able to be writin' fer ya. Have him be writin' a letter to be lettin' me be knowin' ya be a'right. One of Teagan's girls can be reading h'it to me. Ya be askin' that there preacher how to be buyin' a stamp in the big city, so ya can be sendin' that there letter on home to me. I be needing to be knowin' ya be a'right."

"Yas'm," Eamon said as she walked out of the room.

CHAPTER THIRTY
TRAVELING TO THE BIG CITY

The reason I stayed here instead of going with the Angel was to be with Eamon, so I wasn't going to let him go to the city alone. The thought of staying on this mountain without him was too painful to bear, so when he and Lil' Gal left the next morning, Dog and I were sitting behind him on Lil' Gal's back.

He rode all the way to the highway without talking to Lil' Gal, which was unusual for them. The morning fog seemed to give him a place to hide his emotions, but even from behind him, I could tell he was crying. We rode through that fog for several hours, barely able to see the beauty of these mountains that we might never see again. The fog lifted minutes before we reached the highway. Lil' Gal knelt by the side of the highway for Eamon to dismount, and Dog and I were already on the ground when he did.

When Lil' Gal stood, Eamon dried his eyes, grasped the sides of her face and pulled her forehead to his own. As they stood there with their foreheads touching, Eamon said, "I surely will be missin' ya, Lil' Gal. Ya done been a mighty fine friend to me. Ya be goin' on back to MawMaw Tierney's. Nary ever be goin' to Ma and Pa's place again. If'n ya be doin' that, yer life nary be worth livin'. Ya be goin' on back to MawMaw Tierney's, and ya be makin' sure ya be stayin' there. Do ya be understandin' me?

She nodded and neighed.

Tears welled in his eyes as he kissed her on the muzzle and said, "Ya be havin' yerself a right fine life. Ya be goin' on back to MawMaw Tierney's now."

Eamon watched until Lil' Gal was out of sight before he started walking down the highway with his thumb out like MawMaw Tierney told him to do. His limp became noticeably worse quickly, so I feared what would happen if no one gave him a ride. Several cars did pass by before a brand new 1950 Buick Super stopped.

"Where you heading?" the man asked as Eamon opened the passenger door.

"My MawMaw done told me to be findin' myself a ride to the city."

"I'm heading all the way into Cincinnati. That's a city. Do you want to ride along?"

"Yassir."

"Then get on in," the man said. "I'm not going to bite you."

Eamon got in the passenger seat, and Dog and I thought ourselves into the back seat. I couldn't stop staring at the man, because I'd never seen hair so white before. The contrast between his hair and his dark suit looked odd to me.

As the man drove onto the road, he asked, "Why are you going to the city?"

"I be havin' to be gittin' away from here."

The man talked so fast I could hardly understand him as he said, "I can understand that. Let me guess: you just turned twenty-one and became a free man."

"What do ya be meanin'?"

"You're a legal adult when you turn twenty-one."

"I nary be knowin' that," Eamon said. He paused for a long time before he added, "Yassir, I reckon I be twenty-one."

"It's okay if you're not. I'm not going to tell anyone," the man said before he started telling stories. I soon learned he always talked fast, but it got easier to understand him the more he talked. Eamon quietly listened for most of the trip. I guess he didn't have much to say to the city slicker since no one ever acted like his words were valuable.

A couple of hours later, the man stopped telling stories long enough to ask, "When's the last time you ate?"

"MawMaw done fixed me some vittles this mornin'."

"It's past lunch time. Would you like to stop and get something to eat?"

"Ya be havin' family 'round here?"

The man laughed the same short brisk laugh that had punctuated many of his stories before he said, "No, we'll stop at a restaurant and buy some food."

"I nary be havin' money fer that kind of thing."

"I'd be very happy to buy you a hamburger."

"Really?" Eamon asked as he looked at the man and scrunched his eyebrows. "Why would ya be doin' somethin' like that fer me when ya nary be knowin' me?"

"Hasn't anyone ever bought you a hamburger before?" Eamon shook his head as the man asked, "Can I be the first?"

"If'n ya be sure ya nary be mindin'."

"I'd be happy to," the man said before he started telling stories again.

A few miles down the highway, the man turned on his turn signal and took a side road. A few miles down that road was a diner with a neon side that said "Ruby's". He pulled into the parking lot, parked, opened his door and said, "Let's go on in and get us some lunch."

Eamon opened his door slowly and followed the man, and Dog and I followed Eamon. When they entered the restaurant, Eamon stopped and looked all around the room. Bright lights reflected off the shining linoleum floors, the shiny Formica counter, the shiny metal and glass container of pie that hung on the wall behind the counter, the shiny strips of silver metal along the edges of the counters and tables, the shiny metal bases of the round chairs with red cushions that lined the counter, and the shiny benches with red cushions that sat on both sides of the booths that lined the windows. This restaurant was the opposite of the creaky gray house Eamon grew up in, so I understood why his eyes were wide and his mouth hung open as he looked around the room. I thought this must be what heaven looked like, because I'd never seen anything so bright before. That thought made me realize I might not ever know, since I refused to go with the Angel.

The man and Eamon sat on opposite sides of a booth, but Eamon rarely looked at the man. He stared at the tabletop even when the man was speaking to him.

"What are you planning on doing when you get to the city?" the man asked.

"I don't rightly be knowin'."

"How are you going to pay your way if you don't have enough to buy a hamburger?"

Eamon looked at the man long enough to say, "Ya nary be havin' to be buyin' me one if'n ya nary be wantin' to."

"That's not my point. I'm happy to buy you a hamburger. I'm just worried about how you're going to survive after I drop you off in Cincinnati."

"Why ya be worryin' about me? Ya nary be knowin' me."

"I wouldn't want my son out on the road without a plan. You remind me of him."

Eamon looked at the man long enough to ask, "Really?"

"Yes. If you don't have a place to go when you get there, I want you to go to Goodwill®."

"What do Goodwill® be?"

"It's a place where they'll help you find a job and a place to live," the man answered as he pulled a pad and pencil out of his pocket, wrote the name and address of Goodwill® on the top sheet and gave it to Eamon. "Promise me you'll go there."

"I be promisin'. Much obliged."

A waitress who wore a white, knee-length shirtdress came to the table, removed a pad and pencil from her red apron pocket, looked at Eamon and asked if he wanted to order. When Eamon didn't respond, the man asked, "Could we just have two hamburgers and two Cokes?"

"Sure thing," the waitress said and walked away.

Eamon listened to the man's stories until the waitress returned with their hamburgers. The man took small bites, but Eamon ate his in three big bites.

"You must be hungry," the man said before he waved the waitress over to the table and asked for another hamburger for Eamon.

When they were done eating, they went to the shiny cash register that sat on the counter, and the man gave the waitress the check. While she pushed big keys that made big numbers pop up where they could see them, the man looked at Eamon and said, "Maybe we should go to the bathroom before we get back on the road."

When Eamon agreed, the man pointed to a bathroom door in the far corner and said, "It's right over there. You go first while I pay."

"A'right," Eamon said before he walked to the door and entered the bathroom. When Eamon returned, he waited while the man went to the same room.

When they were in the car again, the man asked, "What kind of toilets do you have where you come from?"

"Do that be what them things be called?" Eamon asked as he turned sideways in his seat and looked at the man with the same expression he had on his face when they entered the shiny restaurant. "I be tellin' ya, I nary be seein' nothin' be like that before. I nary be knowin' what to be doin' with h'it exceptin' they be havin' a hole in them like the ones in our outhouses be havin'."

The man laughed and said, "Yes, those are toilets. That's what you're going to be using when you get to the city. Did you know you have to flush them?"

"Do what?" Eamon asked as his brow crinkled.

The man laughed again before he said, "Did you see that silver handle on the tank behind the toilet?"

"Yassir."

"You should push that down after you go, so the next person doesn't see what you did."

"No joshin'?"

"No joshin'."

"I nary be hearin' of nothin' like that before."

The man laughed again and said, "Welcome to the big city."

"I be gosh-darned," Eamon said as he leaned back in his seat. "I be thinkin' I done seen h'it all now."

When they got back on the road, the man continued to tell stories, and Eamon continued to listen politely. Just before they got to Cincinnati, they drove down a big hill that ended at a bridge that crossed the Ohio River. As they drove across the bridge, the man asked, "Have you ever seen anything like all of these lights?"

The last time I saw the look of joy that was on Eamon's face was when Dog was still alive and they played together. He smiled bigger than I'd ever seen him smile when he answered, "Naw, sir!"

After they crossed the river, the man drove down a series of asphalt roads that were lined on both sides with buildings. I'd never seen a place with so little grass and so few trees. The man stopped in front of a big brick building and said, "These people will help you." The sign on the building matched the letters on the piece of paper he gave Eamon in the restaurant.

"Much obliged," Eamon said as he opened the car door.

"Take care of yourself."

"I be doin' that," Eamon said as he got out of the car and watched it drive away, leaving Eamon, Dog and me standing by the side of the road.

Eamon did go in the building, and they did help him. They gave him a job and a place to sleep. He became good friends with his manager. He eventually bought a car. Most important – he fell in love.

She was tall and thin, but sturdy. She had black hair and thick black eyebrows that complemented the big brown eyes underneath them. She was beautiful, but that wasn't what made him fall in love with her. She was reserved like he was while still being friendly, she spoke in an accent similar to his own, she was a hard-working waitress who was trying to make her way in the city after having grown up in the mountains, and she was as kind as Uncle Teagan and MawMaw Tierney. She couldn't talk to a dog the way his mother talked to people. There were people in the neighborhood whispering bad things about her, because she was being kind to an old black man who washed dishes at the restaurant where she worked. That gossip only made him love her more. She was so kind, he couldn't stop himself from falling in love with her.

It might seem like Eamon's story ends here, but this is actually where it begins. His salvation begins with this woman and continues through their daughter. It is a happier story than what you've heard so far, but any story that is prefaced by this one can't possibly be lived free of trials. Fortunately, it will no longer be lived free of love.

Thanks to Religious Recovery Press for publishing this book in 2015.

Religious Recovery Press is now a 501(c)3 Non-Profit Publishing House. We decided that "The Blood Moon Series" is not a 501(c)3 book series, so I changed publishing houses. I still strongly support their literature and recommend it for any readers who need help recovering from religious abuse.

Following are the books currently published from
ReligiousRecoveryPress.org

(available on Amazon)

Every Path Leads Home, Opening to Your Spiritual Journey
By: Wayne Holmes

Strength For The Journey Home
By: Wayne Holmes

Set Your Course
Daily Lessons into Spirituality
For the Religious Recovery Program
By Wayne Holmes

About Rhonda Partin-Sharp

Rhonda comes from an Appalachian lineage. Her memories combined with stories she heard of previous generations have nurtured her as a storyteller. Although she received higher education in literature and writing and worked as a writer in various non-fiction forms, she feels her heart is what made her a storyteller, and her heart is tied to the mountains that were the lifeblood of many generations before her

In her early years, Rhonda often found herself surrounded by troubled people. She had to learn that not all people had needs as great as her parents and the friends from her culture she often helped. She also had to learn that women were not required to put their needs and their family's needs second to other people's wants in order to be right with God. These lessons helped her start learning to stop extending compassion and/or understanding to people who cherished chaos above healthy relationships. This change began when her counselor recognized that Rhonda's personal key to healing was to recognize that people see in others what they are themselves; therefore, Rhonda had to stop assuming all people were as accepting, compassionate, and helpful as her lineage and life experiences had taught her to be.

She hopes that her writing – this book and other books that are in the works – will help others achieve the same successes and happiness. She desires to pay it forward.

Book Two in The Blood Moon Series, "Escape Under A Waning Crescent Moon," will be released in March, 2018.

Book Three in The Blood Moon Series is planned for release in 2019.

www.ingramcontent.com/pod-product-compliance
Lightning Source LLC
Chambersburg PA
CBHW070930180626
46817CB00003B/1228